Praise for the M. L. Buchman:

"Top 10 Romance of 2012, 2015, and 2016."
– Booklist
The Night Is Mine, Hot Point, Heart Strike

"One of our favorite authors."
–RT Book Reviews

"Suzanne Brockmann fans will love this."
–Booklist, *Wait Until Dark*

"A rousing mix of romance and military action thrills...Buchman blends tender feelings with military politics to keep readers riveted."
-Publishers Weekly

"Buchman continues to serve up nonstop action that will keep readers on the edge of their seats."
– Library Journal Xpress

"A must read for fans of military romantic suspense... "
– Fresh Fiction

Praise for the Night Stalkers series:

"The Night Stalkers is a series you'll want to read, in order or not."
– Kirkus Reviews

If you love military romance, you'll love this series.
– *Book Lovers Inc.*

"*happy sigh* Another greatly entertaining and fabulous read from the brain of M.L Buchman. OMG, I love how this guy writes military romantic suspense!!"
– Smitten with Reading, *By Break of Day*

"The Night Stalker series is one of my favorites!"
– Night Owl Reviews

This entire series has been phenomenal.
– Smitten with Reading, A rating

The fabulous Night Stalkers series by military romance genius M.L. Buchman.
– Fresh Fiction, *By Break of Day*

Target of Mine

a Night Stalkers 5E / Titan World romance

by

M. L. Buchman

Published by Buchman Bookworks, Inc.

Sign up for M. L. Buchman's newsletter and
discover more by this author at:
www.mlbuchman.com

Cover images:
Helicopters © Tebnad
Beautiful Athletic Couple Over White © Photobac

Buchman Bookworks

Other works by M. L. Buchman:

The Night Stalkers

MAIN FLIGHT

The Night Is Mine
I Own the Dawn
Wait Until Dark
Take Over at Midnight
Light Up the Night
Bring On the Dusk
By Break of Day

WHITE HOUSE HOLIDAY

Daniel's Christmas
Frank's Independence Day
Peter's Christmas
Zachary's Christmas
Roy's Independence Day
Damien's Christmas

AND THE NAVY

Christmas at Steel Beach
Christmas at Peleliu Cove

5E

Target of the Heart
Target Lock on Love
Target of Mine

Delta Force

Target Engaged
Heart Strike

Dead Chef Thrillers

Swap Out!
One Chef!
Two Chef!

Firehawks

MAIN FLIGHT

Pure Heat
Full Blaze
Hot Point
Flash of Fire
Wild Fire

SMOKEJUMPERS

Wildfire at Dawn
Wildfire at Larch Creek
Wildfire on the Skagit

Deities Anonymous

Cookbook from Hell:
Reheated
Saviors 101

Angelo's Hearth

Where Dreams are Born
Where Dreams Reside
Maria's Christmas Table
Where Dreams Unfold
Where Dreams Are Written

Eagle Cove

Return to Eagle Cove
Recipe for Eagle Cove
Longing for Eagle Cove
Keepsake for Eagle Cove

SF/F Titles

Nara
Monk's Maze
the Me and Elsie Chronicles

Titles of the Titan World Project

Flightpath by Amber Addison

Going Under by Anna Bishop Barker

Target of Mine by M. L. Buchman

Where I Belong by Claudia Connor

Rescued Heart by Tarina Deaton

Deja Vu by Cristin Harber

Twisted Desire by Sharon Kay

Bullets and Bluebonnets by Jessie Lane

Downtime by Karen Lawerence

Edge of Temptation by Gennita Low

Never Mine by Megan Mitcham

Letter from Cristin Harber

Dear Readers,

Welcome to the Titan World books with stories ranging from military romance to paranormal to contemporary romance. There's something for everyone—action-packed romance, swoon-worthy moments, and happily ever after!

When I started the Titan series, I wanted to combine my love of steamy romance and action-packed suspense. I wrote strong men and women who I hoped readers would fall in love with. I can't think of anything more exciting than opening my world up to very talented authors to extend that experience so that you, the reader, can have a deeper connection to more than one book series at a time.

You will meet new characters and see them interact with familiar ones; you will also see the interpretation of the Titan universe through another author's eyes. I hope that you take the time to experience each book in the Titan World series!

I'm thrilled for you to read M. L. Buchman's *Target of Mine,* where the elite military crew from the Night Stalkers 5E meet the Titan Group in an exciting and romantic ride. I first met M. L. in person at a novelist conference, and we began discussing our characters with such passion that I knew that our teams had to meet. He agreed! Our readers are in for a treat as our worlds collide.

Thank you to M. L. Buchman and all the authors who took time out of their busy writing schedules to participate in this project. I think the result is something our military romance readers will find special.

Titan Hugs and Happy Reading,
Cristin Harber

Letter from M. L. Buchman

Greetings!

The main thing I remember about my first conversation with Cristin was that we both spent most of it laughing and saying, "I know!" We had so much fun talking about our characters, our stories, our families…I could have spent the whole conference just sitting and chatting with Cristin and ignored everything else.

Then she suggested that we should collaborate on a project together. I made a few simple suggestions on how we could test the waters. Her answer was to leap in and suggested that I write a novel for her Titan World project.

It's the main thing we found in common. We both love romance, we both love action-packed suspense, but most especially we both love plunging into projects and discovering the joy of the characters and story.

Getting a chance to play with Team Titan has been so much fun. I was captivated by the team leader, Jared Westin, and the woman who sweeps his feet out from under him—sometimes literally—Lily "Sugar" Chase. They were so unlike any character I had ever written, and yet I so enjoyed their story that I just had to tackle them.

Target of Mine takes place shortly after Cristin's *Westin's Chase*. It is also the third title in my Night Stalkers 5E series but, as with all of my books, written completely to stand just fine on its own from either series.

Thank you, Cristin and Team Titan, for letting the Night Stalkers come play!

Hope you enjoy the flight,
M. L. Buchman
2017, the Oregon Coast

Don't Miss a Thing!

Sign up for M. L. Buchman's newsletter today
and receive:
Release News
Free Short Stories
a Free Starter Library

Do it today. Do it now.
http://www.mlbuchman.com/newsletter/

Chapter 1

Rain sucked.

Philippine September-monsoon rain really sucked.

In a full flightsuit and helmet it was thick, hot, and disgustingly sweaty.

Worse, it was creating mayhem with their midnight attack plan.

Drake Roman hung on to his M134 Minigun with both hands as the Night Stalkers' DAP Hawk helicopter *Beatrix* banked hard to avoid a hundred meters of island that came out of nowhere. The tactical readouts were showing nothing but a wall of water thick enough to block most radar signals, and the infrared night vision was totally useless because everything was the same temperature—wet.

His flight harness cut into his shoulders as he leaned against the turn. Levering himself forward, Drake stuck his head out the window, trying to see ahead through the unlit darkness. The rain was coming straight down, but the Hawk moved at over a hundred and fifty knots, so even in the slipstream of the hull, he couldn't see squat as the rain drumbeat on his helmet.

The crew chiefs' seats faced to either side from close behind the two pilots' seats. His Minigun was on a traveler that reached out the side window and gave him a full range of fire from directly sideways to straight ahead and from level to straight down.

Right now he just wanted someone to aim it at.

On the first pass, the other crew chief had taken a hit, a bad one by the sound of it. With Carl out of action, the pilots had twisted sideways, giving Drake the primary action side, so Carl was someone else's problem. He had an aircraft to defend.

Normally able to strike from a thousand meters away, tonight's weather was forcing encounters to be up close and personal.

"I'm in crew chief starboard seat," a new voice announced on the intercom, "I've got Carl patched and sedated." Anyone else, he wouldn't have registered more than the fact that the position was occupied and Carl was alive. But Chief Petty Officer Nikita Hayward spoke with a smooth, soft Southern accent that had messed with him since the day he'd first met her on a mission a year before. Never did him any good, but damn he liked that voice.

The wall of water broke—one instant in the midst of a biblical downpour, the next in clear air—to reveal a narrow beach and a high vertical cliff capped by dark jungle. Probably be dramatic as hell in the daytime. At night it was just another obstacle to not smash into. At the base was huddled a line of small boats.

Less than a hundred meters above the sea and less than that from the soaring cliffs, the tactical readout inside his helmet's visor finally painted a clear image.

Tourist boat. Tourist boat...and another tourist boat. They were tied up just outside the surf line. Abandoned to the nightly monsoon, they'd be washed clean for tomorrow's tourists who came to mob the dramatic beaches of Palawan Island, Philippines, along the South China Sea.

Except it wasn't only tourist boats huddled here tonight and the Night Stalkers of the 5th Battalion E Company had been waiting for just such a night to take care of a problem.

Someone had made it abundantly clear to the Philippine military to not interfere in this region. The AFP had recently lost three helicopters, two boats, and twenty personnel before giving up.

Drug-runner, gun-runner, pirate—it didn't matter. Tonight was the night they were going down.

Technically, the US couldn't help, at least not in any obvious way. They couldn't admit to attacking any Philippine nationals without putting their new military base leases at risk. The Philippine government had given the US military access to five new bases in addition to Subic Bay with the understanding that they'd help defend the country, not attack it.

Regrettably, the local criminal element didn't feel the need to honor any such unspoken agreement. The 5E were her to give them a lesson tonight in the hazards of ignoring that.

The 5th Battalion E Company was here because they specialized in never-having-been-there operations.

Tourist boat…tourist bo—

The next boat flared with heat signatures of ten people on a night when no one in their right mind would be afloat. Hard radar returns, as if their boat was loaded with more than tourists or local fish. There was metal on that boat, a lot of it.

He saw the hot flash of gunfire from yet another boat just emerging out of the curtain-like edge of the deluge. Multiple targets.

The bastards had already taken the first shots, hitting Carl more by chance than skill—which satisfied the 5E's rules of engagement for this mission: *do not fire first.* They hadn't.

But paybacks were about to be delivered.

Big time.

Chapter 2

What the hell did you guys do to my helicopter?" The mechanic was practically screaming. Like he'd never seen a shot-up helo before.

Nikita stood off to the side of the hangar next to a long folding table, checking through her gear. It was late afternoon and the four helicopters of the 5E had just unloaded from the C-5A Galaxy transport. After the long flight home, they'd been reassembled and then hopped to the 5E's private corner of Mother Rucker. Fort Rucker, Alabama, had gained that name for the brutal standards of the Army flight instructors stationed here and, even though Nikita wasn't part of the 5E, she'd adopted the name.

"She only has a few holes in her," Drake Roman protested loudly. "*Beatrix* done good!"

"Thirty-two," another mechanic, this one with a clipboard, spoke up. "Thirty-two holes. Who knows how much damage to internal systems we'll find when we peel off the skins. If it wasn't a Black Hawk, you'd be dead."

By Nikita's estimation, that count was low for a standard mission with the 5E, but mechanics enjoyed whining. Besides, they didn't count the holes that had been put in Carl.

"Told you she done good," Drake patted the side of the damaged helicopter.

The helicopter wasn't the only one who'd done good. Nikita had flown a half dozen missions with the 5E over the last year and they were becoming her favorite assignment. They weren't designated as a Special Mission Unit, unlike her own DEVGRU SEAL Team 6, but they should be. Most of the time Delta Force and DEVGRU didn't get anywhere without tapping the Night Stalkers of the 160th SOAR.

The Special Operations Aviation Regiment delivered her team wherever they needed to go, and always showed up to get them back out no matter what unholy hell was breaking loose. Of them all, the 5E was both the smallest and the most effective. They only had four helicopters: a monstrous twin-rotor Chinook, the lethal DAP Hawk, and a pair of Little Bird attack helos. And they were all stealth rigged—making them some of the rarest helicopters anywhere. They also had one of the most advanced drones yet produced for their exclusive use.

To her knowledge, the only other company who rated any stealth rotorcraft was the 5th Battalion D Company and the 5D only had two. Which was how the 5E rated their own private corner at Ech Stagefield on Mother Rucker whenever they were home. These assets were best kept hidden.

"What is wrong with those people?" Drake stood directly across the folding tables she'd set up to sort her gear. He stood only a few inches taller than her own five-ten. He was lean, but soldier fit with dark eyes and darker hair. And he was pissed.

"Why do you feel so defensive about your aircraft?" Nikita went back to sorting her ammo to determine how much she needed for restock. For some reason, which her commander Luke Altman wasn't sharing, he and she had returned with the 5E. Usually they would do what the rest of the SEAL Team had done, just melt away after a mission. Standard protocol was to go back to the DEVGRU base at Naval Air Station Oceana in Virginia and do a full breakdown of the mission to extract lessons learned. Then start into skills training while waiting for the next call-up.

"Because she did great!" Drake apparently just needed to rant, so she let him. He'd get down to what was actually bothering him eventually. He turned back to glare at the mechanics.

That's when she recognized the stain pattern on the back of his flightsuit. The outline of the crew chief's seat back was marked across the fabric—clean where the seat back had been, dark brown where Drake's arms and shoulders had stuck out beyond the edges of the seat.

Carl's blood-spray pattern. There'd been a lot of it.

She'd stabilized him with a tourniquet around the stump of his mostly missing arm. And a pressure patch to the mess that was his other shoulder. Glue to close a few more holes. He was still listed as critical at the Antonio Bautista Air Base hospital in the Philippines. The chances of Drake Roman's fellow crew chief ever leaving there except in a box were slim.

Nikita remembered what Lieutenant Commander Altman had done for her on a similar occasion.

She walked over to the unlocked weapons cabinet where the team had been stashing their mission weapons. She grabbed a pair of MK11 sniper rifles, slipped on suppressors, and took a couple boxes of ammo.

"Hey, Roman!"

"What?"

When he turned, she threw one of the rifles to him.

He caught it and looked down at it in surprise. "What?"

"You once said that you wish you could shoot like I did."

"Uh huh." He'd been her rear guard during a Peruvian mission a few months ago. Six targets, all out past fifteen hundred meters. She'd taken down all six before they figured out what was happening. It's what SEAL snipers were trained for.

"Well, it's never gonna happen."

That earned her a perplexed smile. "Great. So what's with the rifle?"

"I figure that I can't make you a worse shot than you already are, so anything has to be an improvement."

He laughed. It was bitter, but it was a laugh. He was one of the top helicopter gunners anywhere. But a Minigun wasn't a sniper weapon—it was a blunderbuss.

"Besides," she stepped out of the shadows into the sunlight and so-familiar heavy heat of the late Alabama afternoon, "I figure I should get you out of here before the mechanic shoots you, or the other way round."

"Fine."

* * *

Drake tried to shake off the tightness in his shoulders but wasn't having much luck with it. They felt as if he was turning into the hunchback of Notre Dame. He had no idea why he was being so twitchy.

Even after a year stationed at Mother Rucker, he wasn't used to the Alabama heat. He peeled his flightsuit and chucked it over on the laundry pile. The shorts and t-shirt he'd worn underneath weren't much better. Alabama was a land where sweat didn't evaporate, it clung.

When Nikita did the same, though, he could feel his mood improving.

She was the first and, as far as he knew, only woman to make

DEVGRU through the front door and it showed on her body. She was of a medium build that fit her perfectly. But she wasn't merely strong, she was carved. Not like a bodybuilder with bulging biceps and six-pack abs. She was carved the way an artist would shape her in cool stone or, better yet, warm wood—not an extra ounce of flesh, but what was there was perfect. Soft, smooth…and tough as hell. Her brunette hair was always pulled back in a painfully tight ponytail that made her look panther sleek. And her light brown eyes were always watching.

He followed her out of the hangar and onto the stagefield. Ech was designed for helicopters only. It had five short runways for practicing mass landings and takeoffs, or emergency procedures. The concrete was rough with a thousand scars from auto-rotation practice and helicopters sliding to a grinding halt on steel skids.

But not a single aircraft had landed here other than the 5E since they took over the field last year. Their four rotorcraft were never left out on the apron. Instead they were immediately rolled out of sight into the field's lone hangar. The field purposely looked abandoned and unused, weeds growing up through the cracks in the concrete and the surrounding field in need of a good mowing. At the rate it was growing, maybe they should skip mowing and just bale the area as hay.

The only change to Ech Stagefield in the last year was that the hangar was now highly secure and there was a new two-story housing unit big enough for each of the 5E's fifteen pilots and gunners to have their own tiny apartment in addition to a few guest spaces—those had only ever been used by the SEALs. It included a communal kitchen-dining room-briefing room, but most of their meetings were held out at the small cluster of picnic tables between the offices and the hangar.

Ech was surrounded by thick 'Bama forest on all sides: towering longleaf pine and willow oak, hickory and beech, prickly holly and sweet bay. He'd learned the trees when he found out Nikita was from Alabama—not that he'd ever had a chance to show off that bit of knowledge. Even a year here and it still smelled strange, particularly on the quiet evenings when his nose was expecting the Scotch pine, oak, birch, and maple of the New Hampshire hills where his family kept a summer home up on Squam Lake. The only entry to Ech was by air or a narrow dirt road through the forest.

He tromped along behind Nikita as she led him across the tarmac and out into the grassy field.

"Walk softly," Nikita's voice was barely louder than the banging in the hangar behind them as the mechanics got to work.

"What does walking have to do with shooting?"

Nikita stopped and he almost ran into her.

"What?"

"Are you here to learn or to whine like a little pissant, Roman?" Soft Southern with a razor-edged tongue.

"To whine like a little pissant!" At least *that* felt like he was getting something done.

"Okay," Nikita turned back toward the hangar.

"What? No! Wait."

She stopped.

He closed his eyes but all he could see was the blood all over the DAP Hawk's cargo bay. Just wait until the mechanics had to clean that up. Then they'd be sorry. Maybe as sorry as he already was. He'd done what he could, swabbing out the back of the DAP during the long flight home. He'd nearly punched his pilots Rafe and Julian when they offered to help. Carl had been his fellow crew chief, so it had been his job to do and he'd done it alone.

He managed a deep breath and opened his eyes. Nikita was still standing there, as impassively as ever—more beautiful than a Grecian statue, waiting for him to choose.

"Okay. If it gets my mind off..." he couldn't finish the sentence. "I'll learn anything."

Nikita nodded and continued to lead him out into the field.

"To take your shooting to the next level, you gotta leave emotion behind. Emotion changes heartrate and reaction time. And it breaks concentration. Those are the obvious effects."

"What are the unobvious?"

"Emotion blurs perception. To shoot at truly long distances, out past a thousand meters or more, your entire being must be perceiving the shot flying true far downrange or you'll never hit your target."

"Sounds like mysticism, but put those damn gunrunners back in my sights,"—that's what they had to have been by the scale of the explosions when the 5E had finally destroyed their boats—"and I'll show you what I'm perceiving downrange."

"Look behind us."

He turned. Through the thick growth of the late-summer-tall grass, he could only see one heavily trampled clear line, his own. Nikita Hayward had hardly left any impression at all.

Walk softly, she'd said.

Drake gazed back at the line of helicopters parked in the hangar beyond.

That's what the 5E did: their stealth aircraft walked softly and carried a damn big stick.

"Okay. Show me how to do that."

* * *

"What the hell are we here for?" A big voice boomed across the twilit airfield, making Drake break off in mid-clip to see what was going on. They were deep in the tall grass, so he actually had to rise up on all fours from his prone position beside her in order to see.

Nikita sighed—the man had the attention span of the goddamn gnats that kept hovering about them. Even for someone who was hurting, he was being chaotic. That he had hit the target at all over the last hour was a testament to his skill.

Ever since she was a child, she'd always found shooting was a great way to relax, giving her a simple focus that cleared her mind of other problems.

Not Drake.

"Come on, Roman. I thought you were serious about learning this shit." Drake was a seriously decent shot for a helicopter crew chief. She felt that there was hope of training him to be actually good. Maybe not SEAL Team 6 sniper good, but definitely operator level.

"I am."

"Well, then you're gonna have to learn to focus. You can either be a sniper or see what shiny objects are glittering nearby to distract you."

With practiced speed, the hangar doors were being raced shut before the intruder could round the corner of the hangar and see the line of stealth helicopters.

"Right. Sorry." He turned back and caught her looking toward the stranger continuing to shout out his impatience.

"Chief Petty Officer Nikita Hayward!" Drake's voice was soap opera dramatic. "I'm shocked. You call that maintaining focus?"

"Screw you, Roman." At least she'd stayed lower, looking between stalk and seeds so that she'd be less visible. Drake's head was popped up like some stupid gopher just asking to be shot in the head.

"Anytime."

"Yeah, I already knew that about you." Sergeant First Class Drake Roman was a damn handsome flyboy and knew it. It had taken him under thirty seconds into their first mission together last year to make it clear that the offer was open whenever she was interested. Absolutely not! Though, oddly, he'd never renewed the invitation and that bothered her at times. It was as if he was up to something, but she couldn't figure out what. Normally she had to beat guys like him back down more times than kudzu vines crawling into the vegetable garden.

Her attention stayed on the newcomer standing in front of the now sealed hangar that housed the 5E's four helicopters. Strangers were not supposed to come to this corner of Mother Rucker. This was exclusively the territory of the Night Stalkers 5th Battalion E company. Outsiders not welcome.

He was a big guy, classic broad-shoulder type. Walked with the arrogance of a US Army Ranger, but there was something else about him. Something that didn't fit—completely—aside from the babe at his side.

She'd have looked like an over-built sidewalk hussy with her leather clothes, long brown-black hair, and come-fuck-me boots, if it wasn't for where she was. Mother Rucker was one of the most secure military bases in the country, and Ech Stagefield was perhaps the most secure part of the fort—it was a seriously long way from the Miami strip. Besides, what crazy-as-shit person wore leather this far south of the Mason-Dixon line?

Nikita unclipped the Leupold telescopic sight off the rail of her MK11 rifle and turned to inspect the guy.

He was ignoring Pete and Danielle—the 5E's commander and chief pilot—standing right in front of him. Instead, he was looking right at her. He shouldn't even be able to see their position. They hadn't dug in their shooting site, but the sun was down and the light was getting iffy. Besides, she and Drake were fifty meters out into the tall-growing grass.

The smile he sent her way was chilly at best. It made her wish she wasn't merely using the scope, but had swung her entire rifle his way just to chap his ass. Then he turned his attention to Pete and Danielle. The leather-clad babe had followed his line of sight and now *she* was watching them.

Nikita checked the parking lot. Latest model Ford Expedition SUV, black, top-of-the-line, windows all tinted, fancy chrome wheels—all the geegaws. It fit right in with their flashy style.

"Should we go over?" Drake didn't yet have the sniper instincts that would have made it a whisper. Thankfully, the light breeze was blowing from the hangar toward their position, so their voices weren't likely to carry in that direction.

"You that desperate to get near a busty woman in leather, Roman? Besides, we'd just be sent away again if it's anything important. Command talks to you when they're good and ready—not a moment before." She felt foolish for stating the obvious. After snapping the scope back onto the rail, she double-checked the alignment marks.

"We've got incoming. Whoo-doggies, do we ever," this time Drake whispered, but it sounded more like awe than caution.

"You're not from Texas, Roman, so cut that out. Your Southern sucks even worse than your Yankee."

Nikita glanced over and saw the woman was coming their way with a swing of hip like she really did belong working the Miami strip—though definitely the high-rent end. Drake was gonna be useless until she was gone, so Nikita waited her out.

"Hi, honey. Aren't you the cutest thing?" The woman laser-focused on Drake. Her voice had that sexy, breathless quality that always seemed to grab men by the balls. She had long sleek hair that defied the humidity, fair skin, and dark blue eyes.

Drake was a goner. For a reason that eluded her, Nikita found that irritating. Not that she had any claim, but they had fought together and this woman was—

"You can call me…Sugar."

She had to be kidding. Even her honey-smooth words were lipsticked carmine red. The accent was real though. Maryland or maybe Virginia—somewhere up north.

"What are you shooting today?"

Like the overeager puppy dog he was when faced with a large set of breasts, Drake held up his MK11. "It's a sniper rifle."

"I can see that, Sweet Cheeks. May I?"

Before Nikita could protest, Drake had handed over his weapon.

No SEAL in their right mind would ever relinquish their weapon short of a court martial. He was only a Night Stalker, but still it was no damn excuse.

"Sugar" gave the rifle a quick inspection that showed more familiarity with weapons than Nikita would have expected.

She shouldered it without asking permission.

Nikita jerked her sidearm, but Sugar was aiming downrange toward the target. If she turned it anywhere else, Nikita would take her out first and ask questions later.

Sugar snicked off the safety and unleashed five rounds, two heartbeats between each shot. Nice and steady. Good weapon control. Absorbed the kick of the 7.62 mm round through her shoulder and down into a back-braced leg. Her stance wasn't military, but it was good.

Nikita ducked her head to her own scope and checked downrange. First shot high, the other four rang steel—near enough to dead center to make it impossible to tell if there was any drift. The target was six inches at six hundred meters, so it wasn't a hard shot, even in this light, but it was far better shooting than most civilians could manage. As good as Drake had done.

Sugar handed the rifle back to Drake. "Your scope is set a half mil too low. Watch out for the catch on the trigger at the last pound of pull. If your shots are drifting to the right, that's why. You should have it fixed. I've seen that in the MK11 Mod 0s before." Her accent almost disappeared when she was talking weapons; in its place was a sharp professional.

Drake was clearly past noticing such nuances, or perhaps even past speech.

Sugar looked at Nikita and probably would have cracked her bubblegum if she'd been chewing any. Instead, she slapped a hand on her own leather-wrapped behind with a loud smack as she turned back toward the field. "Book and its cover, dearie, book and its cover. Y'all c'mon in. There's gonna be a powwow if

I know my man." And she strode back the way she'd come, hip swing and all.

Drake didn't look aside for a single second—total brain death. "She sure got your number, Roman."

* * *

In the past, Sugar most certainly would have gotten his number—in a past before Drake had met Nikita Hayward. Built babes in leather shooting high-power rifles were definitely his idea of seriously hot—wasn't a man alive who wouldn't agree. But it was no longer any contest.

Sitting next to him in the tall grass was five-foot-ten of SEAL Team Six in female form. And not just female—she was Lieutenant Commander Luke Altman's right hand. Whatever it took to be that in the male-ruled world of Special Operations, she had it. She embodied it. Nikita was the most amazing woman he'd ever met…not that he'd ever seen her give any man the time of day.

Jason had taken a run at her when the SEALs were along on a mission with them into Russia; he might as well have been running at a brick wall. M&M's attempt to get her attention while they were in the Philippines was so dismal it couldn't even be called a decent try.

Himself, he'd searched for tactics, an *in* on the powerful Nikita. He'd even watched the movie *La Femme Nikita,* the *Point of No Return* Bridget Fonda remake, as well as both television show spin-offs about the exquisitely lethal assassin, in hopes of gaining any insight from the fictitious character that he could apply to the real-deal SEAL.

Every single approach he'd cooked up had sounded stupid in his head and some tiny bit of common sense had left them all unvoiced. But to watch her shoot…it was a thing of true beauty.

Lying together in the tall grass—doing nothing other than target shooting—was more of a start than he'd managed in a year.

No matter how much fun she was to watch, the hip-swinging Sugar wasn't even in the same world. Besides, she had "her man."

"Was she for real?" He'd always thought of himself as a great judge of women, but Nikita was slowly teaching him that he was only a great judge of the subset of women willing to slide into bed with him. Nikita wasn't one of those. He found her wholly unreadable and that, as much as anything, had snagged his attention until even looking the other way was impossible when she was around.

"Give me your weapon."

Nikita aimed his rifle downrange and, even though it was dark enough for the first fireflies to begin showing off, she fired a single round with hardly any hesitation. He heard the bright plink as the bullet hit steel. She handed the weapon back.

"What?"

"She's for real. Thought you knew how to zero a scope. We can cover that next time if you want."

"I know how to zero one. But I'm not used to shooting such piddly little guns. I just shifted down a bit instead." At first he'd thought he'd been missing high because the distance to the target wasn't what he thought it was or because Nikita was so distracting or… He'd run out of excuses and simply compensated by aiming lower. The pull to the right? That he'd missed entirely. Just what he didn't want to do, look like a complete doofus in front of an ST6 SEAL.

"It's better to zero the scope if you're taking multiple shots like this. Less of a distraction. And if you don't know how to fix that trigger, I can show you." She flicked on a flashlight and began collecting her brass from the deep-shadowed grass. He did the same until they could account for all of their rounds, including the five that Sugar had shot.

He actually didn't know how to repair the trigger, but he'd find someone else to show him how to fix it, then swear them to secrecy.

"A sniper in the field never leaves a trace that they were there," and she didn't. When they were done, there was nothing but two flat spots in the grass that would have disappeared soon enough. She leaned down to fluff up the bent grass. After admiring the view of a bent-over Nikita for a moment, he did the same. All evidence of lying close beside her for an hour, erased.

He hefted the MK11. A dozen pounds of rifle good to eight hundred meters and past a thousand in a pinch. The same basic cartridge as his M134 Minigun, though he typically fired eighty rounds per second instead of one every couple heartbeats. Being shot-perfect was less critical when he was throwing two pounds of lead per second versus half an ounce per shot. Personally, he liked the power of his M134, but there was a cleanness, a purity to what Nikita did, shot by shot, that he could appreciate.

As they walked back to the main hangar, he could see by the lights through the high windows above the closed doors that some of the others were gathering in. Most were still in the hangar working over the helicopters and their gear, preparing for whatever came next.

The 5E's commanders Pete and Danielle, who flew the massive Chinook, were front and center. Rafe and Julian, the two pilots from his own Black Hawk crew, also came over. The drone's copilot, Zoe DeMille, rounded out the gathering.

With just four helicopters and one drone, the 5E was the smallest company in the Night Stalkers by far. But they were the only team to be a hundred percent stealth equipped, garnering them the edgiest assignments. Drake wished he knew quite what he'd done right to be here so that he could make sure to keep doing it.

They'd flown against the 5th Battalion D Company in a training exercise, and beat them more by luck than anything. It hadn't hurt that they had "borrowed" two of the 5D's mechanics for their first missions, but the "loaners" recently returned to the 5D. Anything the 5E achieved from now on was completely theirs. He liked that.

A massive black SUV with tinted windows was the unknown vehicle in the parking lot.

"Wondered when you'd notice. Now you're going to have serious truck envy too," Nikita sounded thoroughly disgusted.

He just shrugged nonchalantly, but he thought it was seriously cool. Way better than his ten-year-old battered-blue Ford Ranger.

Another vehicle rolled in, a base Hummer.

"When it rains…" Drake recognized the passenger before he climbed out: Colonel Cass McDermott, the commander of the entire Night Stalkers 160th Special Operations Aviation Regiment. Drake hadn't seen him since the night the 5E was formed up right here at these picnic tables a year ago.

"…Oobleck falls from the sky."

Drake looked over at Nikita.

"I'm a Dr. Seuss fan. So sue me."

He laughed at the sudden image of Nikita Hayward as a little girl intently studying a book about a boy trying to save his kingdom from sticky green goo falling out of the sky. The mission to save the kingdom made sense for a future Navy SEAL, but Nikita as a young girl was almost impossible to imagine. Though if she'd worn pigtails as a kid, he definitely wanted to see a picture.

It was difficult reconciling her looks with who she was. By her looks she could have been the nice girl next door. But he'd seen this "girl" swing on a sixty-pound pack as easily as he could sling a rifle, and he'd watched her shoot to kill.

The casual ease of her soft Southern accent would never have flown at Andover Prep—whereas his own moneyed Boston had fit right in. She was like an education in how narrow his world had been before joining the military. But any thought that Southern meant slow or mild was blown away by one look in her brown eyes—she missed nothing of what was going on around her. He could see her mind working every moment behind those eyes.

At the picnic table, Pete and Danielle sat facing the two strangers. The two couples were eyeing each other in silent suspicion. Even Danielle's unflappable Quebecois politeness appeared strained.

"Who are—" Major Pete Napier and the big guy snarled at each other almost in unison. Then they held a glaring contest before both turned their ire toward the Colonel.

Colonel McDermott pulled up a chair and sat at the end of the table as if joining a jovial party.

Lieutenant Commander Luke Altman, Nikita's boss, came to stand on Drake's other side. Not many men could make him feel small, but Altman was even more physically imposing than the stranger. Luke Altman wasn't even the sort of guy you'd eventually call by his first name—he'd never be "my buddy Luke", he'd simply be "Altman" or maybe Lieutenant Commander.

By the time they were all gathered around the table—five of the fifteen Night Stalkers who made up the 5E, two SEALs, the strangers, and the colonel—full dark had descended and, along with it, an Arctic chill that had nothing to do with the balmy September night. The cicadas and frogs seemed to be the only ones happy at the moment.

Drake did his best to pretend that he wasn't trapped between the two ST6 SEALs, but was standing there because he belonged—lined up like they were a Greek chorus to narrate the drama about to unfold. Someone fetched a Coleman lantern and dropped it on the table, lighting everyone in strange shadows. Someone else dropped a case of beer on the table—which meant no flights tomorrow, no battle flights anyway. He wanted to step forward to take one, but neither of the ST6 operators moved, so he stayed put.

"So tell it," Colonel McDermott said to no one in particular as he twisted a cap off a beer.

* * *

"Why?" The big guy snarled back. And in that moment, Nikita knew what he was because no one who was still military would talk back to a bird colonel that way. He wasn't a US Army Ranger, he was a *former* US Army Ranger.

"Mercenary," it came out as no more than a whisper, but his gaze shot to her. His smile built—it was *not* friendly.

"I'm a *contractor*. Always on behalf of my country. My Titan team takes on the messes you military types couldn't handle if your lives depended on it. What are you, missy?" He grabbed two beers, opening one for the woman beside him. Then he tipped his own toward Nikita like he was aiming a gun.

Titan. Probably the toughest military contractors in the business. They were the baddest-ass door-kickers out there. Their rep was good. But still goddamn vigilantes—just ones with a big budget and a government sanction.

Nikita wouldn't mind telling him exactly who she was, but DEVGRU operators didn't go around announcing themselves to the general public—except for a couple of the guys on the bin Laden raid with no sense of silence. Luke Altman had never said a word about it, though she was fairly sure he'd been in on that mission.

This guy needed a different answer.

"I can tell you what I'm not."

"Oh, bring it on," he thumped his beer on the table, then crossed his arms over his big chest and glared at her. In a pissing contest, you didn't look away, so she couldn't see how the others were reacting except for Sugar. She sat close beside the big man and was slowly shaking her head in amusement—as if she knew what was about to land on her companion's head and couldn't wait to watch. Nikita could almost like her for that.

"I'm not from a team that levels an entire South American

villa in a bang so big that I could hear it while stretched out all comfortable in my bunk at Fort Bragg," which was not her real base. That was at Naval Air Station Oceana in Virginia Beach along with the rest of DEVGRU.

That got his attention. He clearly didn't like that she knew that about him. She'd always kept track of the main "contractors." Ever since— No! She wasn't going to think about that.

"No running attacks back and forth across the hills and hollers outside Charlottesville, Virginia. No gun battles shredding up multiple floors of an Abu Dhabi hotel. Y'all Ranger types are great at kicking down them doors. When I go through one, nobody knows I've been there, asshole." Name calling was lame, but she couldn't stop herself. And where the Southern hick was coming from she had no idea. But Nikita knew where her emotional heat was coming from, had spent most of her adult life trying to ignore it. Now she had her past chilled down to the point where it took someone like this over-confident bastard to drag it back to the surface. She didn't appreciate it.

"How the hell do you know all—" The guy shut his trap and glared at her, his eyes momentarily shifting from merely black to carbonized steel. Then he glanced around the circle and she could see him start thinking—finally. She didn't look aside, but had the impression that all of the others were remaining impassive, revealing nothing.

Sugar started to giggle. She tried to hide it in a swallow of beer but didn't make it.

He glared at her.

Sugar broke into laughter and began poking at the man's ribs with a red manicured nail. "She got you, J-dawg. She so got you. That's exactly who you are."

"Shit!" *J-dawg* scrubbed a hand over his face. A smile actually cracked his stern features. "Between Sugar and Nicole, you think I'd have learned about women who know how to fight."

"Just wait until Asal grows up. Our girl will teach you a thing or two about warrior women."

He pulled his companion in and kissed her on top of the head with a surprising tenderness. "She already has, damned kid."

He eyed the circle of people once more, keeping his arm around Sugar's shoulders a moment longer.

This time Nikita let herself look around as well. Of the five Night Stalkers present, two were women and neither of them looked any happier with this guy than she felt.

"Not my best meet and greet, I suppose."

"No shit, J-dawg!" For a moment Nikita wished she was her movie namesake rather than a SEAL. *La Femme Nikita* wouldn't hesitate for a second to unsling the rifle over her shoulder and see how a mercenary liked staring down the barrel from two meters out. That's how welcome he was.

"Only Lily gets to call me J-dawg. Name is Jared. And I'm the only one who gets to call her that. She's Sugar to the rest of you."

"Lotta rules there, *J-dawg*." Not a chance in hell of her cutting a mercenary any slack.

He inspected the circle again, then pointed at the line of her, Drake, and Altman. "What are you three? You sure aren't flyboys."

"Hello! Not a boy!"

J-dawg ignored her and looked to Colonel McDermott, who had apparently been enjoying the whole scene.

"Who the hell are they?"

"The two on the outsides are the reason you're here." Then McDermott scowled at Drake, "The guy in the middle? We'll be damned if we know what he is."

She couldn't tell if Drake was unhappier with McDermott's tease or her laugh right in his face.

Chapter 3

The base commissary had delivered a stack of pizzas. Drake figured that if you ever wanted to know the location of every top secret outfit on a base—and be welcomed into the compound every time—you just had to get a job as an on-base pizza delivery driver.

Drake had managed to stick close beside Nikita as well as snag three slices of fully-loaded pizza to go with his beer, more than sufficient solace for his battered ego. He'd been razzed for the way he spoke—he was an Army sergeant with the speech befitting a West Point officer—more times than the sirens had called to Odysseus, so it was no big deal. Though he could have done without Nikita laughing at him.

Everyone was calling the guy J-dawg and he bristled just like a junkyard dog every time. If the guy would just chill, it would go away, but Drake expected that chilling wasn't in the guy's repertoire.

Well, it might eventually go away for everyone except Nikita. Something had crawled way under her skin.

Drake always did his best to take his own name's advice: Drake the male duck. He just let it all slide off his back. He'd had to bust his ass to make Night Stalkers, but only because *everyone* did to make it into such an elite outfit and he'd wanted in. The rest of life? He did his best to just swim through, and it came easily—especially the women. The women before Nikita anyway.

He'd never gone for the difficult or tricky women before. Wasn't worth the time. For every one of that type, he could mow down a half dozen or more. But something about the DEVGRU SEAL sitting beside him, and her glowering at J-dawg, made him want to work for it this time. He bet himself a twenty that it would be worth it. He wasn't yet ready to bet money on whether or not he'd succeed. All of his normal lines wouldn't do anything but push her away.

"Now, tell it, Jared," the colonel thumped his bottle on the table for attention. He was the only one who hadn't gone all J-dawg on the guy. "Nikita, keep your mouth shut and let the man speak."

"Nikita?" Sugar looked at her with surprise. "Hayward?"

J-dawg looked at his wife, who continued to watch Nikita. "What?"

Sugar just shook her head, "Times I wonder how it is you manage to stay alive, J-dawg."

"Easy. I'm too ornery to die," he spoke around a mouthful of pizza.

"Next time," Sugar informed him, "think before you argue with the first woman to make the cut into DEVGRU."

He stopped mid-chew and narrowed his eyes at Nikita. "No shit? SEAL Team Six?"

Nikita didn't say a word. It was obvious that she didn't like having her name out there.

Sugar must have noticed, "Don't worry, honey. Your secret is safe with me. I only heard because I have low connections in

"You fix it, shooter," the head of Titan glared at her. "Whatever it takes, you goddamn fix it."

"Sure thing…J-dawg."

Sugar's laugh filled the darkness.

Chapter 4

You look like crap!"

"Thanks, asshole."

Drake wanted a do-over. Too late for that. "Haven't you slept?"

Nikita just shook her head and plinked a finger against the computer screen.

Keeping it casual, he wandered over to the counter and made a cup of coffee. The morning light was shining into the kitchen-dining area, at least enough of it to not turn on the overhead fluorescents. The original stark-white walls were now covered with posters, so many that they were overlapping. There were the hot helicopter shots, of course, but mostly it was travel posters: China, Russia, Laos, the Philippines, a lot of Central and South America. The common theme was that the 5E had been to every one of those places on the quiet.

No need for any pinup posters or hot-girl calendars, not with the stunning women of the 5E in the residence. There were a couple big group shots of the 5E and one of them with the 5D out on the Nevada Test and Training Range—*that* was his kind of pinup. Funny, it was only now he noticed that Nikita wasn't in a single one of them. And the one time they'd caught Altman on film it was only half his face over someone's shoulder.

The main part of the room was filled with a big U-shaped table set up for meals and meetings. A cluster of chairs and couches faced a big-screen TV that was mainly used with battle-game consoles—some nights the entire company would get online together and duke it out. The other sidewall was a bank of computer workstations, at one of which Nikita sat sagging in her chair.

"You want?" He held up a coffee mug.

She shook her head, so he wandered back to her and looked over her shoulder.

"What's the issue?"

"The issue is that these GSI contractors kept crap for records. What Titan gave us hardly tells us a thing. I've scratched up a couple of names and an amateur-hour contact method that came right out of a bad movie. Nothing about who they might be, how many there are, nor even a location. I tracked a whole lot of money and more than a little not-approved-for-export military hardware, including several helos rigged with serious armament, but I can't tell where it goes." She dropped back in her chair with a groan.

"Gaps in the data, or a second set of books?"

"No other records according to their guy Parker, and this work is good enough that he's probably right."

Drake set his coffee mug on the table and dug his fingers into her tight shoulders. She sat up straighter and leaned forward enough to give him access around the chair back. Nikita groaned as he dug in. She twisted her neck right and left; he could feel her spine crackling through his fingertips as he eased clenched muscles. He drove a knuckle under her shoulder blade as he pulled her shoulder back with his other hand. Her muscles fought the motion, so he dug harder…and it finally released.

"Oh, yeah," she groaned softly.

"So," Rafe, the pilot of Drake's Black Hawk, came in and hit the coffeepot. "It's good for her. How is it for you, Duck-man?"

"You make him stop," Nikita answered before Drake could tell Rafe to go screw himself, "and I will replace that useless piece of jelly you use for a brain with a month-old cabbage."

Drake took that as an invitation to run his hands down her triceps. Normally his hands could reach right around a woman's upper arms—not even close on Nikita. He dug into the bound-up muscles there, working back toward her shoulders.

"Hey, I'm next," Zoe called out as she wandered into the room. She was a cute little whip of a thing: Scandinavian blond with dark roots, bright blue eyes, and a constantly cheery attitude. She looked like she should be in social media marketing, not flying fifteen million dollars of Avenger stealth drone.

Out of the corner of his eye, Drake could see Altman roll in. Nikita's commander stopped for a long moment and Drake was careful not to look in his direction. Eventually, he crossed behind Drake—without maiming him, which Drake would count as a plus—and hit the kitchen.

By the time half the crew was in, Drake decided he was pushing his luck. With a final squeeze of her shoulders, which she answered with a slight shrug of thanks up against his palms, he let go. His hands tingled with her warmth. He'd have to remember to thank his big sister next time they spoke. Years ago she'd needed a practice subject for her masseuse license and been between boyfriends. Hennie had discussed what she was doing to his muscles aloud, and over the years since, more than a few girlfriends had succumbed with a happy sigh after he applied what he'd learned.

He hadn't given Nikita the massage with any illusions that it was more than a massage, but he still liked how she felt. Again the contrast of the hidden strength and the beautiful woman. He worked out just as much as the next grunt, but he could feel that she lived at a whole other level of fitness. Maybe he'd start hitting the weights harder.

She picked up his coffee mug and took a sip, "Ack! Crap, Roman! How much sugar did you put in this?"

"Two packets." Army coffee, even when he made it instead of one of his teammates who didn't give a damn, was still the bitterest substance on earth. What it was about Army coffeemakers that always scorched the flavor, he'd never figured out.

"Weenie," she razzed him loudly enough for anyone to hear. But she offered him a smile and kept drinking it, so it was hard to feel bad.

Breakfast came together fast. Drake almost asked what he could get for Nikita, but decided that would be pushing his luck. Normally a woman would like the solicitousness, but maybe not a SEAL. Also, it would be like singling her out for being a female—which he'd just done with his massage. He tried to picture himself digging into Altman's shoulder if the SEAL commander had been the one who'd spent all night in the chair. Wasn't going to happen.

During his indecision, Nikita grabbed a breakfast burrito out of the freezer, tossed it into the microwave, then took it and his coffee over to the table. He went for dumping boiling water over a bowl of instant oatmeal and called it good with a fistful of raisins and a spoon of brown sugar. And a fresh cup of coffee—with two sugar packets, by god—he followed her to the table. But rather than sitting next to her, he went for his normal spot, four seats away from Nikita.

He did it because he wasn't thinking about her, at least not that way. Not the way he might have after giving her a massage, or lying in the tall grass while she showed surprising patience in teaching him gun handling. It had taken half an hour before she'd even let him fire a round; it was all about positioning his grip and mental attitude.

You gotta think slower, Roman, she'd spoken softly and patiently—the gentle trainer inside the tough soldier. *Think slower?* Not about Nikita Hayward, he wasn't.

Nope, he definitely wasn't thinking about how much he wished he'd noticed what she was doing and stayed up with her last night so that he could at least pretend that her lack-of-sleep tousled look had been his doing. Her hair had lost parts of its habitual ponytail and was now a soft, enticing cloud about her face.

None of that. He didn't want to get any teasing from the team. More importantly, he didn't want her to get any.

Rafe kicked Drake's chair, hard enough that it wasn't an accident as he sat down in the next seat over. Julian's elbow as he sat on Drake's other side was just as "mistakenly" and solidly planted in Drake's ribs. So much for plan A.

"Hey, I've got this tight spot right here," Rafe pointed at his shoulder.

"I can tell you where the Duck-man's tight spot is," Julian squawked at him from the other side, following it with crappy fake-duck sounds.

The two were the pilots of the Black Hawk that he was gunner on and were always carrying on like they were the funniest guys in the entire Night Stalkers regiment.

"Yeah," he answered Julian. "Maybe I shouldn't be sitting between you two, because I know right where your tight spot is."

Rafe punched his arm while Julian groaned and then the three of them laughed together.

* * *

Nikita watched the guys messing with Drake. It would have been funny if it hadn't given her some thinking to do.

Drake hadn't been like the others. Most of the male crew had come on to her at one point or another, and one of the women as well. Drake had only tried the one cheap pickup line way back at the China mission and then backed off. She wondered if it had been only a joke to protect his reputation. Since then, he'd been a decent guy.

He was too well bred for her taste. She wanted a challenge and Drake was too smooth and slick in his ways—it was obvious what he was: overeducated Yankee far too used to getting his way with women. He even sounded kind of posh, Boston maybe. Nikita rolled her shoulders—they felt seriously better. She'd have protested when he touched her, but his thumbs had landed right on a hard knot from hunching over the keyboard all night. That and the memory of his hand on her thigh last night. He hadn't asked what was messing her up, he'd just helped her back from that edge. Instead of sliding up her thigh, he'd eventually squeezed once lightly in reassurance and then withdrawn his hand with no one the wiser.

Altman dropped into the seat next to her. "Hayward." He made it a question even though it sounded like a statement.

"Commander?" She made it a statement even though it sounded like a question.

He eyed her over his fried eggs, toast, and sausage. "Got anything to tell me?"

Not about the shit going on in her head. "When the team is all sitting down." *Nothing personal going on here. Just business.*

He eyed her for a long moment before accepting her evasion with a nod. The rest of the crew trickled in. They were on no hard schedule today, but it was just 0600 and the whole crew was up. It actually made sense. They'd been in the Philippine jungle for three weeks, always flying at night and sleeping during the day. Philippines to Mother Rucker, Alabama, was twelve hours time difference. Staying awake all night, she was the only one now out of sync with the clock. Usually they all were out of sync, because the Night Stalkers weren't called that for flying in the sunshine.

As the last of them were settling, she grabbed her laptop and turned on the projection screen.

"Target is Honduras."

"A new poster!" Drake chimed in.

"A new…?" She must be more exhausted than she'd thought if she missed the reference. There was no Honduras travel poster on the walls of the 5E common room.

Others were looking around the room double-checking as if they couldn't remember all of the places they'd fought over the last year. Actually, the 5E's operational tempo was high enough, maybe they couldn't.

She turned back to her report.

"Last year a team of heli-aviation wildland firefighters from Mount Hood Aviation received a contract to fight fires in the Honduran countryside. In the midst of their contract, they were shanghaied by an unknown group of men. One of Mount Hood Aviation's Firehawk helicopters—civilian version of a Black Hawk—became instrumental in halting a coup staged against the duly elected president."

"Duly elected," Drake cut in, again breaking her rhythm, "is a tenuous term for Honduran politics. They've had presidents who were polling below twenty percent win elections, perhaps because they were vocal supporters of the army and the military police who were the ones manning the polls." He was right and she could see that many didn't know about the mess that Honduras called leadership.

"That was a prior president. This one *was* duly elected, with only minor complaints from UN observers and very few riots during the voting process. It's no longer our concern."

Drake nodded his concession on that point. She didn't know what to think of him. Was he trying to be helpful or… She was too tired to think about it now. Focus on the briefing.

"Honduras is also the murder capital of the world. This is not a happy country, nor has it been for a long time—again outside the scope of our rules of engagement. It is estimated that thirty members of the coup attempt died that night. How the civilian team in an unarmed Firehawk did this is unclear, and command has the *who* and the *how* marked as need-to-know. By their methodology, I expect it was a Delta Force action."

That earned her everyone's full attention. If she had said that back at DEVGRU command on Naval Air Station Oceana, it would have incurred a buttload of comments about the SEALs now having to clean up Delta's mess because they couldn't finish a job or some such crap. Ever since DEVGRU's founder Richard Marcinko had declared that if there was water in his canteen, that was close enough to the ocean for a SEAL, ST6 and Delta had coexisted uncomfortably on the same tactical turf of elite counter-terrorism.

"Maybe they used fire," Rafe waved a piece of pancake at the screen.

"That's another way to bring the heat," Julian made finger-flexing motions like an air massage, "or you could—"

"Shut the hell up and let Nikita speak!" Drake took advantage of his position sitting between the two and smacked both of his teammates on the back of the head.

They turned to retaliate and Nikita sighed at the unavoidable interruption. She was never going to get this briefing done and it was pissing her off.

Major Pete Napier spoke for the first time, "You two don't shut up, I'm giving you latrine duty."

"No way, Pete. Who would fly our helicopter?"

"The goddamn base janitors for all I care! Now close your yaps and listen."

* * *

They shut up.

Drake thought everyone knew not to antagonize Major Pete Napier before he'd finished his morning coffee, or ever, for that matter. Drake had been planning on getting the guys back for what they'd said about Nikita being his tight spot. Even better? Having the company commander shutting them down.

He smacked them both on the backs of their heads again, just because it felt good. And they wouldn't dare retaliate after Pete tromped all over them.

He exchanged a look with Nikita. There was a deep chill in her eyes, practically Arctic despite their brown color. Okay, maybe he shouldn't have so enjoyed smacking his two teammates. Or maybe that was simply how much she disliked anything that wasn't squared away military.

She returned to her briefing while Drake resisted the urge to cower under the table.

"The people killed were identified as primarily military: shooters and a general, along with a key member of the opposition party. However, based on what minimal information GSI kept, it appears there was a much broader operation in process than merely a military coup toppling a president. I found traces of smuggling: gold, drugs, weapons, people, you name it. Money laundering is probably part of it too, but there is something much broader going on. The Honduran government is helpless in this. And believe it or not, that's all we have to go on."

"And the US government gave it to us, that means small and quiet. We need an intel team on the ground," Altman declared. "Scout detail: me, Nikita, Drake…who else speaks Spanish?"

A couple hands went up around the table.

"No pilots," all of the hands went back down. None of the other three gunners.

"I need another woman. Zoe," Altman pointed to the drone's copilot, whose hand had been among those initially raised, "you're in."

Drake raised a hand.

"What is it, Sergeant Roman?"

"I don't speak Spanish. My languages are Japanese and German."

Altman scowled at him, "Then why do you know about Honduran politics?"

Drake shrugged, "Just one of those things. I followed a rabbit down an Internet hole and emerged days later. Their politics are among the wildest of any country; it makes for great reading."

"You still current on what's happening down there?"

"Yeah."

"Then you're in because who knows what knowledge we'll need. Just don't speak when we're in-country. You and Zoe, me and Nikita. We'll look like vacationing couples and see what we can find out."

Drake wasn't real thrilled with the team pairing, but he was glad to be along for the ride. And he supposed it made sense. The massive SEAL commander and the little slip of a drone pilot would definitely make an odd couple.

"Pete," Altman was moving on. "Find a way to get your team quietly into place. Costa Rica, offshore, something. That's why I'm not taking any pilots. Nikita, hand off your research to Mr. Honduras there and get some sleep. Drake, you find us a way in and where to start."

Pete nodded, "Everyone make sure that your gear, weapons, and aircraft are fully serviced and restocked. By nightfall, we're ready on zero notice. Sophia, grab a senior instructor with top clearance to cover for Zoe on your Avenger drone. Everyone clear?" No one would dare to do more than nod in agreement when Pete Napier used that tone.

Breakfast was cleaned up and everyone had left for the hangar in under five minutes.

Nikita simply sat at the table, staring down at her plate and half-empty mug long gone cold.

Drake cleared it for her.

By the time he turned around, they were alone and she was asleep with her arms sprawled on the table and her head cricked sideways between them.

"Come along, you," he coaxed her back to her feet.

"Didn't sleep on the damned flight back either," she mumbled. Which meant she'd been awake for at least three straight days, maybe four. The last couple days in the Philippines hadn't exactly been conducive to rest and relaxation.

When she almost face-planted over her chair, he slipped a hand around her waist. She did the same and suddenly they were as close as a couple of teenagers walking along hip to hip. Now he was the one who wanted to stumble.

Thankfully her room was on the main floor, though at the far end of the hall. No stairs to navigate.

"Is there anything special I need to know about the files?" He needed something to think about other than Nikita draped against him. His palm had landed on the curve of her hip where it dipped upward to the soft valley of her waist. It wasn't decent behavior, but he wanted to pull her in closer. Taking advantage of her current state, he did. For just a moment he could pretend.

Then she slipped her hand into his back jeans pocket, raising his blood pressure about a jillion points.

"You've got a nice ass, Roman."

He managed to guide her through the door between the common room and the residence without breaking their connection. Unlike the poster-plastered décor behind them, the hall was standard, unremitting, military-base beige with gray carpet, best practices posters that no one had ever read, and a couple too few lights. The place would pass well as a cheap motel anywhere in the country. It wouldn't normally be wide enough to walk side by side, except for their current sideways clench.

"Look who's talking about having a nice ass. I assume that's the main qualification to become a DEVGRU SEAL." He'd certainly noticed hers, he just never thought he'd get a chance to be talking about it.

"Helps if you can swim. You know, SEAL and all. Sea, air, and land is what we are. Can you swim, Duck-man?"

"Only when I'm trying not to drown."

"You're a sad case, Duck-man."

"How's that?" They reached her door, but she didn't seem to be reaching for her keys. Taking a deep breath, he began checking her pockets because if he didn't get away from her soon he didn't know what was going to happen. A few hand brushes, which he did his best not to enjoy (but failed miserably at), located them in her back left pocket.

"You shoot like a heli-weenie. You've got the hots for busty babes in leather. And you barely swim." She appeared to be talking to a poster on how to recognize athlete's foot.

He slipped his hand into her back left pocket and earned no complaints. By the time he had her keys extracted, he knew for a fact that DEVGRU women absolutely *did* have the best asses in the military—even if Nikita was the only one.

"So damn much I gotta teach you if you're going to be a decent man."

"Like what?" he unlocked the door and guided her into her room. Just like his: double bed, small desk, a hand sink, and a dresser. The difference was that she had five rifle cases stacked in a corner and three field packs that he knew from past experience were armor, ammo, and tons of the tech gizmos that SEALs always seemed to have. Her clothes wouldn't fill a daypack.

"Like," she grabbed him by the belt, spun him around, and shoved him back against the door—slamming it shut, hard. "Like I'm tired, not drunk. You want to cop a feel, you better do it right." She reached around his hips and double-grabbed his butt, then she leaned in and kissed him hard when his mouth opened in surprise.

He certainly wasn't going to argue and leaned in to the kiss. Her mouth was spicy with her breakfast and sweet with a taste that must be her own.

Drake went to slide his hand down her spine. A dip of back muscle made her belt span the gap and his hand slid inside her pants instead of outside. He was rewarded with a handful of delightful, cotton-clad muscle.

She hummed with pleasure for a moment. Long before he was ready to stop, she tipped her head sideways onto his shoulder.

"You're a good kisser, Duck-man. At least I won't have to teach you that," each word tapered softer and softer.

The last one never got its final consonant.

"Oh," she roused for a moment, "the password on the file is 'Sweet Cheeks'. Figured you'd appreciate my using Sugar's nickname for you." Then she was out.

"You're not drunk, but you're not conscious either."

She didn't answer. Her body slowly went limp until she was a deadweight leaning into him and pinning him against the door.

"And here I am with my hand down your pants."

No reaction.

"And talking to myself."

Extracting his hand, he pulled her tightly against his chest to keep her from slipping directly to the floor. Doing his best not to enjoy the moment, Drake slowly walked her backward toward her bed. He had to nudge her legs along with his own. They were in the closest contact possible while still clothed, from toes to her chest pressing against his to her hair brushing against the side of his neck. He wanted to twist around and sit back on the bed, pulling her the rest of the way into his lap.

Controlling himself, he lowered her onto the bed. There was no way in hell he was going to be undressing her. It was September in Alabama; she wasn't going to freeze on top of the covers. He undid her boots, then did his best to arrange her so that she wouldn't wake up a dozen hours from now with an intolerable kink.

Drake studied her for a long moment. He didn't feel like a cad doing so, despite her butt-warmth still very real on his palm. Instead, he looked at her just in case he never had the chance to hold her again—he wanted to remember this moment. He brushed her hair out of her face and resisted running his hand down her lovely neck.

Get out while you still can, Duck-man. It was good advice, which meant that normally he wouldn't follow it, but this time he did.

He was back at Nikita's laptop with a fresh cup of coffee a minute later.

When Altman checked in on him shortly after, he was past blushing about the "Sweet Cheeks" password and deep into the file, enough to have a feel for it.

"Nikita did a lot of good prep here," Drake said without turning. "Give me a couple of hours and I should have a handle on it."

Altman thumped him on the shoulder, a lot harder than would be appropriate for a "well done," but Drake wasn't going to point that out.

He'd sometimes wondered if Luke Altman and Nikita were paired off. They communicated on some other level. It might just be a SEAL thing, but he couldn't be sure.

Then he thought about her kiss and was glad that he was facing away from Altman because he couldn't stop his own smile.

Chapter 5

I uncovered a travel reservation in GSI's name," Drake looked very pleased with himself. "They were headed to a meeting in Honduras and apparently the owner liked to travel in luxury."

"I think you found this because you didn't want me to sleep." Nikita had managed five hours.

Though she could have used fifteen, before Altman was kicking the bottom of her bed. "We leave for Miami in fifteen minutes. Shower, dress summer casual but upscale. A light engagement kit."

Light engagement meant she'd only brought two sidearms and one rifle in addition to her clothes, spare ammo, and a diving knife. Upscale was a problem: her nicest clothes couldn't pass and clearly there wasn't time to go hit a wardrobe supply or go shopping. Well, back-of-her-closet shit would have to do.

Once she could stop blinking against the painful midday sun, she saw that it wasn't a Black Hawk waiting for her either. Instead, it was a sleek Bell 429 in a VIP configuration with comfortable armchairs and a minibar from which she grabbed an energy drink. Nikita had gotten ready in ten minutes and still was the last one on board—its rotors were already spinning up. The five leather chairs faced each other: two turned backward and three forward in the wide-windowed rear cabin. Altman and Drake sat in the back-facing seats, Zoe was across from Altman, which left her across from Drake. Rafe and Julian were up front in the pilots' seats.

Drake's smile shifted from pleased about discovering the travel arrangements to tentative in a way she wasn't used to seeing on his features.

It took her a moment to catch up with why. For ten minutes she'd been at a dead sprint getting showered and ready. Now she remembered a tight ass in her hands paired with a jungle-steamy kiss—he could kiss even better than he could shoot his Minigun, which was saying something. She definitely wanted to try that again when she was conscious. But she wasn't going to be admitting that in front of her commander, so she went with a short nod and didn't trust herself with a "good morning."

"Oh my gawd! What is wrong with you people?" Chief Warrant Zoe DeMille rolled her eyes at Nikita as the helo lifted into the air. Zoe wore fashionable bright yellow shorts and tank top. Her white-blond hair was back in matching clips that emphasized the dark roots and she sported big, thick-rimmed round glasses that Nikita had never seen before so they must be merely decorative. Zoe even carried a ridiculously poufy jacket in the same yellow despite the warm day. She looked as if she'd popped right out of a designer magazine.

"What?" For lack of any other options, Nikita had worn a tight black t-shirt and her only skirt, a summer weight in floral blue that her mother had picked out for her ages ago and she hadn't worn since. She had one pair of strap-on sandals. Her running shoes and boots were in the pack she'd stuffed into the cargo area. It wasn't as if there was a whole lot more back at her apartment in Virginia.

She could tell that Drake liked the way she looked, and she liked how he looked in tan khakis and a simple, sky-blue, button-down men's shirt. Again, keeping that to herself.

Altman had dressed the same as Drake, except in dark pants.

Zoe was still in a snit. "We so have to fix this before we land. You people are a disaster. They're never going to buy in that we're wealthy passengers. You said wealthy, right?" she asked Drake.

"Passage for four in something called an Oceansaway Suite aboard the *Oceanwide Whisperer.*"

"Oceansaway suite on an Oceanwide cruise? Oh my *gawd!*" Zoe's Brooklyn accent was coming on strong in her obvious excitement. "I have a cousin who works booking cruise trips. That is awesome. Oceanwide is one of *the* luxury lines."

"There are luxury lines?" Nikita had never been near a cruise ship except during training exercises for taking down a terrorist attack on one.

Zoe smacked a palm against her forehead. "Where have you been, Nikita? Carnival Cruises are for people who want to party. Disney for families with kids. Princess for people who want to be pampered, treated like, you know, royalty. Holland America draws an older crowd who still want to go out and see the culture and not just whatever party or sports thing is going on. Oceanwide is trying to take on Crystal and Silversea for the luxury niche and doing an awesome job of it."

Nikita blinked as she tried to absorb and categorize all that. But at the speed that Zoe talked, she'd already forgotten two of the cruise lines names. She'd thought a cruise ship was a cruise ship.

Zoe glared about the cabin. "Next you're going to tell me that you are planning on landing at Miami International and all crowding into a taxi to the ship. Please tell me that you guys aren't that dense. Pretty please?"

Nikita could see by the look Altman and Drake exchanged that it was exactly what they were planning.

Zoe grabbed a headset, "Julian, we want to land directly aboard the ship—on the ship, not near it, not on the dock, on it. Get in touch with them and find out how to clear the helideck, these ships all have the capability in case they have to do a medevac at sea. And make it so that we arrive during the very busiest loading time. We want everyone to be looking at us."

"No," it didn't sound right to Nikita. "We're undercover. We want *no one* to be looking at us."

Zoe hung the headset back on its hook without changing her instructions to the pilots. "Look, we are immensely wealthy, arrogant, and probably crooked contractors who have totally bought into our own hype. We're arriving in a very pretty helicopter. We want to make a splash, right? We're undercover, but our characters aren't."

"Right," Altman nodded, ending that part of the discussion. He smiled down at Zoe in approval. She was definitely the pixie in this crowd. At five-four she wouldn't even reach Altman's shoulder and she was one of those vibratingly slender types. She almost seemed to shimmer, blurring her own edges until she might disappear if you glanced aside for a moment.

"They won't see *us*," Zoe fluffed her hair to make her point. "They'll see our arrival. Well, they *will* see us if we can't do something about the way you three look."

Again Nikita scanned their clothes but didn't see the problem.

Zoe rolled her eyes.

Altman scowled down at her.

"Okay, good," Zoe pointed a finger at Altman. "That works. Big, tall, handsome, and dangerous-as-hell." She leaned close to pluck the sunglasses from his pocket and slide them on him. She studied him a moment longer, then undid a button on his white dress shirt, then another.

Nikita was surprised that Altman didn't put her down hard for getting inside his personal space, but he just sat there as she ignored his glower and did what she was doing.

"Delicious," Zoe grinned. "Keep that fierce expression. You're the muscle of this outfit. You're the one all of the women will be looking at…and not a one will remember your face, not when they can see enough to imagine your beautiful chest, Luke."

Nikita had never heard anyone call Altman by just his first name, not even the captain who commanded DEVGRU. Nikita also hadn't ever looked at Lt. Commander Altman in that way. He was simply her commander. But now that she did, he looked amazing: muscular, handsome, and lethal. And when he noticed her inspecting him, very fierce.

"You two," Zoe turned to face her and Drake. "You two are a problem. At least you have the good sense to buy designer shirts, Drake."

Nikita looked at it, but it just looked like a button-down shirt to her.

The only sound during Zoe's silent study was the beating of the rotor. Nikita had never been in a non-military helicopter before. On military helos you needed a headset or helmet just in order to survive. This aircraft must have used up half of its useful payload on sound insulation; they didn't even have to raise their voices to speak.

Outside the window, she could see that they soared over the Chattahoochee River and into Georgia, then moments later crossed into Florida where the river bent to the west. On their current line, they'd pass close over Disney World. Maybe she could get them to drop her off so that she could climb on a roller coaster and get some sleep there—at least that would make more sense than what was happening around her now.

She didn't like feeling slow, but the speed at which things were happening… Zoe seemed to be the only one keeping up with them.

And then there was Drake Roman. Now that Nikita's brain was coming back online, she was starting to second guess her actions last night. She remembered how good he'd felt.

Heat crept toward her face until she ordered it to stop as she considered why what had happened had happened. It had started…when? When Sugar had strode out into the field and fused the nerve endings in Drake's gonads. Nikita had wanted to…mark her territory like a *junkyard dawg?* No! That was the merc's style, not hers. She was a SEAL operator, first, second, and third. But she'd—

"Take off your shirts."

"Say what?"

Zoe did point-and-swap motions at Nikita and Drake. "Trade shirts."

Drake shrugged and began unbuttoning his shirt. He was lean-framed, but his chest and abs were soldier-fit. She remembered how he had felt when they were pressed together last night—this morning—whenever it was. Nikita had wanted to simply curl up against him. Actually, that's exactly what she'd done and he'd felt glorious. Now she could see why.

* * *

Drake noticed Nikita's attention. And Zoe's as well, which was flattering, but it was Nikita he'd been trying to figure out since the start of the flight.

Her good morning nod of acknowledgement had been curt enough that he'd wondered if she indeed didn't remember when she'd pinned him against her bedroom door.

Tired, not drunk.

So maybe irritated and wanting to pretend it hadn't happened, which was about what he'd figured on while he dug through the data, then started chasing the leads that Nikita had bookmarked for further research.

But now she also offered a thin smile. No, she wasn't smiling *at* him, but she was definitely smiling.

That in itself was unusual enough for her and he'd found it very encouraging.

As he took off his shirt, she wasn't taking off her own. Instead she was simply watching. When she realized that he'd caught her at it, she reached back over her head and yanked off her t-shirt in a single pull, then held it out.

"A sports bra?" Zoe sounded aghast.

Drake had seen Nikita strip off a shirt that was soaking wet from a hard workout to change into a fresh one before. He'd seen her peel off a shirt, rank with Burmese swamp water, to wring it out. He'd seen her in just a sports bra any number of times.

But never had it been full frontal while sitting toe to toe in a leather-upholstered luxury helicopter. Whatever Zoe thought was wrong, he couldn't find a thing. Nikita Hayward in a sports bra was a vision. Add that to the memory of her kiss and he was a very happy man at the moment.

Nikita took one look at him and heaved her t-shirt into his face.

He handed over his dress shirt with a formal courtesy and couldn't wait to see her in it. He tugged on her t-shirt. Between her strength, his leanness, and their similar height, it wasn't a bad fit. A little tight, but hopefully that made him look more muscular than he actually was. It was warm with her scent. Maybe he'd never give it back, or wash it.

Nikita started to pull on his dress shirt.

"No. Lose the sports bra." At Nikita's fulminating look and Altman's even darker one, Drake wished he'd kept his mouth shut.

"He's right," Zoe agreed. "It will give you the devil-may-care attitude to make up for—" she waved her hand at the rest of Nikita's outfit in disgust.

Nikita and Altman shifted their scowl to Zoe, which was a relief, but it didn't fluster Zoe for a second. She had more spine than he'd expected, facing down a pair of DEVGRU operators.

"Do it!" He'd never have thought that Zoe had a fierce mode, but she did and it was formidable.

Nikita snarled at Zoe, who continued to be unflappable. Then she turned to face him and Altman, "Both of you close your goddamned eyes."

As much as he hated to, he did.

"Cover them!" It was a DEVGRU death-threat tone not to be argued with.

Then there was a movement of fabric just barely loud enough to hear above the rotor's beat and the engines' muted roar.

"Wow, you've got great breasts."

Zoe's exclamation almost had Drake uncovering his eyes to see but he caught himself in time. Then cursed silently, wishing he hadn't restrained himself.

"Seriously, Nikita. What I wouldn't give to have grown a pair like that." Zoe was lean all the way down. It looked very good on her. Why didn't women get that sometimes lean looked awesome?

To distract himself he tried to imagine Zoe with breasts more on the scale of Nikita's, which actually wasn't distracting him at all.

"No, like this," more fabric sounds before Zoe announced it was okay to open their eyes.

Her transformation was so dramatic that Drake almost didn't recognize the woman across from him. She'd let her hair down. It fell neatly to the open collar of his shirt—open far enough down to reveal a very nice cleavage.

Not the serious kind, like Sugar's, pressed together and ready to burst forth at a moment's notice.

Instead, Nikita's cleavage revealed two soft swells of flesh that invited the eyes to linger and—that's exactly what he couldn't do. The shirttails were tied together above her flat stomach, offering more to admire. And she'd rolled up the skirt's waistband until the bottom of the hem barely reached mid-thigh.

Zoe had produced a filmy yellow scarf from somewhere in her outfit and tied it as a decorative sash to hide the roll-up of the skirt. It emphasized Nikita's narrow waist and made it look like she had even more womanly hips than he already knew she did.

Again, he'd admired her legs plenty of times in workout shorts and running shoes. But in the helicopter—with his shoes only inches from her sandals—her legs were astonishing.

"Ro*man*," Nikita's voice was a threat that he was spending too long checking her out, but he couldn't help himself.

"You're gorgeous."

"I can also open the door and drop you into the Gulf of Mexico from five thousand feet." The bad-ass version of flattery gets you anywhere.

"Better than a mangrove swamp," he glanced outside to see that they were just skirting the Florida Gulf Coast as they headed south and if she threw him out it could go either way. "I've never been a fan of mangrove swamps. They're snarly and smell awful."

"Dead man," she left the threat clear in the cabin.

He made a point of scanning her body and outfit one last time, "Totally worth the price of admission." Even if he never got to touch her again, the way she looked was a memory worth keeping.

Chapter 6

Nikita still wasn't sure what to do about Drake as they slid to a hover above the vast white ship. He gave no indication to Altman that they had kissed, which she was thankful for. He was doing a less than thorough job of not staring at her. Every time she turned from whatever merry chatter Zoe was carrying on, his eyes were riveted on her.

Was she so transformed? It was just clothes. Zoe had tried to apply lipstick and other makeup, but Nikita was having none of that no matter how Zoe alternately whined and cajoled.

At first, the direction of his attention had been thoroughly predictable. But as the flight continued, he'd taken to watching her face. He spoke almost as rarely as Altman and she couldn't read what he was thinking.

Or was Drake still thinking about that same splendid kiss that she was?

She welcomed the distraction of their arrival and stared down at the ship. She'd trained on everything from a five-meter rubber boat to an aircraft carrier, but none of that had prepared her for boarding a cruise ship as an elite passenger.

The *Oceanwide Whisperer* cruise ship was halfway between an Arleigh Burke destroyer and a Nimitz-class aircraft carrier in length, but it rose for eight full decks above its tall freeboard. In a space that would house four thousand navy personnel, there would be six hundred passengers and four hundred crew to take care of their every whim. The minimum stateroom aboard would probably bunk four to six swabbies. By the degree of Zoe's excitement about their suite, it was probably bigger than the admiral's quarters on a carrier group.

"How is this real?"

From above she could see a small swimming pool that had an oversized circular hot tub off each corner. There was lounge seating, shuffleboard, and a miniature golf course all surrounded by a running track. The wood-planked bow of the ship, several stories lower, had been cleared and Rafe and Julian settled the Bell 429 into the relatively tiny space.

A line of people were waiting for them. Four stewards, two male and two female, in natty white uniforms, and a fifth, clearly in the lead, dressed in dark blue.

"Remember," Zoe said just before she opened the door. "It's all in the attitude. Drake, you're in charge, flaunt it. Nikita, you're his gal—you're the most desirable woman around. Luke is the muscle. Sorry, that's just the stereotype looks we have and when they're expecting a cliché, I figure what the hell, let's give it to them."

"And what are you?" Altman grumbled at her, truly living his role.

"Me? I'm just the hanger-on, slave-to-fashion, good-time gal. Maybe if she's lucky, moll to Mr. Senior Hunk Bodyguard Luke," she teased Altman.

Nikita had never in her three years serving with Altman seen a woman tease him. By the surprise on his face, it was something he'd never seen either.

"Four stripes on her epaulettes," Zoe whispered as the ship's officer came over to greet them. "It means she's one of the top people on the ship. We've done good."

A customs official barely glanced at their passports, then left as the officer stepped in to greet them just past the edge of the slowing blades. She was a tall, handsome woman with neatly short blond hair.

"I am Norma, the hotel manager. Please allow me to welcome you aboard the *Oceanwide Whisperer*. I'm so glad that we were able to accommodate your late reservation changes."

By the woman's partially masked grimace, Nikita would guess that the former head of GSI may not have been the most welcome of guests.

"I don't think that you'll have any problems of that nature in the future," Drake had picked up on the cues as well, but he shouldn't be too polite. The team needed him to be the arrogant military contractor.

Out of sight, Nikita slipped a hand down onto his butt and pinched him hard.

He reached back and snagged her hand, "It seems that someone is eager to get to our suite after the long flight. If we may?" He made the statement appropriately lascivious, but he also kept her hand tightly clenched in his so that she couldn't attack him again.

The stewards and luggage were already gone.

Over the side of the boat, Nikita could see the long lines of people just now working their way from dock to ship up a pair of ramps. Some simply walked aboard, others gawked and looked terribly like first timers (a good lesson for her in what not to do), and several strode up the ramp as if they owned the ship. However, she noticed that even they glanced up with curiosity as the helicopter climbed back aloft. Then their gazes slid to her and she stepped back so that the tall railing would block their sightlines.

Drake's tug on her hand led her through a hatchway and into a narrow corridor. It was nicely appointed, the rug a pattern of a Victorian drawing room instead of the more expected nautical theme. The walls were actually wallpapered, not painted. It would have been homey if the hall hadn't stretched apparently on to infinity. She suddenly had the creepy suspicion that she'd just stepped onto the hotel carpeting in *The Shining* and that a pair of identical twin ghost girls would appear at any moment farther along the corridor.

She didn't hear a word that the hotel manager said, but she figured that was appropriate for her role. Zoe was right. Their method of arrival had sold them as worthy of the hotel manager's—Nikita supposed that a floating luxury hotel was an apt description of the ship—direct attention in the middle of a busy boarding process.

Nikita started feeling less like a woman lost in a whirlwind of changes she couldn't keep up with and more like a SEAL. DEVGRU operators were like the Bruce Lee quote: *The superior warrior is a normal person, with a laser-like focus.* This role was no different. They were—

She caught a glimpse of herself in a tinted mirror in the elevator lobby. Nikita did a double-take—what the hell had happened to her?

"I know," Drake leaned in and kissed her lightly, then brushed his fingers through her hair. "I dragged you off your favorite beach on no notice. You can fix yourself up once we're in our suite."

Fix herself up? She'd never been a dress-up kind of girl. Not as co-captain of the volleyball team and captain of the decathlon team in high school, definitely not while working for the bastards at Curtis Contracting, and there'd never been a call for fancy attire as a SEAL.

But the woman in the elevator lobby mirror, with her tousled hair, bare midriff, and long legs, was positively stylish.

In the elevator, as they were whisked upward, her instincts checked for lines of attack or escape. Mirrored access panel directly overhead—hard to spot the seam unless you were looking for it. How open was the elevator shaft on a cruise ship and what places could it be used to access if clandestine motion was needed? Then she focused on what was reflected in the panel—a clear view down her own cleavage practically to her belly button. This shirt didn't hide anyth—

"Here we go," Norma announced as the doors whisked open.

Nikita tried to clamp Drake's loose shirt to her chest, but he still held her hand. She went to clench the shirt closed with her other hand, but Zoe slapped it aside.

Altman held a palm across the gap, holding the elevator doors open to let her go first. He'd never done that for her. He'd always treated her as just another SEAL, except for when an assignment called for an undercover approach; then he treated her like just another *female* SEAL. Now he was standing all formally, waiting for her.

—Until Zoe pinched him!

Altman jolted, glared at her.

Nikita was hard-pressed to hide her laugh. Zoe winked at her.

"Check it out," Drake snapped at Altman.

The lieutenant commander didn't appear to appreciate being reminded of his role as bodyguard—especially not with a hard pinch to his butt. He stepped first out of the elevator and made a show of scanning up and down the hallways before signaling that it was okay to leave the elevator.

* * *

Drake was having fun with the role of chief mercenary. For one thing he got to order around a DEVGRU lieutenant commander like a hired gun. Wasn't a merc in the world who could command that kind of clout. It also gave him an excuse to hang on to Nikita's hand even when she kept trying to extract it. *The arrogant merc is in control.*

"Oh yes, this will do nicely." He been on a couple of cruises with his family, but they were definitely on the inside stateroom budget. This suite would do more than nicely, it would do better than any hotel room he'd ever been in.

Coral and crystal motif—the suite wrapped around the front corner of one of the decks high above the bow. It offered a trio of floor-to-ceiling windows with views both forward and to the port side off their private verandah. He was definitely going to be spending time in those loungers. Inside, leather chairs clustered about a dining table. Another seating group included a couch and offered fine views of both the outdoors and the big screen television. A small marble service bar completed the scene.

Through one door was a connecting suite with bed, bath, and a small seating area. Through the other was a master bedroom *en suite* with its own access to the verandah, a writing nook, a bathroom to die for, and a big walk-in.

The air was pleasantly cool despite the hot, muggy Miami afternoon.

"Honey," he pulled Nikita in and kissed her quickly, though not too quickly. It was a fine balance between playing the part and having Nikita or Altman pummel him to the thick mocha carpet. "I know I didn't give you time to pack properly. Why don't you run down to the boutique and get a couple of nice outfits?"

"Excuse me, Mr. Roman," Norma the hotel manager was still with them. "The shops do not open until we are at sea."

Drake blessed his habit of keeping a couple hundred dollars in his wallet emergency fund ever since he got stranded in Poughkeepsie, New York, once when a broken ATM machine had come between him and the last train out for the night. He drew them out hoping that Norma couldn't see that smaller bills made up the rest of his cash.

"I'm sure you can fix that for a special guest like my Nikita," he passed off the money in what he hoped was a properly discreet handshake.

The manager attempted to demur, but finally accepted that the problem could be solved.

"We simply won't charge your account until we're at sea, Mr. Roman." Norma handed them each their boarding passes. "Use these to charge anything to your room. And you'll need them to register your departure and return through security at any port, if you choose to leave the ship."

Drake was impressed that they bore their names and likenesses though he'd only transferred the reservations five hours ago.

"Fine. Fine. Now go, honey. And get something filmy for… later. You know what I like."

Nikita's warm brown eyes were almost jet black in warning about exactly what line he was on the verge of crossing.

"And take Zoe with you," because she was clearly enjoying the whole scene as much as he was. Drake slapped Nikita's behind lightly, because he felt it was in character. It was only as his hand landed there that he remembered how it had felt to hold her last night, however briefly. His mouth went dry at the memory.

The three women exited the suite.

"Well," he watched the door close. "That went better than I—"

A powerful hand grabbed him by the back of the neck. A moment later he was slammed face-first into the wall. The coral wallpaper didn't look nearly as nice from a half inch away.

His "bodyguard" spun Drake around and pressed his forearm hard enough against Drake's throat that he couldn't speak. It was probably a few careful ounces from the pressure needed to crush his windpipe. He tried to swallow, but there was no getting his Adam's apple past Altman's forearm.

"What the fuck are you playing at, flyboy?" Altman's face was only inches from his own and he looked beyond pissed.

Drake tried to breathe in but only managed a lame squeak.

Altman eased of a fraction of an inch.

"She kissed me," he sounded like Elmer Fudd, or maybe Bruce Springsteen after a hard night of drinking. Either way it hurt like hell to manage the three words.

Altman blinked at him twice, then backed off enough that Drake slid down the wall until his feet hit the floor. It was such a surprise, his knees almost went out from under him as well. He hadn't even known that Altman had lifted him up as easily as Perseus lifting up the Medusa's head after chopping it off. For once Drake could sympathize with the mythic monster—it must have hurt even worse than this.

"Try explaining that one again," Altman was still only inches away.

Drake wrapped his hand around his throat, impressed to find it wasn't, in truth, severed. He didn't risk the pain of repeating himself.

"When?"

"Last night," maybe he sounded more like a frog. One that had been the subject of a roadkill accident. "This morning. Whatever it was when I helped her to bed after the meeting. She was too exhausted to even walk."

Altman's fists bunched hard and Drake wondered if he was about to die.

"And you—" Altman ground to halt. He looked even more dangerous than Major Pete Napier when he was angry, and that was saying something—the commander of the 5E didn't take shit from anyone. "You kissed her back."

"I'm not an idiot, Altman. A woman like that kisses me, damn straight I'm gonna kiss her back." Now that his own expiration didn't appear to be imminent, he was starting to get pissed. "What? Am I treading on ground you want for yourself and she won't give you?"

Altman's growl said that maybe confrontation wasn't the best tactic to take with a DEVGRU SEAL. But…in for a penny, in for a pound.

"By the way, I don't give a good goddamn what you think. If Nikita lets me, I'll damned well kiss her again. Up to her, *not* you or me."

Altman managed five stiff steps away until he was standing at one of the big windows. Beyond him lay the MacArthur Causeway and the sprawl of Miami Harbor.

"You got an issue with me, Altman, spit it out."

"It's not you. It's— Shit!" Altman turned and dropped into one of the chairs.

Drake crossed to the bar. Crown Royal XR—the former head of GSI had expensive taste in whisky. He poured two fingers each into a pair of tumblers, decided that Altman wasn't the ice or splash-of-water type, and then poured a third finger into each one. He walked over and handed one to Altman before sitting down across from him.

The whisky soothed Drake's aching throat. The warmth slid down into his stomach.

"Okay, Lieutenant Commander. Better if we have it out now before the ladies get back."

The SEAL stared at his glass a long time before knocking back half of it. "I'm just trying to protect her."

"From who? Me?"

Altman shook his head and continued to study the thick brown carpet. "From herself."

* * *

"Oh my gawd, girlfriend. You *really* don't get it, do you?" Zoe's wink asked forgiveness after the fact for the familiarity.

"What don't I get?" Nikita looked helplessly about the small boutique. Not a black t-shirt or pair of camo pants in sight. She did most of her civilian clothes shopping at thrift stores because they were cheap and what the hell did she care. She almost swallowed her tongue when she glanced at the price tag on a simple white blouse.

The shopkeeper hovered in the background, doing a very credible job of not being irritated at being called to work early by the hotel manager.

"You're with Drake Roman…*the* Drake Roman," she said it loudly, with a tone of awe.

Nikita wanted to shush her, but Zoe didn't leave her a moment to do so.

"I heard that when the military took out that al-Shabaab camp in Somalia, that it was actually Drake Roman and his boys. And that coup in—"

This time Nikita did shush her, with a hand over Zoe's mouth. But Nikita could feel Zoe's smile against her palm and finally caught on. "We aren't supposed to talk about those things."

Zoe looked properly chagrined and they both glanced guiltily toward the shopkeeper, who was listening avidly and doing her best to pretend she wasn't. *And so the rumor mill gets started.* To what end, she wasn't sure, but Zoe seemed to know what she was doing.

"So," Nikita did her best to put her nose in the air. "If I'm with *the* Drake Roman, what should I get?"

"Oh, I'd start here," Zoe's grin was wicked as she reached for a lacy bit of nothing. The La Perla bodysuit didn't even pretend to cover anything. In fact, it was designed to *not* cover *anything.* It also had a four-figure price tag.

"Not a chance!" Then to mask her out-of-character reaction, "I think that Mr. Roman needs to be much nicer to me before he deserves me in that."

"How about for me and the luscious Luke then?"

Nikita couldn't have heard that correctly. "You aren't seriously thinking about…" Or was she?

Zoe put the bit of lingerie back on the rack and shook her head. “No. But it might be fun to shock him with it anyway.”

“Can we be serious about this?”

“Oh, Nikki,” Zoe shook her head. “Clothes shopping is never serious.”

The nickname from her past stopped Nikita’s protests by overwhelming her with memories she didn’t want.

Zoe began walking among the racks and pulling off item after item. When she had an armful, she guided Nikita back to the small changing room. “Start with these.”

“Start?” There were more fancy clothes here than she’d worn in an entire lifetime.

Zoe ignored her as she pushed her into the changing room. Thankfully, she didn’t stay after hanging up the items she’d grabbed. Nikita had been sufficiently mortified by the comment about her breasts on the helicopter.

At the threshold, Zoe looked back over her shoulder. “It’s obvious you haven’t slept together yet.” Thank god she kept her voice down this time.

Nikita resisted the urge to ask how she knew that.

“How good a kisser is Mr. Drake Roman?”

Nikita sighed, “Very good.” She could still remember the fire that had lashed between them as they’d held each other hard. Judging by that, sex with Drake would be very rough and tumble, and very good.

“Crap! I should have known. Sooo envious!” And she was gone.

Nikita picked up a flowing silk caftan of tropical colors with a plunging neckline; definitely no bra could be worn with this one, that would be barely long enough to cover her underwear. How was a woman supposed to sit in such a dress?

It turned out, that wasn’t the worst of the options Zoe had chosen. Behind the caftan hung the black La Perla bodysuit.

* * *

"It's not my story to tell."

"Bullshit!" Then Drake wished he'd spoken more softly. The whisky hadn't numbed his sore throat nearly enough. "You try to kill me, then tell me I don't get to know why. Spill it, Altman."

"You this much of a pain in the ass to your commander, Roman?"

"Are you kidding? You've flown with Pete Napier. Do you think I'd be still walking around if I talked back to him?"

"But *I* get your shit?"

"He never tried to kill me either. So he gets a pass. You don't."

Altman stared down into his glass. He hadn't touched it after that first big swallow.

Drake sat back and took another sip of his. Was this what it felt like to be Altman or Napier? Assured, calm, drinking a quiet whisky in a luxury suite? Well, maybe not the last. And looking at Altman, maybe not the first two either. But an odd contentment had come over him, as if for only the second time in his life he was in the right place at the right time.

The first time had gotten him into the Night Stalkers. He'd been a decent gunner for the 101st Airborne. Then the Night Stalkers had come up short a man when one of their crew chiefs stepped off his bird and onto a landmine in an area that had supposedly been cleared. They'd needed a new gunner for a mission that night and he'd been available. Once he'd had a taste of what it was like to fly with them, he'd fought like a madman to get in. They were the best people he'd ever flown with. It took him two more years before he flew with them again, but he'd made it.

He wondered where that feeling of rightness would lead this time. He'd only had it that once, so banking on it turning out well might be presumptuous, but he'd bet on a good hand until someone forced him to fold.

"Nikita comes from a shit past," Altman finally ground out.

Drake's contentment froze in that moment and the whisky suddenly churned in his guts. Someone touching her who wasn't—

"Not like that," Altman was looking right at him. "Though I like seeing that you're the kind of man that would piss off."

"Damn straight!"

Altman just nodded before continuing. "Got in with a merc outfit. A bad one. One that didn't like spending the extra money on intel, even though she had the lead right in her hand but needed a payoff they wouldn't give her. Got her dad and her fiancé killed in a single mission."

"Oh, crap!" That sure explained her reaction to the GSI guys.

"They were a lean outfit, *so* lean that she was also on the comms when they went down. Talk about a lady who's had a world of hurt…" Altman knocked back another big swallow of his drink.

"That's what gave her the drive to take on ST6 selection." Drake knew it was true even as he said it.

Altman nodded. "Volunteered Navy. SEAL track from day one. Before she made it through boot camp, someone gave me the heads-up to come watch her. I did. You know from making it into the Night Stalkers that it's ninety percent mental."

"And ninety percent brutal." For the Special Operations teams, being motivated or excellent wasn't enough—you had to be both.

"You got that right. She's got it, that indefinable *it*. But I wasn't kidding when I said to watch your goddamn step with her. There's something inside that's hurt and angry, and real goddamn dangerous. She's got a hard control of the former and can use it to direct the latter where I need it. You crack that barrier and screw up one of my best people and you've got me to answer to. We clear?"

Drake considered the idea that Nikita wasn't as tough as she looked. That wasn't right. She was tougher. Her strength ran all the way to the core, or SEAL Team 6 wouldn't have let her in to begin with.

"We're clear. But she's—"

And he heard the door open behind him. He glanced over his shoulder as sandals slapped across the suite's marble foyer. Two women laughing together. At least someone had been having a good time.

They stepped into view and Drake jolted to his feet.

Nikita wore a…he didn't know what to call it except amazing. Two sweeps of pleated white fabric swept around either side from behind her neck. They rode over her breasts and crisscrossed on her abdomen before disappearing around the back. A flirty black skirt barely reached mid-thigh. She was completely covered, but with deep cleavage, a bare midriff, and long legs.

"You were right, Zoe. Look at them."

Drake couldn't turn away to see Altman's reaction.

"Do a spin," Zoe instructed Nikita with an elfin laugh.

Nikita twirled about. The only thing covering her back was her hair, reaching only a few inches onto her shoulders. The two sweeps of fabric actually melded into the dark skirt at the base of her spine.

Drake strode up to her, "Remember how I said you were gorgeous?"

Nikita nodded uncertainly.

He slipped his hands around her waist and onto that beautiful bare back. He whispered for her alone, "I lied. You're way beyond gorgeous."

* * *

Nikita didn't know what to do with him.

Drake had always been a pleasant enough, smooth-mover of a guy who had the added benefit of being an excellent gunner and crew chief. But the man confidently holding her in the cruise ship's luxury suite was someone else entirely.

Without forethought or intent, she leaned into him. She'd never needed anyone to lean on, but somehow, leaning on Drake Roman felt…safe. Not that she'd ever needed safe.

When he kissed her, she eased into it. Unlike last night's hot and heavy, there was a sweet tenderness to it.

"Yes!" Zoe's whispered cheer, which she probably would have accompanied with a fist pump if her arms weren't full, was enough to pull her back from it. But the warmth and peace stayed with her as she eased away.

Altman was watching her carefully. She couldn't read his thoughts but his look made her want to hide her face against Drake's shoulder, so instead she retreated another step.

"There's more," she said to fill the awkward silence and signaled to the shopkeeper, who had been thrilled to help Zoe carry the purchases. They'd probably made the shop's quota for the whole trip in a single go. She'd finally thrown the last of her caution to the wind when Zoe had suggested they could just bill the whole shopping trip back to Titan and J-dawg wouldn't dare argue. She'd liked the sound of that. Even better, he'd probably whine the whole way, and then they could sic Sugar on him to get him back in line. On that premise, they'd made a few purchases for Zoe as well.

"This way," Zoe flashed a big smile, then led the shopkeeper into the master suite.

"I'll take the top one," Nikita snagged the first of several dress bags out of the shopkeeper's hands. "I got this for you, Drake."

She'd bought it as part of the role they were playing, but now it seemed more intimate and personal. Nikita slipped the white Armani jacket from the black plastic and held it out, open and ready for him.

Drake turned and slipped his arms in. She tugged it up onto his shoulders and ran her hand down the lines of the back. They'd guessed at his size and done well.

When he turned, he was dazzling. He still wore her tight black t-shirt and tan khakis. Combined with the white jacket, he looked both wealthy and dangerous. With the power of his light kiss still on her lips, she was having trouble meeting his eyes.

"Oh, the fit is perfect, I am so glad," the shopkeeper inspected Drake with a professional eye as she came back into the room. "No need to take it to our tailor." But it wasn't only the jacket she was looking at. Whether it was because of how handsome he looked in the jacket or if she wanted to see the *notorious Drake Roman* was unclear. But he definitely made an impression.

Drake reached for his wallet.

"Oh, there is no need, Mr. Roman. Your lady-friend has been most generous already." She'd signed a big tip on to the room charge just for J-dawg.

As she left the suite, there was a small gasp of surprise, then the shopkeeper spoke softly. "Good afternoon, Arthur." Her tone, which had warmed up the instant Zoe had gathered a third of the shop into the dressing room and had remained cheerful and friendly throughout, went distinctly cool.

"Arthur" rapped his knuckles on the open door. "Good afternoon," he stepped into the suite without so much as an invitation. He was a lean man in a sharp suit that looked inappropriate for the setting—as if he was trying too hard. His overly cheery smile faded as he inspected the four of them carefully, instantly dismissing everyone except Drake.

"Yes?" Drake managed a decent mix of arrogant and curious.

"I'm sorry. I was expecting someone else. I had understood that this was Global Security's suite." But he didn't back out. Global Security International, GSI. Arthur had just said the magic pass phrase.

"*Was* is the *operative* word," Drake replied without even an eyeblink of hesitation. His voice chilled like the haughty person he was supposed to be and Nikita wanted to warn him about doing too much.

She'd spent the night deep in GSI's files, so she knew the source of Drake's reaction. Not only mercs, but by the end they'd added kidnapping of women and children to their list as part of a blackmail attempt.

She slipped her hand around Drake's arm to caution him, but decided that playing the dumb brunette was to her advantage at the moment.

Arthur blinked slowly though she could see his mind working quickly. "A...change in circumstances?"

"Let me just say that after our...*acquisition* of GSI, their people are no longer a factor. I'm now looking out for their business interests." Who was this man she was holding on to? It certainly wasn't Drake Roman the pleasantly thoughtful Night Stalker gunner. This was a dangerous man who could easily command an entourage and stage a lethal takeover of a competitor.

A part of her wanted to shove him away, disgusted with the merc attitude she knew all too well from her days at Curtis Contracting. But another part of her wanted to hold on tight and stay close to his unexpected power.

The ship's horn blared to life somewhere above them, a muted roar through the closed windows.

"Excuse me. Departure is always an exciting time aboard a cruise ship and I should leave you to enjoy it. Especially as you are traveling," he nodded toward Nikita, "with a friend. But perhaps I may interest you in attending an art auction during your cruise," he produced a card. "The gallery is always open for viewing and the first auction will be tomorrow evening."

Drake took the card, glanced at it, then dropped it on the bar counter instead of pocketing it.

"We'll consider it," then his dark and dangerous mood shifted. He kissed her lightly on the cheek. "I am completely at the mercy of whatever whim takes my lovely lady."

"Of course, sir," Arthur agreed smoothly and then withdrew.

Drake led them all out onto the wrap-around verandah. He leaned heavily on the forward railing, which offered a sweeping view of the dock and the many islands that dotted Miami's harbor. Blue sky, shining water, islands packed with luxury homes, it was quite the scene. A glance down revealed dozens upon dozens of other passengers doing the same thing they were, leaning on their own suite's verandah railings to watch the busy harbor.

"Did I do okay?" There was the Drake Roman she knew. She'd been right to hang on to him.

She kissed him on the cheek this time and whispered, "You did great!" It was an intimate moment, and one she rather enjoyed.

* * *

Altman's slap on his back didn't dislodge Nikita's hold on his arm, which was good or it would have knocked him over the railing and into the ocean far below.

"Next time I need an undercover badass, you're my boy," Altman almost smiled.

"Amazing what three years in the Yale drama department can do for you."

"If you went to Yale, why aren't you an officer?" Zoe was standing on Altman's other side.

"Because I never went back for year four. I enjoyed acting. I enjoyed actresses especially," then he felt stupid for saying that aloud. He was going to need to negotiate an unlimited do-overs license with Nikita. "But I wasn't anything special and I spent an entire summer getting cut at auditions in Seattle just to prove it. That's a major theater town and I didn't get a single casting—only got a handful of callbacks."

"Theater to military?" Nikita's voice had changed. It wasn't just like she was continuing the role from the suite; it was warmer. As if she was genuinely interested.

"Granddad on my mom's side flew Hueys in Vietnam. Was flying lumber in Seattle—picking hard-to-reach timber out of the deep forest with an Erickson Aircrane. While I was losing all those auditions, I stayed with him and Grandma. Every night he'd tell me stories over a beer. On the days I couldn't line up a tryout, he'd take me aloft with him. Liked it better than a whole lot of stage doors slamming in my face."

A trio of dockhands were gathered on the concrete dock in bright yellow vests and hardhats. Nearby was a massive bollard with a six-inch-diameter line run around it and back to the ship. The dockhands were just waiting. Finally one answered a radio call, then the three of them walked up to the heavy line and flipped it off the bollard and into the water. The ship began cranking it aboard.

Then with another horn blast and a low rumble that he could feel through the handrail, the dock began moving away. The cruise ship was so massive that it felt as if the island was gliding aside and not them. But he was. For better or worse, he was trapped in his new role.

"And now I've gone from military to mercenary."

"Military contractor," Nikita corrected him. "They never call themselves mercenaries."

"You mean *we* never call ourselves that."

In answer she continued to watch the dock moving away from the ship but squeezed his arm where she clasped it, either in friendly conspiracy or as if seeking strength against something she despised.

"What do you make of your new friend Arthur?" Zoe was clearly used to the departure process and didn't spare it a glance.

"He's hitting the Internet on us right now," he and Nikita practically spoke in unison. "That's why he pulled back and retreated," Drake finished.

"Nope," Zoe shook her head. "Not us. He's researching *you,* the great Drake Roman. He doesn't know the rest of us from a hole in the wall."

"Or care," Altman agreed. "You saw how he ignored us, which is good. Let's keep it that way."

"Perfect! Is it too late to get the helo back?" Drake searched the sky though they were probably halfway back to Rucker by now.

"What's wrong?"

"What's wrong? Arthur is going to run a search and it will go *ping!* Sergeant First Class Drake Roman, 160th SOAR, 5th Battalion—"

"Dishonorably discharged eleven months ago," Altman cut off his rant. "Misappropriation of government property, to wit: four million in sanctioned military hardware including air-to-ground Hellfire missiles and Miniguns."

"I did what?" Drake tried to breathe. "A dishonorable what? But I never—"

"Apparently you pulled a lot of high-end strings and called in favors so that you didn't go to Leavenworth along with your fellow conspirators. He can check the back news articles, it actually did happen and there were parties unnamed who were 'arrested and released.'"

"But—"

"Instead you formed DR, Inc. According to your hype, Drake Roman can *doctor* anything anywhere as long as it's military. Parker, Titan's data geek, has been planting wild and nefarious exploits for DR, Inc. in all of the wrong places. You also have a website. If Arthur knows where to look, he'll find out that you can be very bad news."

Nikita bumped his shoulder with hers, "It's not our first rodeo, Drake. We know how to set up a cover fast."

"Couldn't you at least have changed my goddamn name?"

Altman shrugged, "Easier to work with your own name. Your civilian passport remains valid. Due to the short notice, there wasn't time to change it anyway."

Drake stared out at that the blinding waves of Government Cut and the Atlantic Ocean beyond.

Easier? If Granddad heard about this, he would stroke out.

"Ye-ah!" Zoe placed her vote and Nikita knew it was a lost cause.

Drake looked both sophisticated and, with the shadow of a beard, rugged. It made her remember more about his kiss some forever time ago like this morning. Hot and rugged.

"My question though," Drake leaned toward Altman in a conspiratorial whisper, "is how did we luck out to get to escort the two most beautiful women on the ship?"

Altman's answer was an equally conspiratorial fist in the ribs—except Drake winced like it actually hurt.

* * *

The pre-dinner mixer in the Wave lounge included the occupants of the ship's eight high-end luxury suites, the captain, and Norma the hotel manager. It also included a hosted, high-octane bar and a small flock of stewards constantly circulating with tiny *amuse-bouches:* oysters served in those white Chinese soup spoons with a Thai salsa, prosciutto-wrapped shrimp on tiny metal Neptune's tridents, eggrolls the size of his pinky with more flavor than any he'd ever had before.

Drake opted for whisky, in keeping with the Crown Royal XR that had been delivered to his room, and handed Nikita a flute of effervescent champagne that practically made her giggle. Altman had somehow talked a beer out of the bartender, and Zoe had the champagne as well.

He wasn't sure what he was supposed to be saying to anyone. Oddly, it was the deeply reserved Nikita who took the lead in the introductions.

"Drake is in project management, specializing in conflict resolution at the international level."

"Oh, Drake took me to Rio last month. He had work there, not for me to know about, of course. I stayed in the Fasano Rio spa—really, you must go. The Filipino face massage is to die for.

After that we went to one of those nature reserves and stayed in a treehouse where the only way in or out was on a zipline."

"Drake is in international transport of specialized equipment. We just returned from Kenya. If you ever need to get away, you simply must rent Kilulu Island. The villa is charming. It has a pool, a full staff, and the whole island is so very private." She actually managed a coy look and a blush as she told that one.

He wasn't the only one with an acting background. Nikita was practically dripping with brainless, fawning jetsetter—until he wondered quite who she was.

By the time he could get her aside, he'd been introduced twelve different ways to stockbrokers, bankers, an airline executive, mistresses, and somebody's boy-toy. He could overhear Zoe doing the same thing in her effervescent tone as she sometimes hovered at Nikita's side and other times at the silent Luke's.

"What happens when they compare notes?" He kept his whisper urgent.

"They already are," Nikita replied with a perfect placidity, slipping back into her normal self, which was a relief. At least the cool and soft-spoken SEAL he knew, even if he didn't understand her any better than the flirty airhead.

"But—" Drake had been saying that a lot lately. "I'm not—" But he was. Every description had, in a way, said the same thing. However, Nikita had said it so many different ways that it was making his head spin. He looked at his glass. Still half full, he'd been careful to pace himself. Maybe drowning his woes in a glass would be a better choice.

"Everyone here now knows that you're an international man of mystery who is wealthy, can afford to send me to the highest-end spas and resorts—which I know about because Mom likes watching the travel channels and we do it together whenever I'm home—while you do dangerous, secret work. We're giving you an instant reputation."

"For what reason? Wait," the pieces began clicking into place. "Because word has a chance of getting back to Arthur, the art auctioneer, and whoever his cronies are."

"Precisely; can you imagine a circle of people more likely to buy his 'art'?"

Drake scanned the room. His mom was a banker and his dad a named partner in one of the major Boston law firms. Dad came from old money, which had opened the doors to Boston society. The joke was that none of the four of them had enjoyed the society events, but Dad's parents were deeply enough rooted in it that his family couldn't avoid attending.

Drake could practically hear his sister Hennie giving them a running commentary on each person.

I know *that black coral is illegal, but I just had to have it. So I had Henry purchase a vintage piece at ten times the market value.*

My yacht may be twenty feet shorter than yours, but mine has a chef trained by Mario Batali himself.

Oh, the tourists on Martha's Vineyard are just hideous this year, so we've rented a villa in Nice.

Their family was always the slightly odd group giggling among themselves during the various mandatory outings.

Hennie would have a blast with this crowd. Old men with jewel-bedecked twenty-somethings. Widows and widowers on the prowl for someone of the proper class—*money.* One bruiser who just had to be with the Russian mob. There were only two couples who looked happy to be together and were making a real point of ignoring everyone else in the room. Under normal circumstances, they would be the ones that Drake would gravitate toward.

These were not normal conditions.

"Mr. Roman?" Drake tried desperately to remember who was the man now shaking his hand.

Banker—Ranker— "Mr. Rankin." Drake resisted the urge to

crush down on the hearty handshake of someone who had never picked up anything heavier than a martini glass.

"I wonder if we might have a moment," he glanced sideways at Nikita. When they'd first been introduced, he'd barely glanced at Nikita despite how incredible she looked. Maybe the man only made love to his money.

Drake tried to think of a way to keep Nikita at his side, but her presentation of being his mistress-of-the-moment had been so thorough that he couldn't come up with one. At a loss, he kissed her briefly, patted her bottom just to mess with her head, and told her to go mingle.

"I have a competitor that I was hoping I might talk to you about."

And I have an FBI contact that I'm probably going to be reporting you to.

* * *

Nikita was going to have to do something about Drake's fascination with her behind. The gentle pat to send her on her way, the playful slap to send her shopping, and the way he'd grabbed it hard when they were kissing in her room back at Mother Rucker. He was confusing the crap out of her…which was half the reason she'd been playing the empty airhead. He wanted to treat her like that in public, *fine!* She'd *be* that in public.

It fit her chosen role, so why was it irritating her?

Only partly because it now meant that she couldn't accompany him as he and Rankin moved off to stand at a window and look out at the sunset as they talked.

It also thrust her once more into the social whirl that was like nothing she'd ever been through. Without Drake to hang on to, she felt lost—adrift on a sea that had rules she didn't begin to understand. Her attempts to latch herself on to Zoe were intercepted by many of the men. Several of whom had no compunction about talking to her breasts. What they wanted was only too clear. She barely resisted correcting their habits with a hard body slam to the floor.

Others talked to her breasts but they talked about Roman, seeking more stories. She reached into her research of GSI's files and embellished liberally until she felt like she was spilling tales of fictional supervillains. Nikita made sure that her stories at least half the time conflicted with the first round of stories.

You're going to treat me like an airhead, Roman, that's what I'll deliver. On the plus side of that role, it meant that everyone would underestimate or even totally ignore her until it was too late.

She finally forged her way to Zoe.

"Refuge!" she pleaded.

"You bet, Nikki." Zoe slipped her hand around her waist, causing Nikita to put her arm around Zoe's shoulders and feel the comfort of a friend. "What do all of those bad boys want? I mean, I saw how they were looking at you."

"Half want to dial my escort service, even with their wives or mistresses or whatever they are standing right next to them."

"No brainer with the way you look. How about the other half?"

Nikita looked about the room. There were a number of very pretty women in the room. Though much of the beauty seemed overly studied. The only reason she stood out in this crowd was that she wasn't bone thin. "The other half want to know what Roman really is."

"And what is he?" Zoe's voice was teasing. "Other than hunk handsome?"

"He certainly seems to like patting my behind."

"Smart man," Zoe agreed as if that wasn't somehow outrageous. "Your boss won't touch me."

For a moment she thought Zoe meant Drake and decided it was a damn good thing he didn't take any liberties there or she'd bust him a good one. Then she realized that Zoe meant Luke, which was totally outrageous to even think about.

She had to look around the lounge twice to spot him.

It was a SEAL tactic, finding exactly the right tempo of the room, then match it to become invisible. He stood close by one of the exits looking quietly casual by himself. But Nikita knew the stance: he was on alert for anything out of place. From his position by the exit, he had a clear view of the entire space as well as the two other entry points, both currently blocked by brass standards and a loop of red velvet rope to keep this a private party.

His eyes locked on her for a moment in one of his scans, then he barely nodded before continuing on about the room. Altman was lucky. Of them all, his role alone matched who he was. Whether it was the bodyguard or the SEAL watching the entire room, the feel was the same.

Nikita was feeling much closer to a psychotic break.

Dinner was no better. Normally when she was undercover, she and another SEAL were paired to simply look normal walking down a street together, observing security they were going to have to bypass, defenses to surmount, and targets to infiltrate.

At the dinner table she had to play the merry hostess and would have failed miserably without Zoe's assistance. Drake appeared completely at ease with the situation. Fine, let the two of them take the lead role and she'd go sit beside Altman in his forbiddingly too-dangerous-to-even-approach guise. Except she couldn't.

Dinner led to reserved seats in the large auditorium that could seat half the ship's guests to listen to a horrendous mashup of Cubano salsa and Jamaican steel drums that everyone seemed to inhale as the new sound of the century. Then quiet drinks at the late night piano bar—seats around the piano instead of back at one of the shadowed tables, of course.

"What are we doing, Drake?" She'd had five hours of sleep in four days, more drinks than she typically had in a year other than a friendly beer or two after a mission, and she was ready to collapse.

"Being visible," he whispered under a predictable but not unpleasant version of *What a Wonderful World.*

"Can we be invisible now?"

"Sure thing, sweetheart."

"You sound like Will Smith in *Men in Black.*"

"I was trying to sound like Humphrey Bogart."

Nikita considered laying her head down on the grand piano they were seated around and weeping.

"Got it. Come along." Drake slid his arm around her waist and helped her to her feet.

Nikita didn't know what was going on. Endless corridors, elevators, more corridors. Normally she could dig deep and gut out anything. With Drake taking control, she didn't need to maintain. As a result, she ended up in a head-wobbling space.

When she looked at the woman in the lobby mirror this time, she was practically lying against the handsome stranger that had replaced her Night Stalkers crew chief. Her head rested on his shoulder and, surprisingly, was content to remain there. His reflection turned enough to kiss her on top of the head before the elevator arrived.

If she hadn't known the sunny and sexy woman of this afternoon, she knew the elegant, clingy woman even less, but couldn't rouse herself to protest.

When the acceleration of the elevator threatened to take out her knees, she let it. The handsome warrior swept her into his arms.

In the mirror in the elevator's ceiling, she appeared helpless yet content to merely nestle.

"We pushed her too far. Damn it but I'm an idiot!" she could as much feel as hear what he said. "Five hours sleep in four days. I just wasn't thinking."

"We all should have seen it," another gruff male voice replied.

"Almost there, Nikki," someone whispered encouragement from close by. Nikki. The last person to call her Nikki was…

"I don't want to remember," she turned her face into the shoulder of the warrior who carried her and hung on.

"Then don't."

A door, another. In moments the dress was gone and a nightshirt had taken its place. One last time strong arms lifted her and lay her down on soft sheets.

The last thing she remembered was a kiss on her forehead.

Chapter 8

Where am I?" Nikita was used to waking up in strange places: barracks, barns, blown-out buildings they were hiding in, African huts, and the backs of military transports on sea, air, and land. She couldn't begin to make sense of luxurious sheets, fine wood furniture, and the crystal vase on her night table—she had a night table—filled with tropical flowers. That was the strangest thing of all.

She flopped over and was greeted with a sweeping view of an island and turquoise-colored waters. Sheer curtains fluttered in a sea-scented breeze. And when they fluttered aside, she could see Zoe stretched out on a lounger in the sun, wearing a bikini that was as scant as she was.

Nikita grabbed sunglasses, then stumbled out and flopped into a chair on the suite's verandah. It offered her a bird's-eye view of Key West. She'd flown out of the Naval Air Station here on any number of missions and recognized the unique look of the town from above. The cruise ship was far and away the tallest building in town. The palm-lined streets were a breezy and comfortably warm mid-seventies—because that's the temperature the town always was.

"How long was I out?"

"What day is this?"

"Ha, ha, ha."

"Well, you've missed Key West. They'll be reboarding in an hour or so. You've been out for fifteen."

Nikita plucked at her long nightshirt, "Who?"

"Drake, but I made him promise not to peek."

"But he did anyway."

"I'm not so sure. He was so busy being pissed at himself for running you into the ground like that, I'm not sure he was noticing anything."

"At least it wasn't Altman. That would have been too mortifying."

"Besides, you don't get to have both men."

Nikita raised her head enough to inspect Zoe, but she was still flat on her back, working on her tan. "You're going to burn." That was a safer topic than whether or not Zoe was actually interested in doing more than joking about LCDR Altman.

"Wearing SPF-gazillion. Don't get much sun in a drone coffin."

The cargo containers that housed the ground-station controls for flying drones had always been called coffins, which Nikita tried not to see as morbid.

"Besides, I always was super-fair skinned. That's why I finally gave in and went blonde, at least mostly. I know healthy tans are out, but pasty white is a sad way to be, too."

"Where are the men?"

Zoe flapped a hand toward shore, "Drake didn't want to leave you, but I've seen Key West a couple of times. So, I kicked him out before he woke you to ask if you were sleeping. If they're doing their jobs, they're out there being manly and spreading more rumors. If they pick up any women who aren't us, I'm going to be very upset."

Nikita decided that she would be, too. Very upset. And that was an irrational enough thought to force her back to her feet.

"I need a run."

"They have a track here, up on the top deck. A hundred and fifty meters."

"Twenty seconds a lap? I'd get dizzy."

"It's a jogging track, probably cluttered with couples strolling hand in hand and calling it exercise. They do have weights and treadmills."

"A gym. Excellent!"

"A fitness center."

"Doesn't matter," Nikita yanked on Zoe's ankle hard enough to almost pull her off the lounger. "You're going, too."

"No! I want to become fat and lazy. That's what cruise ships are about."

"I thought they were about Arthur and the Honduran bad guys."

"Crap!" Zoe clambered to her feet. "Reality sucks."

* * *

Drake didn't know when he'd ever been so happy.

Zoe's three-letter text, "Gym," when he was just back aboard through security, sent him scrambling upstairs to change. Once their suite's butler had told him where to find the fitness center, he'd tracked them down.

After a day like today, doing a workout with Nikita was exactly what the doctor ordered—maybe, if the gods were smiling on him, they'd have a wrestling mat. Then again, she was SEAL-trained in hand-to-hand combat, so maybe not.

Because the project was so compartmentalized, McDermott hadn't wanted to involve the other agencies directly. So he'd sent a very simple request for any information on outstanding GSI operations in Central America. That was enough to make someone in intel look at what had actually been going on—then Internal Affairs had taken over and slammed a lockdown on all information requests. Some oversight committee landed at the center of a witch hunt, which had shuttered all further information that might have flowed to the 5E.

The only message to escape the fray was a single and utterly useless note: *No Global Security International operations authorized outside Southwest Asia region.* All that told him was just how far off the reservation GSI had gone. Actually, it also told him they were entering the Minotaur's Labyrinth of the wholly unknown monster. Now it was only a question of how soon the beast GSI had created would try to devour them.

Deciding that they'd be better off drawing out the beast, he and Altman had spent the entire day probing the ship's elite passengers under the casual circumstances of Key West. Drake had never spouted so much drivel in his life, not even when playing the mad and ridiculous constable in a summer stock production of Shakespeare's *Much Ado About Nothing*. They'd learned nothing. Not from Rankin the banker, the Russian mobster, or any of the others.

As to the cruise line's officers, his fabricated reputation had proceeded him and they all clammed up tighter than a submarine about to dive for cover. Hopefully Altman on his own would do better, though Drake doubted it.

He finally locate the Fitness Center in the stern of the ship a couple of decks down. He had to go through the spa—past beauty salon, massage tables, the "thermal center" with its hard tile couches, treatment rooms where women lay with gray or green facial masks—to find the workout room. Along the way he'd had to dodge several particularly fit men and women in ship's uniforms asking if he wanted this treatment or that. Perhaps a sauna.

In the exercise room, after being briefly dazzled by the sweeping view of Key West, he spotted Zoe spinning a cycle exerciser faster than a hummingbird's wingbeat.

"Where's Luke?" was her idea of a greeting.

"Still ashore, drinking with a group of the ship's officers. Telling stories and spreading lies." Then he turned and got an eyeful. There were a few other people in the gym doing workouts—civilian workouts. Stair-stepping to the beat of some Broadway show tune, or rowing slowly enough that even Washington's fully laden boats could have beat them across the Potomac.

And then there was Nikita with her back to him.

Five-ten in silken running shorts and a black t-shirt. Her ponytail swinging side to side as she ran in what he recognized as a military ground-eater. Sweat was just starting to make her shine as her long legs ate up the distance that the treadmill was handing out. She wasn't watching the CNN broadcast on one screen or the advertisements for the next port's exciting excursions on the other. Nikita was staring straight ahead at the blue ocean and just now shifting from a warm-up pace to a light run—good, he was only a few minutes behind her. She ran as if she was loping easily through the primeval forests, not working out on a luxury cruise ship.

"You going to watch her or do something about it?"

He gave Zoe the finger without bothering to look away from the magnificent athlete before him.

She merely laughed and kept spinning.

The treadmill beside Nikita opened up and he stepped onto it. Glancing at the program she was running, he hit the same.

She was so focused on her run that she didn't even notice him. Well, when she was ready to, he'd be here. Meanwhile he would run out some tiny portion of his desperate need for the woman he'd cradled in his arms last night.

Women never cost him a night's rest—it just didn't happen. Well, it did, but only when they were sharing a bed and neither of them were interested in using it for sleep.

Last night, after he'd finally finished berating himself for forgetting that even a SEAL had limits, he'd been stuck with the feel of her in his arms. That, far more than how Nikita Hayward looked wearing nothing but underpants, had cost him the night. Women were to be enjoyed, not cherished. But when he'd held her tight to his chest carrying her down the hallway, he'd felt so strong.

When she'd begged him to not let her remember, in a voice so sad that it didn't seem possible it had been uttered by Nikita Hayward, he had felt truly helpless.

And all through the night he wished he was still holding her, to somehow protect her against her own past.

* * *

Nikita powered ahead.

She hadn't needed Zoe's laugh to tell her that Drake had shown up. She hadn't even needed the hint of his reflection off the TV screen—she'd felt him when he'd entered the room. There had been a ripple as other women had turned and paused long enough to admire. Men suddenly moved more briskly on their machines as if needing to show themselves to be up to a standard they'd never meet.

Her mind was turning to mush on the subject of Drake Roman and she didn't like it. They ran for three kilometers before she wondered if she might be losing her mind.

"I'm not a woman designed for cruise ships," she snarled at no one in particular and pushed the speed button up another two klicks an hour.

"Nope," Drake agreed happily, and punched his own pace to match.

She told herself she wasn't going to look at him, but she did. He'd already stripped off his t-shirt and flipped it over a handhold. His skin was just a shade darker than hers, to go with his black hair. And his chest—

Nikita looked away. She remembered that chest and what it felt like to curl up against it. Between the exhaustion and the atypical amount to drink, her barriers had crashed down. The anger, the fear, the grief had threatened to overwhelm her. Until a voice like a benediction called down upon her desire to not remember, "Then don't."

And she hadn't. Instead she had buried her face in his chest and allowed herself to be taken care of with none of the hard time she'd given the docs and physical therapists the couple of times she'd been injured in the line of duty.

"I'm waiting," she managed between two breaths.

"For what?"

"For the great...Drake Roman to tell...me exactly what... he thinks...I'm good for...if not cruise ships." Her breath was starting to run short, but she'd just given him a bad straight line. She punched in another kilometer an hour.

"I'll ignore the obvious," Drake managed in a single breath as he again matched her speed.

Nikita leaned into the run and waited him out.

"Instead I'll tell you why I've been...so attracted to you since the first moment I saw you."

At least the bastard had the decency to take a breath in there. She considered pushing up another klick per hour, but wouldn't be able to speak if she did. Besides, now she was curious.

"My mom and my sister are both...seriously strong women. In spirit and mind...if not athletic."

It was nice that he was finally running short of breath as well.

"You are the only woman...I've ever met...who makes them look average."

Nikita stumbled and almost lost her pace as she looked over at him. Nothing about her body or her face or some other thin compliment.

Drake glanced at her for a moment, his dark eyes not looking aside as he held the pace. Sweat was dripping down his forehead and off his chest. He seemed to grow even taller as he ran beside her. Then he looked away and punched for another notch of speed as if he could somehow run away from what he'd just said.

Nikita matched him. "Why…never say…any…thing?" She managed against the blistering pace.

Drake shrugged and cricked his neck to one side as if he didn't know either.

He hit the speed button once more, which precluded all conversation.

She matched him and they simply ran. There was no glancing aside. Not at this speed. There was only the pounding of feet on rubber tread. The hot burning of legs driving ahead, fighting to hold their pace. Sweat stung her eyes and they burned, but she didn't care.

She could do a fifty-kilometer hike with a full field pack. She could jog along for hours with a light kit and her rifle. At this pace, all she could do was lean into it and go.

Five minutes…ten? She couldn't tell. The television screen changed from Key West to Belize to Coxen Hole, Roatán Island, Honduras. Overly perky hosts "reported" on screens filled with reef diving, parasailing, dune buggies, and ziplines.

Somewhere in the distance the ship's horn bellowed a warning—*get aboard or be left behind.* And still they ran.

There was no question of talking now. Their breath rasped in and out. Disharmonious, desperate.

Impossibly, Drake slapped the pace up once more.

With no idea how she could maintain it, she did the same. The setting was now for a four-minute mile—a record no woman had yet achieved.

It was unsustainable, but she'd be damned if some gorgeous flyboy was going to outrun a DEVGRU SEAL. There was honor to maintain.

Her arms were pumping so hard to keep her balance that they, too, ached with lactic acid buildup.

He groaned aloud against the agony of their run.

And still it built.

Thirty seconds.

A minute.

One and a half.

The scream of frustration ripped from her throat as her body fought to deliver what she demanded of it.

One forty-five.

One fifty.

Drake's snarl beside her was furious as he slammed ahead, struggling to sustain the pace.

One fifty-five.

Two minutes!

In final agony they cried out together as they both slammed down fists on the emergency stop buttons.

The treadmills slowed rapidly.

Two steps.

One more.

She let it carry her to the end of the belt. Stepping down onto the floor was almost impossible because her legs were shaking so hard.

Drake grabbed her hand and dragged her along, stumbling behind him, through the crowd that had gathered to watch their contest.

Flashing impressions: a dozen passengers, spa attendants, a trainer, Zoe's smile.

"No one comes in!" Drake snarled at somebody, then pulled her through a door marked "Men's Showers".

He yanked her forward, then tugged her about so that her back slammed against the cedar paneling.

He crashed into her. Kissing her as she groaned with need for breath and for Drake. She hooked an aching leg behind him to pull him in tighter and she dug her hands into his hair.

His hands were on her. There was nothing gentle. None of the surprising tenderness of last night. She didn't want it.

She wanted him. The way she'd never wanted anyone.

His hand dug under her t-shirt, under her bra, and he was the one who groaned with pleasure.

Her own hands dove into his shorts and clenched on his butt just as they had in her room at Mother Rucker.

* * *

Nikita hauled him so tightly against her that he thought he might break through the fabric between them.

He hadn't asked permission.

His need had him manhandling her. He couldn't stop himself.

"Now! Goddamn it, Roman! Now!"

So much for asking.

He yanked down her shorts and underwear. He retrieved the protection that an angel of grace had made him stuff in his pocket when he left the suite to come find her.

There wasn't time to be gentle. He wanted to caress, to appreciate, to please.

Not a chance.

He wanted to take and Nikita was offering it with as much desperation as she'd run. Gods, how she'd run. He'd never pushed himself so far past his limits, and still he hadn't been able to match her. She was beyond magnificent.

So he sheathed himself and he took.

No finesse. No grace.

He simply took her.

Everything that had built in him, he poured into her body.

She wrapped both legs around his hips and let him plunder. When she cried out, he swallowed the cry and added his own.

Never had a release so pounded through him as the one he

found in Nikita. She clung and shuddered against him until he was shakier than even the run had made him feel.

When the releases stopped slamming through both of their bodies, he still couldn't let her go. His arms wouldn't unwrap from their tight clench about her ribs. Her legs, still ankle-locked behind him, kept pulling his hips even harder against hers—to be answered each time with a soft moan of delight.

He buried his face against her neck and breathed her in.

Heat, sweat, and a smell as rich and elusive as the Alabama forest at sunset.

Maybe he'd never let go.

Drake had simply "taken" women before. A fast consensual screw and goodbye. Once there hadn't been so much as a kiss. He'd received a very surprising send-off as the Elvis Presley character going to war in the musical *Bye Bye Birdie.* During the final scene break on closing night, the innocent "Kim" had delivered exactly what the lusty "Birdie" had been wanting, and she'd managed to fit it in between the finale and the curtain call. Fast and furious on her bedroom set, which had been rolled deep into the backstage shadows—she'd never even had to lift her skirt when she knelt down over him as she wore nothing beneath. He always thought of her whenever he gave the line about liking actresses.

Now he couldn't let Nikita go. His heartrate finally settled. Her legs slipped from around his waist until she was supporting her own weight, and still he held on.

"That was…something," Nikita whispered it softly.

"Something," he agreed. "Though I'll be damned if I know what."

She wiggled a little. "You're still holding on to me."

He was. "I am." Not breast or butt, not dug into her hair, just wrapped around her and holding on.

Nikita wiggled again, "Aren't you going to—"

He kissed her to keep her quiet. Didn't she know that there were moments when a guy needed time to figure out what the hell had just happened? The blood reaching his brain was still minimal for survival.

"Drake," she pressed her hands to his cheeks. "You can let go of me now."

He could.

Except…he wasn't ready to.

"Nope. I'm not that stupid." He eased back a half step, ready to pull her deeper into the locker room—and collapsed into a wall. His shorts and underwear were still around his ankles.

Nikita was also totally disheveled. He'd gotten her pants down and off one leg by nearly ripping off one of her running shoes. One leg had a sock, the other still had shoe, sock, and her own shorts and underwear. Her t-shirt was shoved up enough to see that he'd freed one breast from her sports bra but not the other. She didn't appear to have noticed that yet.

He righted himself and pulled off the rest of her clothes over her ineffective and not terribly strenuous protests.

A naked Nikita was a breathtaking sight. Curves hinted at by her sportswear, suggested by her first outfit from the cruise ship's boutique, and so promised by last night's dress, were astonishing when unadorned.

"Shower," he explained, which stilled the last of her protests. He definitely had to get this woman into a shower with him.

Then he stepped out to drag her toward the nearest stall—and collapsed into the wall again. His own ankles were still snarled up in his shorts.

* * *

Nikita allowed herself to be coaxed beneath the steaming spray, partly because she didn't want to walk through the ship reeking of sweat and sex. But where she'd thought to get herself cleaned up, Drake had other ideas.

Sex with him had been just as rough and satisfying as she'd expected. Sex was meant to be enjoyable and it had been. Though with Drake it had also been much more. To have someone like him totally lose self-control over her as a woman was a revelation.

But a different man awaited her in the shower. He worked shampoo into her hair with a deep scalp massage. With soap and a washcloth, he made sure that not a square inch of her skin was untended, even the bottoms of her feet, which had turned out to be ticklish in a way she'd never been with anyone else. She didn't need any spa treatment when she had Drake Roman to take care of her. She braced her hands against the wall to keep herself upright as he worked over her body. It was so soothing that she was slow to pick up on what else he was doing until it was too late.

She was already halfway to gone before she noticed. He was so gentle that she couldn't find the energy to protest until he delivered another wave of release that stole her breath as it rippled through her body.

He washed himself off before she could recover enough to even think about returning the favor.

"Let's go. We don't want to be late for dinner. Or the art auction."

She leaned against the wall a minute longer before she could dredge up any interest in getting dressed. Men in her experience might give pleasure as long as they were receiving it as well, but for one to make an experience completely about her was unheard of. She was having trouble reconciling the man who had slammed her back against the wall and taken her with such delicious power with the one who had gently coaxed her body to a second release in many ways as overwhelming as the first.

Tender was not something she expected from Drake, nor any man in her experience. Poor Barry always had come to her bed like a soldier—hot and ready for action. He'd been kind and fun, but there was no question about who was having the sex and who was receiving it.

Drake was—

"The clothes fairy has left us a present," Drake announced. He held up a pair of clothes bags.

He was still splendidly naked and already recovering.

"If only we had time, lovely Nikita, but duty calls." His protests did nothing to stop his body's continuing reaction. Taking a deep breath and releasing it as a very complimentary groan of frustration, he pulled a towel off the rack and heaved it at her face. "At least cover up something before you kill me."

Nikita had never been shy. She'd been one of the only women around Curtis Contracting. Nobody messed with her because her dad was Curtis' Number Two, but shy didn't stand a chance. Living with a SEAL team of ultra-fit, ultra-raunchy males? Modesty didn't stand a chance either.

"Aww. Is poor Drake having trouble controlling himself around sexy women?" Not that she'd ever been called that—at least not by anyone who didn't land hard on his ass half a second later. She tossed the towel over her shoulder and let it drape down between her breasts, but not cover them.

Drake's eyes went darker and his expression was very intent.

She eased across the wooden slats of the shower area with the light tread of a sniper stalking its prey until barely a breath separated them.

She could see that Drake was nearly blind with need for her and his body confirmed the assessment.

Was she channeling Sugar somehow? Maybe she understood the woman, so competent in her craft but still sidelined for being female in a male world. So Sugar made a point of packing a physical punch that no man in his right mind could ignore.

And yet Drake had. Oh, he'd watched Sugar surely enough, but he'd watched Nikita far more—even without the tight leather.

Before she'd left, Sugar had said something to her that Nikita hadn't understood at the time. "That boy is just so gone."

When she'd asked gone on what, Sugar had just offered one of her merry laughs and followed J-dawg back to his monster SUV. Well, now Nikita knew. Drake wasn't merely gone on her, he was "so gone." She could feel the incredible rush that she could have Drake forget about everything in this instant if she wanted to. She'd never had such a sense of power over a male, especially not one like the "great" Drake Roman. It was a gloriously heady feeling right up there with sex.

But he'd said that they didn't have time. Pity.

He still held the two clothing bags in one hand. She unzipped the first one, spotted a dress, and plucked it from his fingers.

"Later, Roman."

When she turned to walk away, he grabbed her arm and pulled her back. For half a second she thought he'd take her right there and then. Instead, he dumped his own clothes bag at his feet and held on to her upper arms with both hands. He wasn't looking at her chest or hips. He was studying her eyes from just inches away.

"Say it like you mean it," his voice was so rough that she barely recognized it.

She tried shifting her arms, but his grip didn't ease. She was suddenly a little afraid. There wasn't a chance that he'd try to hurt her, besides, she could take him down a hundred different ways if he tried. But his intensity was so all-consuming. She could feel its shadow all around her. "Drake…"

"I'm serious!" He shook her lightly. "Say that there is a later, because I don't want whatever this is to just be about pounding one another up against some handy door or wall."

Nikita tried to see her own reflection in his dark eyes. He wouldn't allow any flippant answer. But she didn't know what else to give. Only once in her life had she promised there would be more and she'd lied. Instead she'd sent Barry out on a mission with too little information and he'd been captured, then tortured to death in the Congo—and not even for information, just for sport.

Yet for Drake—how was she supposed to make an acceptable answer for Drake Roman?

A part of her wanted to, needed to. A part of her didn't dare.

Fear. That was one thing that had been trained into a Special Operations fighter more than anything else: fear was to be recognized and addressed.

Whatever it was that she feared in this moment couldn't be allowed to stop her. Caution her? Yes. Stop her? Not without a damned good reason.

The gaping wound of her past said she had a good reason. That she should just turn and walk away.

But Drake's look wasn't only demanding, it was also pleading with her.

That she couldn't ignore.

She leaned in just enough to rest her lips on his, but not enough for their bodies to brush together. "There will be a later," she whispered against his soft kiss.

"Okay," he nodded slowly to himself and she could see the tension ease slowly back out of him. "Okay," he repeated it like he hadn't heard himself say it the first time.

He finally let her go and reached down for his clothes bag.

She began drying herself off.

Nikita just hoped that this time her promise didn't kill him.

* * *

Dinner passed in a blur.

He'd barely a moment to appreciate Nikita in the dark blue sheath dress that draped around her and swept to the floor. It must be one of the formal nights aboard. His good charcoal two-piece and freshly polished shoes had appeared from his own bag.

He held the door open to the men's shower as formally as he could for her to step out. Thankfully, only three people were waiting. He handed off the two bags, which now only bore their gym clothes, with a "Make sure these get to my suite" to the first ship steward he passed.

Zoe wore a huge grin as she eyed Nikita—until the moment she spotted Nikita's hair. They'd done what they could with it and Drake didn't feel guilty for a second about what he'd done to it. With a characteristic "Oh my gawd!", Zoe grabbed Nikita's hand, then rushed her along the corridor to the beauty salon.

Altman stood in a simple black suit with a black turtleneck. His arms were crossed over his chest and he was glaring at Drake.

Drake figured his luck was holding when, before Altman could kill him, a steward arrived to guide him off to drinks before dinner.

He thought he had a good handle on the situation. Everything with Nikita was moving too fast and not fast enough, which he hoped meant they were in the middle ground and were progressing at exactly the right speed. He had no idea to where, but that described most missions in his life, so he was okay with that. Knowing he simply wanted more was enough for now.

His professional reputation was sufficiently menacing now that a small bubble of space had formed around him at the bar, even when Altman wasn't adding his looming presence. The Russian mobster crossed the space to size him up and pass the time of day. An Italian prince—were their still princes in Italy? He didn't think so—well-gone on a bright blue drink, barged through the invisible barrier to offer him a price well into six figures for Nikita. He'd have to remember to tell her that one. He also double-checked his wallet and wristwatch to make sure he still had them when the man departed.

He watched the odd dance, as badly arranged as an unchoreographed stage play, reflected by a mirrored wall placed to make the bar seem larger than it was. Everyone was backlit by the failing day. Without thinking, his theater training had him standing in the center of one of the few spotlights so that he stood out from the crowd all the more. Everyone here was merely a mirage except—

Then he'd forgotten everything.

He spotted Zoe first, very attractive in a green jewel-tone gown that revealed almost nothing on the top, but offered an eye-catching slit that showed a very nice leg and spiked matching sandals. He tried to see if Altman noticed, but it was hard to tell if he focused on her specifically or just as a new addition to the crowd. Maybe he had someone at home, but Nikita had said she didn't think so.

Then Drake spotted her. He'd only had a glimpse of the long, deep ocean blue gown earlier. As she stepped into the room, chatter dropped by half and he couldn't hear the other half because his ears were ringing.

The gown was a long sheath that gathered asymmetrically above her waist in a bow. The beaded top emphasized her figure and the semi-transparent mesh across her cleavage declared her exceptional form. It was sleeveless, allowing her powerful shoulders to humble all pretenders. And the salon had done a feather cut to her hair, tapering from front to back, exposing her face.

He didn't remember crossing to her until he was holding her hands and staring into her face.

"You know that it will never pull back in a ponytail again?"

"Shit! I didn't think of that when Zoe was pushing." Then she glanced around and almost blushed. "That wasn't exactly in character, was it?"

"No, but it was infinitely reassuring. I like knowing that you're still Nikita Hayward despite how amazing you look."

She studied his eyes for a long moment, then leaned in and kissed him lightly.

That's when the evening blurred on him. Such a simple gesture. His looks had afforded him a kiss whenever he wanted one. But one from Nikita in such a public setting, and he could suddenly see them as a couple.

Beyond this setting. After escaping his grandparents' social agenda, he'd never thought to be in such a place again. No. He and Nikita would be out hiking, sailing, shooting, something active. And he could picture it like it was already true.

"Someone offered me a lot of money for you."

"Show me who and I'll kill the bastard." Again, the powerful woman emerging from the beautiful one.

"No. I don't want you so much as tearing a fingernail. You're worth over six figures to me already. And in that gown, I'll bet the price has gone up to seven."

"You mean out of this gown." With the harshness of her tone, he was almost tempted to point out the "Italian prince" to see what happened.

"That," he whispered in her ear, "is for nobody but me."

Again, that long, unreadable SEAL gaze.

He'd meant it as a joke.

Then she nodded her assent.

It was his last coherent thought.

She no longer clung to his arm, but instead held his hand, releasing it only at dinner so that they could eat.

Chapter 9

Arthur slid up to them so smoothly as they arrived at the art auction that Nikita almost looked to see if he was on wheels. His smile widened as he inspected her from clasped hands to sheerly masked cleavage.

Drake's hands slowly tightened in hers until his grip was as powerful as the moment he'd dragged her into the men's shower, except this time it was shaking with raw fury. Maybe she could get used to having someone feel protective about her, even if she didn't actually need it.

She considered making an effort to push her chest out further just to see if Drake would test the strength of his fist against the man's jaw. Now probably wasn't the moment.

"We're so glad you could come. It is early in the cruise," he alternated between talking to Drake's face and her chest, "therefore we will be auctioning only a few choice pieces tonight."

Three dozen paintings had been moved from the tiny shipboard gallery to the piano bar. A pair of easels and a podium had been set up at the far end of the room. Out the window, the Caribbean sunset was ending in rusty skies and black waters.

Nikita scanned the room for potential weapons and spotted very few. Tables were screwed to the floor. The bar was open, but clearly rigged for rough seas. Each liquor bottle was clamped into inverted brackets with press-to-pour spigots. The piano sported a massive chain from the base of the sound box down to a U-connector mounted to the floor. This place was fully prepped for stormy sailing.

Of course she could brain Arthur with the edge of her hand, if she dared strike out while wearing this dress. For fear that her chest would fall out of it and give Arthur a thrill, she didn't even dare to raise her arms in order to check out her strange new haircut that tickled her neck.

No one had ever looked at her the way Drake had at that first moment.

When Barry had "staked his claim" on her, he'd simply made it clear he'd shoot anyone who touched her.

Drake didn't boast or warn. Instead he looked at her as if she were the most captivating woman in history and he was the lucky one in this situation.

Which didn't mean he wouldn't pound the crap out of Arthur if she didn't do something soon.

"I know so little about art," she paused long enough for Arthur to have to look up at her face. "If I were to start collecting, what do you suggest I begin with?"

"Mr. Roman's predecessor was always partial to the work of Myora Folsum," he waved a thin-fingered hand toward a particularly awful nude.

Nikita supposed the work was well enough executed, but it was more a *Hustler* centerfold sort of image than even a *Playboy* one—there wasn't even a pretense of artful. It was just a woman's body. The artist hadn't even included her full face, letting it trail off the edge of the canvas so that she existed only from her lips down as if that was all that mattered.

"My predecessor's taste is not mine, I assure you." Drake's dangerous snarl warmed her heart.

Arthur didn't pitch a different painting, instead he looked suddenly worried. Was it loss of a commission or— She double-squeezed Drake's hand as a warning, as much as she could against his still powerful grip.

He glared over at her. The tiniest shake of his head said that he got the message but didn't give a damn.

She knew there was a reason she liked him.

"I think we will pass, Arthur," Nikita offered, not trusting Drake to speak. "Take me dancing, Drake. Won't you please?"

Drake didn't move, instead staring at the man until Arthur seemed to shrink before him.

"If you or the people you represent wish to proceed, know that I am a man of business—not pandering and prurient whims. Approach me directly or not at all. No messages or codes tucked into canvases—I couldn't care. My business succeeds just as well in one locale as another." He waved a hand at a small painting of an African family group in tribal dress that was only spared from being racist by the sympathetic eye of the artist.

Not giving Arthur time to answer, Drake turned aside and would have walked off without her if they hadn't been holding hands.

"When can I get back to my goddamn helicopter?" He snarled as soon as they were beyond earshot.

She let him steamroller along until they reached the very bow of the ship and stepped out onto the foredeck. He led her all the way to the rail. The sunset had left the evening cool, which was refreshing on her face, though she shivered at the unexpected contact with her shoulders. Strapless wasn't exactly her style.

Moments later Drake slipped his jacket over her bare shoulders like a cape. And while she didn't need the warmth, feeling his body heat wrap around her was such a pleasure she might never give it back.

The constellations Capricorn and Aquarius shown in the sky, higher than she was used to. Rather than flying straight overhead, Cygnus the swan was hidden behind the upper stories of the cruise ship as they headed south toward Belize, their next port of call.

"What's our next step?" She didn't trust herself to think more about Drake the man. So she'd focus on Drake the warrior.

"How the hell would I know?" He leaned on the railing and stared out over the bow so she couldn't see his face.

The open ocean always surprised her at how much it didn't smell like anything. Dead algae and seaweed gave beaches their fishy smell. Breaking waves churned salt into the air. Yet the four-foot rollers of the Gulf of Mexico added nothing to the air and only the slightest motion to the ship. This was no Navy ship—it ran with stabilizers that could flatten out the least roll for its passenger's comfort.

The last of the day's light had turned the sky blood orange. A land mass lay low to the south and east. It must be Cuba, the only major island for a long way south of Key West. They would pass it in the night on their way to Belize in Central America.

That left them two ports of call to solve the riddle or this whole trip would have been a waste. She leaned back against the railing close by Drake and looked up at the towering ship, outlined against the glowing sky. It rose four more decks above them, the control bridge a single sweep of glass like a dark eyebrow immediately above their own suite.

Looking at their suite's verandah, she could see Altman and Zoe standing side by side, outlined by the light behind them. Both looking down at her and Drake.

What did Altman see? What did he imagine had become of his prize pupil, the first female SEAL, as she lounged next to her lover in a thousand-dollar gown that she'd just as soon throw overboard?

"I don't know how to do this," she told the fading light.

"That makes two of us," Drake's whisper was a caress that she couldn't stand to turn and face.

"Are we talking about the mission?" Nikita kept her voice low as if Arthur or one of his cronies might hear.

"Or are we talking about us?" Drake's voice was hushed as if he was afraid the world would hear.

"I wasn't," she swallowed hard. "But I guess we are now."

"What happens when the mission is done?"

"Shit, Roman. We've never even shared a bed."

"We will tonight," his tone left no doubt. "Then what?"

Nikita spotted a flash of light on the uppermost deck, no brighter than a cigarette lighter.

A highly trained instinct about the color and shape of the flare had her slamming a fist into Drake's arm. She let half the momentum knock him sideways and used the other half to push herself away from him.

She felt a sharp slice of pain in her upper arm—and the distinctive hard *plonk!* of a bullet hitting the rail.

"Incoming!" She hissed at Drake. He'd been facing the wrong way to see it. "Observation Deck," she called out loudly, hoping that Altman was still at the suite's rail and would hear her.

She dove behind a large steel anchor capstan. Drake went down behind a bench, which was lousy protection, then glanced back at her. She pointed up toward where she'd seen the flash of light.

Another round came in. There was a loud *clang!* This time it hit on the back side of the capstan she was crouched behind. No sharp crack of a supersonic round. The small flash she'd spotted indicated a silenced weapon, which would act as a flash suppressor as well.

She was never going to leave her rifle in the suite again, not if she had to wear it under her dress at a fancy dinner.

Drake took advantage of the moment and rolled to a more secure spot close behind a large anchor resting on the deck.

Unless they could get beneath the overhang of the bridge, they were defenseless.

Five breaths, ten, she held her position.

She was considering a bolt for cover, but knew that patience was her friend and the shooter's enemy.

"Wait it out!" Drake hissed at her. "Do you see the shooter?"

"Just the flash."

If only—

A sharp whistle cut the night. It was high and far away, but it was easily heard.

Long-short-long-short. Pause. Repeat.

Altman. The letter C in Morse Code for All Clear.

He'd heard her and reached the Observation Deck in record time.

As a test, she snagged Roman's jacket from where it had fallen as she rolled to safety and held it out.

The letter C sounded again.

She peeked cautiously through a gap in the steel fixture that had saved her from the second shot.

The silhouette of a man stood right where she'd seen the flash of light.

Against the now red sky, he held his arm up in silhouette, fingers shaped like a pistol. Then he circled a hand over his head to rally up, then pointed straight down at the suite two decks below his position and two decks above theirs, indicating that they should meet there.

She raised a hand to pump a Hurry Up in acknowledgement, but only managed a sharp curse.

"Goddamn it!"

"What?" Drake whispered from where he still lay, not having understood or seen Altman's signals.

"I hate being shot."

* * *

"What do you mean she was shot?"

"That does seem to be the question of the evening," Drake said drily. He'd been the first to ask it. Then by the first steward he'd found and demanded to know the way to the infirmary. Then by the doctor and now by Norma the hotel manager as they each joined the growing crowd in the tiny two-bed infirmary on Deck 2, two levels below the normal passenger areas.

Down here the corridors were steel and windowless. A token bit of carpet stretched between the elevator and the infirmary, but the rest was gray-and-white painted steel. Luxury was for passengers, not crew. The doctor was out of his depth with a gunshot wound; he was more geared for seasickness and elderly patients suffering heart attacks.

Thankfully it was only a clean meat shot on the upper arm. The bullet hadn't made much of a hole going in or out, so a dab of glue, a wrap bandage, and an antibiotic were all that was called for and the doc was able to manage that—though he and Nikita had kept a close eye on him.

Altman came in.

"She okay?"

"I'm fine," Nikita growled from where the doctor was making her lie still, or trying to.

"She's just fine," Drake answered for her.

"Hey, I was *shot,*" Nikita changed from dismissive to seeking sympathy with all of the agility of a Spec Ops warrior.

Drake ignored her, "What did you find?"

Altman held out a pair of brass casings. "Two rounds, .22LR. You said there was no supersonic crack, so they were fired from a handgun, not a rifle. I also followed your lead. I got only fragments from the capstan, but I dug this out of the wooden railing."

"You did what?" Norma the hotelier still wasn't up to speed.

He'd give her more time.

"You'll need to fix it; I had to dig a little," Altman held up a six-inch MK 3 knife.

"Those aren't allowed on board," Norma was still out of the loop, trying to make sense of what had just happened.

Altman's smile said that he was sick of the cruising life and was having fun keeping her off balance.

Drake ignored them both, plucking the round and casings out of Altman's palm and turning to show them to Nikita. Beautiful woman, lovely gown, lying back just as he'd hoped—except on a hospital gurney, not a luxury bed. Somebody was a dead man and he was going to start with Arthur.

They inspected the hardware together.

The bullet was heavily deformed by the impact with the wood, but was definitely a .22 round. No way to get rifling marks, not that it would tell them much without a lab and the weapon. The shooter had gone, or blended back into the crowd by the time Altman showed up. Short of frisking every passenger in the Observation Lounge, he hadn't had a whole range of options.

"I think that's a bit of blood caught in the furling," Nikita pointed.

"Who the hell besides us has weapons on this boat?" Drake spun back to Norma as the rage shot back to life inside him.

"You have weapons on the boat? Those are forbidden. You can't…" she trailed off and swallowed hard. She was the one who had let them board directly from their helicopter—exactly as she'd probably always let GSI board. The pieces were starting to connect together for her.

"Who else besides us?" Drake repeated, resisting the urge to shake the answer out of her.

But Norma was shaking her head in a dazed fashion. "No one else bypassed security. The Captain's safe should have the only weapons on board."

"Does he have silenced .22s?"

"Silenced? Like with…" she made a helpless gesture in the form that might have been an extended gun barrel.

"Like this," Altman pulled out a six-inch silencer from his shoulder holster, holding the lapel aside just long enough for her to get an eyeful of his Glock 19 with laser sight.

"No," Norma managed in a strangled tone. "No, the captain doesn't."

Altman grunted. For the first time on the voyage he was smiling. "Somebody is being bad besides us. Lousy damn shot, though, to miss you both from no more than fifty meters." He tucked the silencer away.

"Didn't miss completely," Drake returned the bullet and casings to Altman. "And someone is going to go to hell for that one."

Zoe came in. "You okay, Nikki?"

"I'm fine, if the doctor would just stop hovering."

"Doctor," Zoe rested her hand on his arm. "We're done with you now, thank you so much."

"But she—" then he winced.

Drake hadn't seen Zoe tighten her fingers about his arm, but they were right over a nerve cluster that was going to leave his hand numb for hours if she didn't back off quickly.

"And you're not going to say a word to anyone about this without our permission, right?"

His knees buckled slightly for a moment, then she let go and patted his arm in a friendly fashion.

"Uh," he stumbled backward into a cabinet that rattled with equipment but freed him from the clench of the harmless-looking blonde in the green evening gown. "If you need me—" He didn't complete the sentence as he raced out of the tiny infirmary.

"She okay?" This time Zoe was asking about the hotel manager.

"Yes," Drake decided that Norma was either the best actress in the world or was actually in shock that such a thing could happen on her cruise ship.

Altman apparently agreed as he closed the door, with the four of them and Norma still crowded into the small space.

Nikita swung to a sitting position and went to stand, but Zoe pushed her back to stay seated on the bed. Then, to forestall argument, Zoe hopped up to sit beside her, her feet swinging in the air. It was just as well; if they all five were standing they'd have to all be hugging to fit.

"Norma," Drake had to repeat her name before she focused on him. "We're US Special Operations Forces here undercover. No one can know, not even your captain. You certainly shouldn't, but we can't have you throwing us off the ship either."

"But someone shot…" she waved a hand at Nikita. "And you have a gun…" the other hand waved helplessly toward Altman.

Drake would bet that LCDR Luke Altman was armed with a lot more than one. It wouldn't surprise him if Zoe was as well, though he couldn't see where she'd hide it in that clingy gown.

"You're going to have to treat us just the way you did the members of GSI. Courtesy and caution. Can you do that?"

He could see the experienced hotelier in Norma slowly pulling herself together. Her spine straightened. She tugged at the hem of her immaculate jacket. A quick hand checked her short blond hair. Then, with a blink of her blue eyes, she was present.

"But who shot you?"

"It wasn't Arthur," Zoe chimed in. "He's still at his auction. I asked around and he hasn't left the podium since you were there."

"Arthur?" Norma looked close to losing her poise again, but she held on.

"Yes. You'll want to line up a new art handler. We'll leave him in place for now, but if they were desperate enough to move against us, I don't expect that he'll be with your cruise line much longer."

"You can't be right about Arthur," it almost sounded as if she was begging.

"Next time they'll need a better shooter," Altman bounced the bullet and casings against his palm before tucking them away.

"Or maybe they already have one," Nikita was squinting into the distance, looking at something far outside the room. "Steady seas. Deck lights were low but bright enough. Two misses…"

"Two misses?" Drake tried not to explode. Tried not to let loose the terror that his suit was going to end up with another splatter pattern on its back, but not with Carl's blood this time. "You were shot!"

Altman hissed at him to keep his voice down.

"I think…" she tipped her head sideways, then nodded once and looked directly at him. "It was an accident."

"People don't get accidentally shot on cruise ships."

"I think I was," she held up a hand to stop him before he could fume more. "I saw the muzzle flash. I knew I only had a split second and I punched you to drive us apart and out of the way."

Drake ran a hand over his upper arm; it hurt like hell when he pressed on it. "Good punch." He hadn't noticed it until this moment.

"Thanks. But we were standing far enough apart for me to be able to punch you. I think I put my arm in the way of the bullet. What if they were aiming *between* us?"

"The second shot was dead center on the capstan," Altman confirmed. "As if the shooter wanted to be sure they missed."

"Scare tactics," Nikita confirmed.

Drake managed a smile for her sake. "Damn good thing they don't know what kind of a woman they're trying to scare."

Nikita's smile was far more genuine than his, "Damn good thing."

He brushed a finger down her cheek, "Remind me never to get on your wrong side, Nikita Hayward."

"Deal, Drake Roman," she leaned into his caress.

Chapter 10

Nikita could never get tired of Drake's caresses. If only there'd been a chance to last night.

Along with the precautionary antibiotic and the local anesthetic—that the doctor had needed more than she did to dress her wound—he'd apparently given her a shot with enough painkiller to level a horse. She'd been staggering by the time they reached the suite, with Drake's jacket once more draped over her shoulders to hide the bandage.

This time she was still conscious enough to remove her own dress. Though she'd need Zoe's help to put on the t-shirt, because she couldn't feel her own arm.

No powerful arms lifted her into the bed, but that didn't matter. By the time she hit the pillow, she was out.

"C'mon, sleepyhead," someone was tugging on her foot. "You don't want to miss every port of call."

She managed to open her eyes.

Drake was smiling down at her.

"How is it that you always look so good and I feel like shit?" He looked far better than good back in his black t-shirt and tan chinos.

"Good living and I stay off the drugs."

Her head was still muzzy with whatever the doctor had pumped into her last night. She tested the arm. Sore as hell, but not anything worth writing home about.

Drake was busy throwing open curtains. She didn't even know if he or Zoe had slept beside her last night.

"Come to bed and maybe we'll discuss the good living part of that."

He circled close and once more brushed a finger across her cheek. His easy smile disappeared and his expression became deeply intent and serious. "If the next boat ashore wasn't in fifteen minutes, I'd take you up on that."

"Let's miss a boat."

"Zoe found out through Norma that Arthur signed up for permission to go ashore. He'll be on that boat as well and I'd like to have a chat with him." He dropped into a chair to wait for her.

She'd like a few words with him as well. Nikita rolled out of bed and onto her feet. She had to close her eyes for a moment as the world wavered sharply, but then it steadied. Stripping off her shirt, she headed for the walk-in closet. Disgusted that she was still probably "the babe" of the outfit, she went for the light cotton blouse whose price had so shocked her when she first entered the boutique, and capris in a dark lavender. Two minutes flat she was back in the bedroom with her hair and teeth brushed. And—damn Drake for being right—all her efforts at a ponytail were completely foiled.

Drake was sitting in the armchair with his feet propped on the bed.

He was shaking his head, but his eyes didn't move from looking at her.

"Damn, woman. I could really get used to being around you."

Right. He'd been in the room when she'd stripped on her way to the closet.

She kicked his leg hard enough to hurt, "Thought you were in a hurry."

"You're enough to make a man think very slow thoughts." But he clambered to his feet. "Metal detectors at the ramp. No weapons bigger than a four-inch knife allowed."

"Shit!" She untucked her shirt and pulled the nice little Glock 36 Subcompact Slimline out of the small of her back and returned to the closet to lock it in her rifle case.

"Extra rounds?"

She pulled the two clips out of her back pocket and tossed them in as well.

"My kinda gal," he took her hand and led her out into the suite.

"That didn't take the two of you nearly long enough," Zoe protested from the chair she'd been slouched in.

"Don't you ever think about anything other than sex?"

"Hunter-killer drones. But other than that? Why bother."

Altman was already by the door.

* * *

Arthur didn't look happy when Drake led his entourage as the last ones on the open taxi boat, but he was too buried in the crowd to make an excuse and rush for the exit.

Belize City harbor was too shallow for the big cruise ships. Even their mid-sized model couldn't make it in. But the city had a jitney service of hundred-passenger open boats that had rushed out to unload the cruise ship and take them the twenty minutes to shore. For twenty minutes, Arthur wasn't going anywhere, so Drake sat in his seat and ignored him.

A very curved lady with skin the color of warm chocolate and hair curling well past her shoulders stood up front. In charming British English she told the passengers about the wonderful opportunities to be found in Belize. There were apparently still open slots in diving, caving, river rafting, and Mayan temple jungle tours. He let her liquid accent lull him into a comfortable semi-trance state as they powered toward shore.

Nikita curled up against him and appeared to be just as content as he was to take in the sunshine, the sea air, and the twenty minutes of peace.

"We are now arriving in the Tourist Village. There are many shops and restaurants to explore here if you are not traveling farther afield on one of our tours. We do wish to caution you to be careful beyond the boundaries of this area. There are clear signs posted. There are parts of Belize City that I regret to say are not very safe and you certainly don't want to be caught there after dark."

After weaving through various anchored boats—mostly luxury yachts in the eighty- to hundred-and-fifty-foot range—the jitney nudged up to a dock and unloaded from the same ramp. They'd been last on, so they were first off.

A glance to Altman, and he and Zoe hung back. Drake led Nikita slowly up the dock and toward town. So slowly that Arthur would have no choice but to catch up with them as the crowd cleared. Zoe and Altman would make sure that he was herded along.

They were three quarters of the way down the nearly empty pier when they all came together. Zoe's idle chatter warned him that the gap between them was now under a dozen meters. He turned aside.

The big industrial piers with their cargo containers were in another section of the city, away to the south. This was a tourist transit pier, colorfully decorated with a scattering of old maritime equipment tucked here and there under the well-spaced palm trees that he supposed would be considered a festive air.

Arthur had to know he was in a pincer, so he followed them until all five of them were in a tall palm's shade.

"It would have been easier if you had bought the painting," Arthur sighed. "I had to go to rather a lot of difficulty to avoid selling it last night."

"So you had us shot at to make up for it?"

"Shot at?" that surprised him enough that he tipped his head down to look at Drake over the top of his sunglasses. "Who shot at you?"

Altman's curse was emphatic.

"*You* are supposed to be the one telling *us*," Drake couldn't believe this was happening. He'd had it all figured out in his head; or part of it anyway. He hadn't behaved the way GSI historically had, so Arthur's people were applying pressure to make them behave. A decidedly weak scenario, but that was all he'd been expecting from these people. Paintings of nudes and patently obvious art dealers struck him as awfully lame fieldcraft.

"Okay," maybe Nikita had some ideas. "If you didn't shoot me—"

"You were actually shot?" Arthur's astonishment didn't look faked, but Nikita ignored him.

"Who else do you have aboard for this operation?"

"No one," Arthur started looking around as if someone other than Drake was about to shoot him. "There isn't an operation. What kind of an operation? Did you need one for being shot?"

Drake grabbed him by the lapels of his summer jacket and forced him to focus. "Who the fuck tried to kill Nikita?" He agreed with her that it had been an accident that she was shot, but she could have just as easily leaned in to kiss him, or he her, and taken a bullet to the head.

"I swear to god I don't know," the man's voice actually squeaked.

"Shit!" Drake cast him aside hard enough that he'd have crashed to the ground if Altman hadn't jammed a hand against this back.

Either he was just as clueless as he appeared, or he was in deep. Head of an operation could perhaps pull it off, but that was too movie-villain evil to be credible. He'd vote for sniveling weasel in over his head—but watch out for scheming bastard.

If it was the former…

He grabbed Arthur's lapel and yanked him in again until their noses were just an inch apart.

"You want to get out of this in one piece, you find out who else is on that boat. And you don't tell them, you tell me or her," he nodded toward Nikita. "On second thought, don't go near her. She'd be far more likely to throw your sorry ass overboard than I am."

This time when he shoved Arthur away, Altman simply stepped to the side and let him stumble to catch his balance before racing off.

"Any bets?" Drake asked the others.

"Twenty says that he's just as useless as he looks," Nikita pulled out a bill to make her point.

Altman eyed her, "I'm still on the fence about him."

"Personally, I thought he was going to pee himself," Zoe sounded delighted. "This is so much more entertaining than sitting at a drone's ground-control station. You," she poked a finger against Altman's chest, "definitely have to show me more, Luke. Much more."

Altman looked down at her finger as if it was a dangerous weapon to be treated with great caution.

The four of them were the last ones off the pier other than a pair of poor crew from the ship who were standing beneath a small white awning in full uniform just in case someone had a question three hours from now.

At the head of the pier, Drake spotted a familiar face—a pair of them.

"You've got to be shitting me."

* * *

Nikita startled. She'd never heard Drake swear, except about her being shot.

There, just outside of security, in front of a row of glitzy tourist shops thick with bad ugly t-shirts and tiny collectors' plates with pictures of a palm tree, stood Jared Westin and Sugar.

Drake blew past the pier's security guards. In a dozen steps he had grabbed J-dawg with a pincer grip around his windpipe and pinned his back against a palm tree even though the guy was a couple inches taller and several times broader than he was.

"Do you have a shooter on the boat?" Drake was practically spitting in his face.

"What are you talking about?"

"Do you have a goddamn team on board our boat?"

J-dawg narrowed his eyes and looked down at Drake, not appearing to even notice the death grip on his throat. "Did you say a shooter?"

"Just answer the goddamn question!" Wherever the mild-mannered Drake Roman had gone, he was awfully far away.

Nikita noted that the rest of the team had circled up, masking the action as much as possible. The waterfront was mostly quiet; the initial blast of cruise passengers had moved farther into the city. The only local paying them any mind was a little girl in an *I Heart Belize* t-shirt and eating a chocolate ice cream cone. She was watching with avid interest.

"No," J-dawg sounded like he was talking to an idiot schoolboy. "I do not have a team on your boat. Now answer my goddamn question. Did you say shooter?"

In answer, Drake released his hold on J-dawg's throat. He shot out a hand so fast that it surprised even her instincts. He grabbed her good arm and pulled her to him. Then he slid up the sleeve on the other one and showed him her bandage. There hadn't been time to change it, so there were some spots of blood seepage from last night.

J-dawg's eyes went as dark as Drake's had last night.

"Somebody did that to Sugar, I'd annihilate the bastard." His voice went just as rough and scary, too.

The two men shared their agreement with very mano-a-mano looks.

"What is it with over-protective men?" Nikita had to yank a bit to recover her arm from Drake's grasp.

"Aren't they just the sweetest little things when they do that?" Sugar was smiling up at her husband.

Nikita wasn't sure about sweet. She was getting sick and tired of being "the babe" of this whole operation.

"When I find him," Drake wasn't over it yet, "annihilation is the least of what I'm going to do."

"I'll hold him down for you," J-dawg muttered and pulled Sugar close. "Any guesses?"

Drake just shook his head. "It must be someone who really doesn't want GSI returning to Honduras, but that's all we've been able to come up with. Up half the night sketching out scenarios, didn't find squat that made sense. Shooter is aboard. Silenced .22. That's all we know."

Nikita looked at her three teammates and saw the dark circles of their sleepless night. And she'd been asleep, well drugged, but she didn't like feeling useless.

The kid who'd been watching them all so intently while she ate her ice cream leaned against Sugar's other side and earned a hand around her shoulders. She'd watched Drake attack J-dawg as if such things happened every day.

"Yes, Swimmer Girl, she's mine." Sugar noticed the direction of Nikita's attention. "Asal saved my life on an Afghan hillside and I jes' figured that returning the favor was about the only thing I could do."

"She fought like a demon for the kid," J-dawg said with obvious pride. He turned back to Drake. "You've got a good grip. Glad you didn't use it." There were still five red fingerprints on his neck but he hadn't even flinched. How strong *was* this guy?

It was time she took control of the situation.

"If you don't have a team on the boat, *J-dawg*," Nikita dragged it out, "what the hell are you doing here?"

Asal answered for him in a high, girl voice and acceptable English, "Checking up on his invesrent."

"His investment?"

The girl nodded and then began practicing the word to herself.

"What investment?"

J-dawg shrugged, "When we took over GSI, we took over all of their bank accounts, too. I get all the bills for everything charged to them, including this trip." Then he looked her up and down, once, assessment with no trace of a leer. "Hope the rest of what you bought looks this good on you. It better, it was a hell of a bill."

"Good!" She still didn't want to like the guy.

"You've got taste. Keep it all."

"*I've* got the taste," Zoe piped up. "She's hopeless. Black t-shirt and camo pants is her idea of a Sunday formal."

"With a McMillan Tac-50 over my shoulder. I always wear a good rifle with my Sunday best."

J-dawg roared with laughter at her joke. "Now that is my kinda woman. You pay attention, Asal," he reached over to scrub the kid's hair. "You wanta grow up to be just like Lily or this lady here."

Asal studied her for a long moment, then nodded as if she'd seen something in Nikita.

"Are you deluded enough to think that the clothes would be a bribe, J-dawg?" Zoe asked. "What are you expecting in return?"

Nikita appreciated that Zoe was reminding her of just who they were dealing with.

"A gift, Pint-size. Just a gift."

"So, what are you doing here? A family vacation snorkeling on the reef?" Zoe waved a hand at the waterfront. It had a case of the late-morning sleepies, not even a cat was stirring. The only boat on the move was a water taxi scuttling across the wide mouth of Haulover Creek—the river that cut the city in half.

"Not so much."

Nikita felt slightly nauseous and didn't think it was the last of the drugs seeping out of her system. "You've got assets on the ground in Honduras? A bunch of trigger-happy goons that we're going to stumble on where we least want to?"

J-dawg finally stood up from where he'd been slouching against the palm tree Drake had slammed him into. "Colonel Be-damned McDermott said I'd never get another government contract as long as I lived if I put someone on the ground there."

"So where are they?"

Nikita saw his eyes flicker aside for a second at her question. They all turned to look while J-dawg cursed at being caught out. A couple hundred meters off the harbor wall, among the anchored motor yachts, was a long, dangerous looking one. Black, sleek, and at least a hundred feet long—it looked as dangerous as its owner.

"Real subtle, J-dawg. Real subtle."

* * *

J-dawg had led them to a place called Baymen's Tavern. It was actually an outdoor restaurant at the Radisson Hotel with a sweeping view from the north side of the peninsula that formed Belize City. They sat beneath the shade of a massive umbrella. The tall palms around the edge of the patio rustled lightly in the sea breeze. The waitresses were efficient and a pleasure to look at. All very high-end.

"This place is upright, respectable—"

"Family friendly," J-dawg cut him off.

Drake could only laugh.

"Come down here with just the team, I can show you where to get real food, but it's deep in a bad quarter. Food is worth it though."

Drake would bet on more than just the food by his expression, though with the way he acted about Sugar, it was probably for memories past, not futures planned. He didn't like what Titan did, but he understood Jared's need to protect, even if Nikita didn't. It wasn't a conscious, thought out, or innately macho plan. It was simply a fact of life—nobody was getting to her without going through him first. He could see that whatever else was going on, he and Jared were in a hundred percent agreement on that point.

"Family changes a man in surprising ways," J-dawg looked at Sugar and Asal discussing the meal with the contentment of a man well pleased with the way his life was going.

Asal was working her way through an appetizer of chicken tenders like she'd never stop.

"Kid hasn't slowed down eating since we pulled her off that mountain six months ago. Stays thin as a rail, just keeps getting taller. Most of the way to starved when we found her, probably set her metabolism for life."

Asal had ended up between Sugar and Zoe. Drake had made sure Nikita sat between him and Altman. J-dawg was across the table with a lazy arm on the back of Sugar's chair. Without even noticing, Drake had mirrored J-dawg's position with an arm behind Nikita. It was surprising that Nikita hadn't chopped it off and fed it to a piranha or whatever Belize had. Maybe he'd leave it there and see how long before she noticed. The open spot at the end of the table was in glaring sunlight and not even the mad-for-sun Zoe had taken it.

"So, Jared."

"Finally gonna use my damned name. About time someone in your outfit did."

"What *are* you doing here?" Drake had opted for ice tea instead of Belikin Beer, much to Jared's disgust.

"Already told you that."

"I don't buy *checking on your invesrent*. Try again."

"My mess to clean up."

"Not according to Colonel McDermott," even Nikita's tone seemed to be easing around Jared. She only sounded disgusted rather than her usual murderous.

"Still mine. I should have taken them down years ago. Would have saved a lot of people a lot of pain. You want someone who should have been shot by his own men in the field, head of GSI was the poster boy."

"How can you—" Nikita flopped back, clearly angry again, and knocked Drake's arm off the back of the chair without even noticing.

Jared leaned in hard and fast enough that Drake leaned forward ready to block any attack on Nikita. "Because a lot more of my unit would have come back alive it wasn't for him."

Nikita shot to her feet. Her face wasn't red with anger, instead it was the palest white, as if all the life and blood had been drained out of her.

When Drake tried to rise, she placed a hand on his shoulder, keeping him in his chair. Then she simply turned and walked away.

"J-dawg," Sugar said sharply as she rose. "You did not just say that to her of all people." She sounded pissed as hell, as primal a force as Jared. For the first time Drake could see that, despite how she might look, she was actually a good match for him.

Also, she obviously knew exactly what trigger Jared had just hammered his fist down on.

"Zoe, would you mind staying with Asal?" Sugar didn't wait for an answer.

When the two of them were gone, Jared looked across the table at him.

"What the hell did I say?"

Drake tried to figure out how to say it without punching Jared a good one, but Altman saved them both by speaking up first.

"Did you hear about the mess that took down Curtis Contracting?"

"Sure, cheap bastard strung his own men out to dry. Wouldn't authorize the fee for the intel some chick had a lead on. Chas Hayward and Barry… Wait. Didn't Nikita say her last name was Hayward?"

"Chas was her dad. The other guy was her fiancé. She was the 'chick' stuck holding the bag." Altman's voice was grim.

"And I just said… Aw, shit."

* * *

"Whoa, Swimmer Girl. Just whoa some."

Nikita didn't want to *whoa.* She wanted to break her fist in some man's face. She wanted to take down Marcus Curtis so hard that he'd never do more than crawl again.

She hadn't even had the satisfaction of taking him down herself. He'd gotten drunk that night and decided to prove how tough he was. Apparently not as tough as the switchblade that slit his throat after he beat a whore halfway to death. That had been the end of Curtis Contracting as well.

Sugar finally rested a hand on her arm, "My legs aren't as long as yours. At least slow down enough that I don't have to run in this heat."

"You're the one who wears leather all the time." But Nikita slowed her stride. Finally grinding to a halt somewhere a lot less nice than the Baymen's Tavern. But the sign said "Tavern", so she turned in.

It wasn't like a 'Bama bar, all battered pickups and neon beer signs out front. Inside also wasn't all battered tables and country boys nursing long-neck Budweisers.

The only thing lined up out front were poor people. The only thing inside were people with enough money to buy a beer and maybe a bowl of chicken escabeche soup. Shorts, short-sleeve shirts, and flip-flops were the dress code. She and Sugar must look like aliens from another planet.

The walls had once been white and the floor was still concrete. But the beer bottle handed across when she asked was just as beaded with sweat as the one in the peeling poster of a bikini-clad babe holding it between her breasts.

She dropped into a wooden chair at a table that rocked a good ten degrees when she set her bottle on it.

Sugar sat down across from her.

"Why *do* you wear leather?"

"You already know that."

Nikita nodded. She did.

Sugar answered anyway. "Thought I was defining self-worth with the way I could draw those boys. Showing them I was just as tough as they were never seemed to make any difference. They just saw these," she cupped her breasts, "so I gave them that. No one saw more, not until Jared. He taught me there was more to me than I knew."

"But still you wear leather."

"Jared *is* male. He likes it plenty, he just sees the woman behind the leather as well. Asides, it's a part of who I am now. Not gonna be leaving that behind just because I fell in love with the man."

Nikita sipped the cold beer, which soothed her parched throat.

"Just like you being all in love with Sweet Cheeks doesn't change who you are. It makes you better."

"It makes me get shot and doubt my sanity."

Sugar smiled, "Yes on both accounts. Though I got shot when I was still in the ATF, back before Jared."

"You were a field agent for Alcohol, Tobacco, and Firearms?"

"A few of my low connections in high places. At least I was until Jared blew my cover trying to save one of his crew's life. Still not sure if I've forgiven him for that. Now I'm mostly just a guncrafter."

"You're Lily Chase?" There couldn't be that many top gunsmiths named Lily.

"Was. Took Jared's name, mostly because we adopted Asal."

Nikita wondered if you could ever really know anyone. One of the best gunsmiths working was a busty babe in the modern version of designer buckskin.

Sugar handed her another beer while Nikita looked at Miss Belikin Beer Bikini Girl in the poster again. She could have been the twin of the jitney boat tour guide. Maybe she was the same woman. Or maybe she was a banker making extra cash on the side.

Drake was like two different people. Or maybe more. The womanizer gunner. The angry man who wouldn't let anyone help him clean up his fellow crew chief's blood. The glorious male who had pounded into her against the shower wall yet whispered so gently that it was okay to not remember while he carried her in his arms.

"Can you ever really know someone?"

"Where would be the fun in that?"

She didn't know. But she wished she couldn't remember.

* * *

"You sure you don't know what's going on down there in Honduras? We land tomorrow—next port of call is Roatán. Anything would help." Drake wasn't sure when he'd switched from ice tea to beer. Altman had as well. Zoe and Asal had gone off to the hotel pool, leaving the three of them at the table with their beers.

"Why didn't you just buy the damned picture?"

"It was tasteless, crass..."

"So was the bastard who ran GSI. It was a goddamn lead. Get the painting."

"Why? You like nudes?"

"Yes, as long as her name is Lily Westin. You?"

Drake had to admit there was a nude he was very partial to himself. "But that stupid painting—I don't like playing games."

Jared crashed a fist down on the table. "Dammit! Listen, GI

Joe. This whole goddamn thing is a game. You think that half the shit I did while I was on the inside made any sense? You think even that much makes sense on the outside? Do you have any idea how much they pay me for what I do? It sure shouldn't be so much more than you make. What kind of sense is in that?"

It was one of the reasons that the people who served didn't like the mercs, but only one of them. Few were like Jared and Titan. A lot more were like GSI and Curtis.

"How does it make sense that you guys are cleaning up GSI's mess and not me," Jared growled at his beer bottle as he worked at peeling off the label with a thumbnail.

"Are you still harping on that?"

Jared shrugged but didn't look up.

"When Titan can launch people like SEAL Team 6 and the Night Stalkers 5E, you let me know."

"Okay. Point taken. Can you at least explain to me why I never even heard about the 5E until I drove onto Fort Rucker a couple days ago?"

"Because," Drake could see Altman eyeing him, but Drake wasn't drunk. Well, not drunk enough to reveal state secrets. "Because like Nikita said, when we go through a door, no one knows we've been there."

* * *

"What are you fighting so hard against, Swimmer Girl?"

"Don't want to repeat the past." Nikita considered another beer even though she hadn't finished her current bottle. She considered getting blind drunk and missing the boat's midnight departure.

"Doesn't work that way," Sugar pushed aside the empty plate of Belize Rice and Beans. That again changed the balance of their wobbly table and Sugar had to grab to rescue her beer.

"Sure it does." For a crappy bar in a bad quarter, they served an amazing version of the traditional dish. It was rich from the coconut milk used instead of water. The heavy spices and the thick gravy from the stewed gibnut meat—whatever kind of local animal that was, Nikita didn't want to know—soaked up some of the beer in her belly, but not too much.

"How is your past going to repeat?"

Almost everything. Maybe she could just stay in the present because the past and future were whacked-out worse than a plugged cesspool. She leaned back to stare up at the fan whispering overhead. It was close to sunset and the few bare bulbs above the bar did little to light the space. In this semi-twilight moment, it almost looked merely disreputable.

As she looked back down to answer Sugar's question, a big man sat at their table and a hand clamped around Sugar's wrist.

And it wasn't J-dawg.

"You two will come with me," his English was as thick as a swamp with Spanish.

"Fuck off!" Nikita had been about to say something important, but now couldn't remember what it was. "Private conversation."

With his hand that wasn't pinning Sugar's wrist, he did one of those flashy gang moves to flick out a switchblade instead of just opening it.

Nikita glanced at Sugar, who just grimaced. *Amateur!*

The way Sugar's eyes flickered up behind Nikita told her that she was wrong.

Amateurs! More than one.

Sugar jerked her arm toward her chest, dragging the man closer by his grasp on her wrist. Under the table, she planted one of her spike-heeled boots between his legs and hard into his crotch.

His scream hurt Nikita's ears.

She felt hands come to rest on her shoulders from behind. With a hard shove off the floor, using all the leverage her SEAL-strong legs could give her, she flipped her chair over backward.

Her attacker stumbled away, knocked aside by the back of the chair.

When her back hit the floor, Nikita used her momentum to continue into a backward somersault. Halfway through she lashed out with her feet and caught the guy's kneecap. There was a satisfying crunch up through the leather of her sandal as his knee broke and doubled over in the wrong direction.

Her continued roll knocked him onto his back with his leg doubled up under him. She rammed a punch into his sternum. Her aim was off but she was in a hurry. Instead of just knocking the wind out of him, she might have broken a couple of ribs as well.

A third attacker had Sugar by the hair, dragging her head back hard.

Somehow, Nikita still had her beer bottle in her other hand. She heaved it into the guy's face hard enough to startle him into easing his grip on Sugar, maybe breaking his nose as a bonus.

It was all Sugar needed.

With a sweep kick, Sugar knocked his legs out from under him. As he fell forward, Sugar managed to get her hands behind the guy's head.

Nikita kicked the table closer and Sugar rammed him down, chin-first onto it. By the look of the blood coming out of his mouth when Sugar let him fall to the floor, he was going to need a new jaw and some teeth to go with it.

They surveyed the scene.

The first attacker was still on the floor holding his crotch with one hand, but groping for his knife with the other.

Rather than kicking his knife aside, Sugar planted the pointed toe of her boot into his temple with a hard enough kick that he stopped having interest in anything other than bleeding. His cellphone lay close beside him and Sugar put a spiked heel through its heart with a satisfying crunch of glass and metal.

It had happened so fast that the other patrons hadn't had a chance to do anything other than draw back and look aghast.

They looked at each other, then down at the table still standing between them.

Sugar laughed. "Table is stronger than it looks."

Nikita nodded.

"The past isn't," Sugar's suddenly fierce, dark-blue eyes were studying Nikita.

Maybe.

* * *

"Why don't I like that sound?" Jared had Asal riding on his shoulders.

Drake didn't like it either.

The women had been gone for hours, long enough that it had become an itch, so they'd all gone looking for them—Altman and Zoe starting to the north, Drake and Jared with Asal working from the south. The problem was that the trail had gone cold and there were five hundred cruise passengers reconvening on Belize City from their adventures, all in time for a pre-sailing dinner. Asking shopkeepers if they'd recently seen two pretty women in nice clothes didn't work.

They'd rapidly worked their way out of the Tourist Village and into the rougher section of Belize City.

There were a lot of sounds that were strange in this city, but the whoop of a police siren was a very distinctive one.

Drake spotted it racing by two blocks over, closely followed by a wailing ambulance.

"Really don't like that sound." They broke into a jog, Asal clamping both hands around Jared's forehead like a stoic captain weathering the tossing seas.

Around the corner and two more blocks up were a trio of flashing cop cars and a second ambulance.

Altman and Zoe came out of a side street and joined them as they reached the police perimeter.

"There," Asal pointed from her perch atop Jared's shoulders.

They forged forward as a unit, brushing aside the few policemen foolish enough to get in their way.

In the midst of it all, Sugar and Nikita were standing at ease, as if merely watching a parade go by. It might have worked as a ploy if not for the three cops hovering close beside them with their notepads out. They'd been at the center of whatever was going on.

Drake barged through, knocking a protesting sergeant and his notebook to the side.

"You okay, honey?"

"Honey?" Nikita looked at him in surprise. "When did I give you honey privileges?"

"Your apartment in Alabama? In a men's shower maybe?" Drake was just glad to have found her. He'd missed her through the long slow afternoon—actually missed her. That was a strangeness he hadn't noticed until this moment when he suddenly felt so happy to be standing next to her again.

"Maybe," Nikita sounded as if she was in a much better mood than she'd been in days.

That's when the gurneys started rolling out of the hole-in-the-wall tavern. Three big guys, looking awfully battered.

Drake glanced at Nikita and Sugar. Neither of them looked the least bit hurt, though they were making a point of straightening their clothes and finger-brushing back their hair.

When he met Jared's gaze, the man's smile was electric. *Don't you just love these women?*

He did. Drake slipped a hand around Nikita's waist and she let herself be pulled against him. He truly did.

* * *

Once the police let them go, they strolled together back toward the ship's pier. Just three couples and a kid talking softly among themselves.

Other couples and groups were wending their way through the warm evening back to the ship, none close enough to hear quite how bizarre the conversation of their group might be.

Nikita had always liked that feeling of being special, being elite. It was her dad's doing. Chas Hayward had taught her young about the high of being better than everyone around her. Better at martial arts, better at shooting, better at noticing details that no one else did. Curtis Contracting had fed that too, at least until it all came apart. Being a Team Six SEAL absolutely did that. But being in this little circle of specialists was something else. Here she wasn't *better than*—she was *part of*. That was something else ST6 had taught her to understand, but this moment was somehow stronger and more powerful.

"I chatted with the bartender before the police arrived," Sugar was explaining. "These guys were complete strangers. And a couple of the patrons said that their Spanish accent was wrong. Any Belizean would have more Creole or British influence."

"Wish we could ID the bastards." J-dawg's growl said that whatever else he might be, he cared deeply about Sugar. Nikita could hear it in his voice.

Even mercenary bastards had feelings. Who knew. And now that she'd count Sugar as a friend, did that mean she had to accept J-dawg as well? That concept she didn't like so much.

"I forgot to ask the damn cops how long it would take to get IDs."

"Oh, we already know that without asking," Nikita said in an offhand way.

Sugar's smile said that Nikita was doing a fair job of channeling Sugar's strong-woman attitude.

"It's going to take them a *long* time. Those three didn't seem like the chatty types."

Their group had reached the head of the pier, where J-dawg and Sugar wouldn't be able to follow past security.

While J-dawg and Drake cursed over the news, she turned aside to where the lights on the pier made a dark, shadowed area behind a wide palm. It was also out of sight of the pier's security watch.

She and Sugar reached down their blouses and pulled out the three men's wallets and passports.

"It may take them a *very* long time without these," Nikita held them up.

The others' laughter made it feel like she was taking a bow at the end of one of Drake's stage performances.

"Careful with those," Nikita stopped Jared from flipping one open. "We took fingerprints of each person on the inside flap."

Jared peeled it open carefully, "What did you use for ink?"

"They each seemed to be leaving a lot of blood around. We also smeared a dollar bill on each of them so that there'd be plenty for a DNA sample."

"IDs look fake as hell. Whatever port authority let these aboard should have his eyes examined." Jared took all three wallets, "I'll get these to Parker right away."

"Hold it," Altman reached out to stop him, but Jared fended him off.

"You people have a boat to catch. And don't worry. Parker can get to any database he needs to."

"*That's* what worries me," but Altman desisted.

"What worries me is this." Nikita reached into the edge of her bra where the damn cards had been poking her.

She held out the men's three cruise ship passes.

"And this," she nodded to Sugar.

Sugar opened her leather vest and lifted her blouse enough to extract the long barrel of a silenced Ruger 22/45 LITE. It was a lean, nasty gun accurate out to seventy meters plus—well past the distance from observation deck to bow. The shooter had put those two shots exactly where he'd intended.

"Scare tactics with the gun. Then a kidnapping attempt. Someone is trying to spook your team," Sugar concluded.

Nikita took it from her. They hadn't had time to inspect it carefully before. She dropped the magazine and held it up to the light.

"Full," Drake said looking over her shoulder.

"So no way to tell if this was the weapon that shot at us, but the model and silencer make it likely."

"Please tell me you hurt the man bad."

"Well, I can tell you one thing, Sweet Cheeks," Nikita leaned in and kissed Drake on the nose. "After what Sugar did to him, he may never have sex again."

Chapter 11

They waited until the ship was dark and quiet before they went on the hunt. They were two hours out to sea and the ship was rolling a bit in the heavy side sea, but not enough to make them misstep.

This time they were all armed. For the sake of the security cameras, they made a show of going out as couples, two couples acting like they were just going for a walk to stretch their legs. Down one long deck to the grand staircase near the end—all red carpeted and brass hand railed.

On Deck 8 they turned away from their quarry and made a point of window shopping along the corridor past the closed boutiques where they'd spent so much of Titan's money.

On Deck 7 they explored the selections in the library. Drake took a Connelly thriller he'd been wanting to read. He couldn't imagine that Nikita had actually been paying attention when she'd a selected diet plan title that promised to burn away fat without exercise.

"It looks like the kind of book my empty-headed self might select," she explained. Then, as if embarrassed by herself, she dropped it on a chair as they left. He set the Connelly with it, liking the juxtaposition—the two sides of Nikita Hayward.

On Deck 6 they meandered most of the way back to the bow.

At side-by-side suites, 612 and 614, they traded nods with Altman and Zoe that would look as if they were wishing each other good night. Both doors had "Do Not Disturb" signs dangling from their door handles.

Zoe slipped the keycard into 614, which had belonged to two of the three henchmen. Nikita did the same on 612.

The electronic locks released at the same moment and flashed green.

In unison they jammed down on the handles, swung open the doors, and pulled their weapons as they moved inside.

Drake was first in.

"Daylin?" A sleepy woman's voice.

A step behind him, Nikita hit the lights.

A lean woman stared at him wide-eyed for the length of two heartbeats, then drove a hand under her pillow.

There was a sharp click and spit close by Drake's ear. The woman yelped as the round punched into the pillow and there was a loud clank as her bullet hit metal.

The woman flinched and jerked her hand back to her chest. As she did, she knocked aside the pillow, revealing a twin to the gun that Sugar had taken in the bar and delivered to Jared.

The prone woman was smart enough to not go for this gun again.

Altman came in through the connecting door with Zoe close behind and picked up the weapon while Nikita kept her covered. He dropped the magazine and nodded, "Two rounds shy of full."

Drake didn't remember moving until his face was inches from the woman's. "Why did you shoot her?" he pointed back at Nikita.

"I did not! I missed," her accent was thickly Spanish.

"Same accent as our three *hombres,*" Nikita confirmed where she still had the woman centered in her sights. "And you didn't miss. My arm still hurts like hell."

The woman looked aghast. "I was ordered to shoot you. A final test it might be...have been. They never said I would be shooting American woman. I was not ready for such things. So I aim away."

Drake glanced back at Nikita and earned an I-told-you-so look for his troubles.

"Daylin know I am crack shot. Now they no longer trust me. That is why they leave me on ship today."

"Sure," Zoe chimed in. "They trust you so little, they gave you gun Number Two."

"They also give this," she went to raise her other arm.

Drake saw a flash of metal and was all set to dive away when there was a sharp clank and her arm stopped abruptly. She was handcuffed to the bed.

"With just the handcuff, I could scream for help. With a *pistola* on a cruise ship, I would be in very much trouble if I was found." Then her dark eyes went wider as she looked at the four of them grouped around her bed. "Or am I now in more troubles? Did you kill Daylin and the others? Now me, too? Are you kill squad like Daylin say?" Her voice kept rising.

Drake did his best to shush her. He would have to admit it was an odd setting. A cruise ship suite at two in the morning, softly aglow with indirect light. A slender woman with dark skin, black hair that spilled in a soft wave to well-curved breasts that were barely hidden by the thin blue nightgown—handcuffed to the bed while four fully dressed Special Operations soldiers looked down at her.

"We are not a murder squad," Nikita said with disgust.

"What about when Daylin comes back? He will be very angry. Where is he?"

"I expect he will be in a Belizean jail for quite some time. We're arranging for the three of them to be extradited to the US on the charge of attempted kidnapping of Americans."

Her shoulders sagged in relief. "He cannot kill me from there. Then maybe you could unlock these cuff. Daylin make it too tight and my hand it…*zumbar*…tingle? Yes? All day."

"Do you have a key?"

"Daylin put it in the safe, but he does not give me the combination."

When Drake looked at him, Altman shrugged. "I could pick the handcuff lock. But since we need to see what's in the safe anyway, you should just cozy up to our friendly neighborhood hotel manager."

"Shouldn't we search first?"

"You cozy, we'll search. Not a lot of hiding places in a standard suite." It was a much simpler arrangement than their own. There were only five spaces: bathroom, walk-in closet, bedroom with big-screen TV, small sitting area with big-screen TV, and a verandah barely large enough for two loungers.

Drake picked up the phone, punched for the operator, and began convincing her that he in truth did want to talk to the hotel manager despite the hour. Stating his name turned out to be the key in the lock—he was on some sort of preferred passenger list. If they only knew.

"Hi Norma. Drake Roman here. Sorry to wake you, but could you join us in Suite 614…Yes, 614." He should have called from Room 614's phone. He didn't want to greet her with the handcuffed woman wearing only a skimpy negligee in 612.

"Don't forget to tell her to bring a master key for the room safe," Nikita said as she came out of the closet and headed for the bath.

He passed on the message, making it clear that she should come alone.

Norma made it in record time, every inch of her ship officer's uniform in its proper place.

The safe turned up nothing except more ammunition, the woman's passport, which matched the fake ID they'd found in her purse, and the crucial handcuff key. Zoe pointed out a charger, but there was no cellphone. It must still be in Daylin's pocket.

"Sugar spiked it with a boot heel. Very dead," Nikita explained as she searched under the mattress.

When they showed Norma the gun, she nearly wilted under the burden. "In a decade of cruising, I have never had a gun on a ship before."

Her suspicions began turning on them until Drake suggested that she deliver the weapon—along with the contents of the safe, except the woman's passport—to the Captain to keep under lock and key, preferably until they were again in Miami in four days' time. Nikita also handed over the three men's cruise ship passes.

"What about her?" Norma nodded to the woman. She now had one of the ship's complimentary white terrycloth robes over her shoulders and was massaging her wrist. "We have a lockup, but the crew would see her and there would be many questions."

"For the moment," Drake took the handcuffs and the key, "she will be staying with us."

* * *

"My name is Esly Escarra and yes, I know my passport says Joan Smith. I was DNIC sergeant in San Pedro Sula. As *policia* sergeant in crime and drugs division, I tried to be honest."

Not what Nikita was expecting. A gang member, a hired thug, but not a cop.

The five of them were seated in the lounge area of their big suite. She and Drake on one sofa, Altman, Zoe, and Esly in the three armchairs across a low coffee table. Esly was now dressed in simple clothes that made her barely passable by cruising standards—wouldn't have without her good figure and nice, though still tentative, smile.

"Daylin, he was my captain and my lover before he change sides. Now he is…how do you say?"

"On the take?" Nikita decided that just maybe there was someone worse than mercenaries: those pretending to do one job while actually doing another.

"On the take? English idiom is very strange. The *take* was very nice and we live very well. Eventually I must arrest him or join him. The decision is not hard in Honduras, especially not in San Pedro where much of Venezuela's cocaine leave for Mexico and America. Honest police have very short lives there. But I never shoot one. Daylin? Maybe he did. I do not know. I am more Daylin's protection, his…he is with woman so he look like a good man? Yes? The other two were his lieutenants." Then her eyes gazed into the distance for a few moments. "He was always nice to me, but the money changed him very much. If he is truly gone, I will miss him only little amount."

"Why shoot at Nikita?" Drake still sounded pissed as hell about that.

Esly shook her head. "I do not know very much. There is a big project—'more money than drugs' Daylin tells me and very much less dangerous. But we must scare away American contractor. GSI, he told me, were no longer needed for this big project. First we attack their women—he say they always travel with many women. Then, if that does not make them to go away, we attack them. That is all I know."

Nikita shook her head. "Your Daylin was not a smart man. The best way to make a mercenary like the head of GSI angry is to attack his women."

"Works for me, too," Drake's growl was so very male.

Esly sighed, "No, he is not very smart. But he was kind to me and better than many as lover. Are you good lover?" She aimed her sudden tease at Altman. Her self-confidence was amazing for a woman who had faced a "death squad" after being handcuffed throughout the day.

Nikita couldn't resist smiling, but Luke Altman's face didn't shift in the slightest as he turned to her.

"So, Esly shoots to miss and loses Daylin's trust. Daylin goes for staging a kidnapping in Belize City."

"Daylin," Nikita confirmed, "ends up bloody when Sugar rams her spiked boot heel into his crotch."

Esly covered a quick burst of laughter with a hand over her mouth.

"Somebody in Honduras…" Drake took Nikita's hand and held on to it as if that would protect her from whatever came next.

It was silly, they were safe in their suite, but still she was charmed.

"…took every bit of weaponry and tactical advice that GSI would sell them and now wants to cut them out of the profits. Which would have made GSI even angrier and more dangerous."

"Wait," Esly looked from one face to another, "you are not this GSI?"

"No," Nikita decided to keep it simple. "No, we're not."

An hour later they were none the wiser.

Daylin, and through him Esly, had been hired to scare off GSI. They weren't likely to be scared off, especially not after the amount of capital they'd invested in Honduras. They'd been paid for it, very well, making an outfit as greedy as GSI hungry for more, not less.

"At least we can all agree on one thing," Nikita finally summed it up.

"What's that?" Zoe finally managed to take the bait. Drake and Altman were beyond speech.

"This is certainly the single most screwed-up, frustrating, really-pissing-me-off project I've worked on since—" she almost said *joining ST6,* but Esly was still there with them, "—the last time I was on a screwed-up, frustrating, really-pissing-me-off project."

That earned her grunts of agreement from the two men.

They had sent Esly's fingerprints, taken with the help of Zoe's mascara, to Parker along with the suggestion to look in the Honduran police files. Esly and the three jailed kidnappers came back with positive IDs almost immediately—exactly matching Esly's story right down to each one's rank and matching picture. He also provided home addresses; Esly's and Daylin's were the same.

Daylin had apparently kept the broader scope of the plan to himself, and his destroyed cellphone had probably been swept out with the rest of the trash in the bar.

They handcuffed Esly to the bed in the back suite—this time less painfully and with her cooperation: "I am the unknown. I understand."

Altman pulled a chair close enough to the bed to prop his feet on the mattress. He'd wake up if Esly so much as rolled over.

Zoe was out cold on the couch in the second bedroom's sitting area.

Nikita slouched lower on the couch in the main room and rested her head on Drake's shoulder. She'd never been so comfortable around a man. She could go to sleep leaning on him, and maybe not even wake if he moved. He felt that safe to be around.

Drake rose to his feet and looked down at her. He tugged lightly on her hand.

"What?"

At Drake's eye roll, she let him pull her to her feet, though she was unsure what was happening, at least for the first three steps. He was leading her toward the master bedroom.

"But—"

"I'm tired…"

And Nikita was surprised by the rush of disappointment that he was leading her to the bedroom to sleep. It was so strong that it almost took her breath away.

"…of not having you in my bed."

Drake Roman in a bed was the best idea she'd heard all day, "But this is my bed. Yours has a pretty Latina handcuffed to it."

"Po-ta-to. Po-tah-to. Besides, I want my Southern belle, not some dangerous Latina." Drake closed and locked the door.

"You're saying I'm not dangerous?"

"There's a difference between dangerous and lethal. You slay me, Nikita."

The room was lit by the bright wash of a nearly full moon shining off the ocean and through the wide-open verandah doors. Plenty enough to see by.

She moved away from the door quickly because the urge to take him here and now was nearly overwhelming, but she'd had enough of vertical surfaces. She agreed: bed. Definitely. Nikita peeled off her shirt and bra as she followed him across the carpet.

"Hey, cut that out," Drake was glaring at her as she shucked shoes, pants, and underwear.

"I thought the point was to get naked," she tossed her socks on the pile of clothes.

"I was looking forward to undressing you myself."

"Why?"

While Drake puzzled over how to answer that one, she grabbed the hem of his own t-shirt and yanked it upward. He mumbled a protest as she peeled it over his head and off his arms.

She had his pants undone before he grabbed her wrists.

"Hold on there, little lady! Just slow down for a second." Drake's John Wayne was better than his Southern, marginally. His pants hung enticingly loose on his hips but didn't slide down. She reached, but his strong grip kept her hands inches from his waistband.

"I thought you wanted sex," she tried again and failed. Drake was far stronger than he looked—though she already knew that.

"Did I say that I wanted sex?"

"Well, we're not going to just get naked and then sleep."

"I didn't say that either."

"Then what?"

After another moment, he slowly released her hands.

"Then what?"

In answer, he raised a hand to her face, cupping her cheek

in his palm. Then he leaned in to kiss her, so softly and gently that she couldn't tell when it shifted from mere contact to warm kiss. His other hand slid around her waist and pulled her tightly against him.

His dangling belt buckle dug into her hip, so she moved back enough to bat his pants and underwear off his hips, then let herself be pulled against him once more after he kicked the last of his clothes free. Drake's chest was just as much a revelation this time as it had been during their first kiss. She pressed against it more and more, every inch of contact a new discovery. The simple sensation of touch had never been so desirable, so necessary. She felt as if she'd go mad if she didn't get—

Overbalanced, Drake collapsed backward onto the bed, his tight grip taking her with him.

"At least we made it to the bed this time," she rubbed her face against his chest as his hands dug into her hair. He didn't guide her, no pressure to aim her attention at his crotch. Instead he seemed to be merely playing with her hair. When she lay her ear on his chest to listen to his racing heart, his hands went quiet and merely cradled her head against him. She listened to it for a long time—seconds, minutes, ten beats, a hundred…she didn't count, didn't try to keep track.

Drake coaxed her the rest of the way onto the bed and onto her back. While he shed his socks, then backtracked to his pants for protection, she lay back, closed her eyes, and prepared herself for the wild ride to come. Sex with Drake was so good. They'd only had the one opportunity, but it had been wonderful, hot, and steamy.

The hand that brushed down her neck was so unexpectedly gentle that she could only gasp at the contact. She felt a shiver that had nothing to do with temperature.

Nikita lay there and could only let her awareness follow that single point of contact. Down her neck, tracing back and forth across her collarbone, down between her breasts until her stomach muscles clenched tighter than after doing a hundred crunches when he rested his palm there.

She managed to open her eyes and look at Drake. The moonlight was bright enough to reveal his face but not his expression. His attention wasn't following the line of his touch. He wasn't staring at her breasts. He was watching her face.

"What are you doing?" Nikita didn't recognize her own voice it was so breathy with surprise.

"Enjoying myself. What are you doing?"

She hissed at the sensation of his fingertips tracing up the side of her breast, then circling around. "Feeling," she managed. She was feeling the sensations as they rippled over her skin like tiny waves lapping on a tropical beach. For years she'd learned about focused attention down range, on the target. Now her focus was narrowing inward until she was aware of no more than the exact path of Drake's touch, a point of fiery sensation and a trailing wake of pleasant tingles.

Then an underwater explosion's worth of heat lashed through the point where his mouth took her breast. A groan escaped her. The more her body reacted, the slower and gentler Drake became. He delivered no fiery heat, instead he coaxed it out of her until she burned for more.

"Drake," she managed on a broken breath.

"Hmm," he responded a lazy time later after nuzzling her neck.

"If you don't do something more and damn soon, I'm going to have to kill you."

"Hmm," he kissed her on the mouth while his hand slid down her body and returned—traveling somewhere between dead slow and full stop.

Her body was begging for engines full ahead. Her life always begged for that. She'd been born her father's daughter and never looked back—charging into the fray whether it was playground tag or full-force suppression of a terrorist training camp.

"I don't know how to do this." Nikita curled against his hand as he slid it between her legs. She could feel his smile against her temple when his lips brushed there.

"Just be yourself, Nikita."

"Myself," she breathed in deep, pressing herself harder against his hand, "is expecting the men's shower wall."

But he didn't give her that. He coaxed and teased and enticed until she finally gave up, having no idea what was happening next—not from him, not from her.

Instead, for only the second time in her life, she was completely out of control. The first time was when everything went south during the operation in the Congo and the bastards had turned the radio on continuous transmit so that she couldn't leave, couldn't do anything but listen. It never stopped though she begged it to. No one could hear her with the transmit key locked down on the other end.

And now with Drake, she was past reason. Her body and her emotions were in as helpless a whirl, but this time she spent every second begging that he *wouldn't* stop. She rose to meet his every touch, ached for him until it was a full-body sensation.

When he finally entered her, there was a rightness, a completeness that she'd never found before. As if, for just this once, she was somehow whole.

* * *

Drake didn't know what to do with the tears soaking his shoulder. He tried to brush them away, but Nikita clung to him so tightly that he couldn't do anything more than hold her in turn.

She didn't weep or sob, but the salty tang of her tears was a thousand times stronger than the mid-ocean air drifting in through the open doorway to the verandah.

"What's with the tears, honey?" He cradled her gently. Never had a woman so responded to him. He'd meant to make love to her, but had become so involved that it was more as if "making love" was a third thing that would have interfered if it had been in bed with them. There had only been him and the magnificent woman now clinging to him so tightly.

"What tears?" Nikita's voice was rough with them. "I'm crying? But I never do that. Not since—"

And he held her tighter as she froze. She didn't struggle to get free, but she didn't relax either.

"Not since… It's been a long time," she faded to a whisper.

"Then I'll take it as a compliment that you felt safe enough to cry on me."

"Felt safe? That is not at all what I felt. Well maybe it is. But that's not all it was. It was—I'm rambling."

"Don't stop now," it never did his ego any harm to hear how he'd made a woman feel. And he truly and deeply wanted to know how he'd made this particular one feel.

His answer was a gentle fist in the ribs. "Not feeding your fantasies of male prowess, Duck-man."

"But they're such good fantasies."

This time she pushed away, not hard, just as if she was ready to go. He didn't want her to, but he never argued with what a woman wanted. She didn't turn on a light, or head to the bathroom while scooping up her clothes. Instead she went to the edge of the verandah and leaned on the doorframe, looking east over the ocean, silhouetted in moonlight.

She looked strong and mysterious. Warm despite the cool light.

He slid out of the bed and wrapped his arms around her from behind. She leaned back against him, wrapping her arms over his.

"I heard every word of their deaths. Every cry. My father must have known they were transmitting. The only words he ever said were, 'I love you, Nikki. Tell your mom that you two are the best thing that ever happened to me.' Other than that, he never made a single sound, even when his torturers promised they'd stop if he did."

There were no tears in her voice or sliding down her cheeks now. Somehow he was now holding both his lover and an ST6 SEAL at the same time.

"Barry never said my name once. For all the pleading and begging and crying he did, he never once said my name." Then she turned slowly in his arms and looked up at him from a breath away. "I haven't let anyone past my guard since."

Drake studied her in the moonlight, memorized every feature from the curve of her cheek to the shape of her lips as well as he could.

She waited and he knew what she was asking.

It should be a hard question. It was certainly one that he'd been an expert at avoiding for an entire lifetime. A lifetime that so far had been filled with no one like Chief Petty Officer Nikita Hayward.

He had wanted to make love to her to bring her closer to him. It had worked. The catch was that it had worked both ways and now he couldn't imagine letting her go.

"I would say your name: first, middle, and last." And once he said it, he knew it was true.

And still the SEAL watched him as the woman held him.

He slipped sideways onto one of the wide loungers and tugged her down beside him. There was a shelf with handy blankets and he pulled one over them.

She curled up against him and together they watched the night sky.

He had nothing to say. His life had been so easy compared to hers. All he could offer was to hold her.

There was only one word that would describe how incredible she felt. How important she felt. He kissed the top of her head where it rested on his shoulder and whispered it into the night.

"Nikita."

Chapter 12

Storm's coming."

Nikita raised her head enough to look over Drake's chest and out the master bedroom's doors. She didn't remember exactly when they had moved indoors. Cygnus had flown out of sight over the other side of the ship and Pegasus had proclaimed the zenith when they shifted locations.

Now, the rising sun was masked by deep red clouds. The sky above was still blue, but the old sailor's adage had more truth than not: *Red at night, sailors delight. Red in the morning, sailors take warning.* A storm arriving from the east across the open reaches of the Caribbean Sea.

That wasn't the only storm coming. Last night Drake had awakened something in her.

Not merely an insatiable need, but the firm conviction that her need had only one focus: Drake Roman. Up on one elbow and looking down on him as he sleepily rolled his head to look at her, she was captured as well as any swamp bullfrog staring into a flashlight.

His smile for her was soft and gentle, but she could feel where her leg lay thrown over his hips that *his* need for *her* was awakening fast—even faster than he was.

No complaints from her. This time, when she straddled over him, there was none of the confusing tenderness of last night. No new experiences that she'd never imagined possible. But neither was there the frantic satisfying of their bodies like after their race.

Yes, the sex was fast, hard, and ripped through her body with mind-wiping pleasure. But afterward he pulled her down until she lay full upon his chest and she had her face tucked into his neck so that all she could smell was the rich warmth that was so distinctly Drake's. That too was amazing. More amazing than the sex in many ways.

There was no hurry to get up and get dressed. No impatience. She'd learned that when men were done, they were done. Not Drake. He stroked her body from her knee—still tucked up in kneeling position—down thigh to hip, up and over her back, into her hair or brushing her cheek, even tugging lightly on her ear, before returning via her shoulder, the side of her breast, her ribs, and back to her hips. It was soothing, gentle, loving…

"Wait!" she mumbled into his neck.

"Wait what?"

"What are you doing to me?" She pushed up onto her elbows and looked down at him.

"What do you mean?" But there was a smile tugging at his lips that said he knew exactly what he was doing.

She was never, ever the slow one in the room. SEAL training had only enhanced her natural tendencies to observe and analyze any situation. "You're trying to slip something by me?"

"Me?" Now he was definitely smiling, no attempt at innocence other than his tone. "When would I ever be able to slip something by the incredible Nikita?"

"Wait a minute! There was something…last night…" and then she had it. She'd asked without asking if he cared enough about her that her name would have been somewhere on his lips if he'd been in Barry's position.

First, middle, and last.

"I was only asking if you'd think of me if—" somehow everything went that wrong.

"I would," his smile shifted toward leer. "I'd think about your breasts," she had pushed herself up high enough that he managed to get his hands on them. "I'd think about the incredible things you can do with those beautiful hips," he wriggled his own beneath her.

"Ro*man*."

"I'd think of your beautiful, ever so expressive face that shows exactly what you're thinking and feeling no matter how much you think it doesn't."

She put her face back into his shoulder to hide whatever it was saying without her permission. That forced his hands back to her ribs.

"And," his voice shifted to completely serious, "I'd spend my last moments thanking the lucky stars for every instant I got to be with you."

Nikita pushed back up to glare down at him. "I don't need poetry. I need truth."

"Oh. I can do both. I know for a fact that I will never meet another woman like you. Known that since the first moment you stepped onto my aircraft a year ago. And now that I've discovered that making love to you is beyond spectacular," he wriggled his hips again, but his tone remained oddly serious. "I'm completely sold. All in. Sign me up."

"Making love to me? Is that what last night was?" Compared to Drake Roman, even everything with Barry had been merely sex. But she wasn't comfortable with—

"That's what I'd thought to do."

"But instead?"

"Instead," he shifted his hands up to cradle her face, then kissed her ever so lightly. "Instead I made love *with* you. There will never be another woman for me other than Nikita Hayward. You're stuck with me now."

"Sure, until the Duck-man finds another willing babe."

"I've been with three women since I first met you. I didn't even bother sleeping with the last one, which pissed her off quite a bit, and that was nine months ago. None of them were up to your standard."

"But *you* are?" Nikita wasn't sure where the tease came from. And for the first time this morning, Drake frowned.

"No. No I'm not," he looked aside for a long moment before looking back into her eyes. His had gone almost black and his expression was once more shifting to the powerful warrior she hadn't met before their treadmill race. "But I'm sure as hell going to do my best to live up to your standard from this moment forward."

She wanted to make a joke about all the grunts who aspire to DEVGRU standards but didn't stand a chance. She could have teased Duck-man the gunner about that. But Drake Roman the warrior? No. The tease dried up in her throat as she looked down at him. Him she believed.

This time, when she leaned down to kiss him, it had all of the power of last night's gentleness as well as this morning's heat. How could she not believe in a man like him?

It was even more true than she first understood as his arms slid around her.

She didn't believe in men, had trained herself not to. Oh, she believed in Luke Altman, but as her SEAL commander, not as a man.

But Drake Roman? Him she believed in with all her heart.

* * *

"This is our last shot at figuring out what's going on. Our ship is in Roatán Harbor only for today. We sail at midnight."

Not sure what to do with Esly in public just yet, Drake had ordered morning coffee into the suite as the ship docked. The butler had delivered it along with fresh croissants, then been quite put out that he hadn't been allowed to stay and hover. Apparently, high-roller guests would never deign to pour their own second cup of coffee.

"I'm hoping that going out and being very public will attract someone's attention. That's why I didn't order breakfast; we'll eat ashore as well. As much as I'd like to leave the women behind—"

"Screw that!" Zoe managed to beat Nikita's protest by only milliseconds. Esly may have kept her mouth shut but her look said plenty.

"But as I don't want to be lynched by my own mob," he offered Altman a shrug and received a grimace of commiseration. "You do understand that so far you women have been the main targets?"

"Part of that was my fault. Again, Nikita, I am very truly sorry I shoot at you," Esly apologized sincerely and the other two seemed to forgive her with easy smiles. God help him, he was never going to understand women.

"So here are our rules of engagement today. *No one* leaves the group. Zoe, you're glued to Altman. Nikita, you to me. Even if J-dawg shows up across the street and Asal is choking on a French fry—no one leaves the group."

He glared around the table until he received nods from both of them.

"What about me?" Esly stared straight at him with her impenetrably dark eyes. "I do not want another day handcuffed to a bed."

"How do I trust that I'm talking to police sergeant Escarra and not Daylin's lover?"

Actually her face said a lot about the latter no longer being true.

She had said she would miss Daylin only "a very little amount" and she seemed to be over that already.

Esly shrugged. She was smart enough to know that no amount of promises would count.

Drake saw Zoe and Nikita exchange glances and knew the decision was already made. He could fight it or go with the flow.

"You're with us," he said it before the women could say it for him. "Anyone asks, you are extra protection for Drake Roman because you walk like a policeman."

"Policewoman," Zoe and Esly said together.

Drake sighed, then looked at her across the table. "If anything happens to Zoe or Nikita while you're with us, whether by you or because anyone else gets past you, I'm going to take it out of your hide personally. *Comprende?*"

Nikita destroyed the moment by remarking drily, "See! I knew that you spoke some Spanish."

She'd clearly been hanging around with Zoe too much.

* * *

Nikita, in all her missions, had never wandered about a tropical island like a tourist before. A well-heeled tourist.

Drake had simply called back the butler, who had been ecstatic to have something to do. By the time they reached the dock, a late model Toyota Hiace van, complete with driver and a bilingual tour guide, was waiting for them. They were an older couple, but it was clear that the wife, Mercedez, had once been a great beauty.

"I am fourth generation in Roatán. I will show you the best of everything." Her energy was cheerful without being overbearing. Before they even traveled the few kilometers to the far side of the island, she had already made it clear that they were all one friendly group for the day.

"Where is the fifth generation, Mercedez?" Zoe asked.

And the brilliance of her light dimmed for a moment. "My daughter was murdered during the riots following the 2009 coup. I have no future generation. I now live through my sister's son. His father is mayor of the island and a good man. They both are good men."

Nikita knew full well that kind of pain. To lose a daughter must be even worse. She offered her sympathy, but couldn't think to do anything more.

"We wish to see the island, Mercedez," Drake replied when she asked. "And as odd as this may seem, we wish to be *particularly* visible while we are doing it."

That earned them all a long, assessing look, which she then covered with a radiant smile. "Of course. To fellow tourists or to…locals?" She was sharp and was making it clear what kind of locals she was talking about.

"I wish I knew, Mercedez. I wish I knew."

She nodded firmly, "Then we must start with breakfast at the Lobster Pot on Sandy Bay."

Crab and lobster omelettes were served under big umbrellas. The sandy beach at the Lobster Pot was fine and white. The score of sailboats anchored close ashore explained the dozen other tables with couples and families enjoying a casual meal—and their table was *particularly* prominent.

For a few lazy hours they seemed to pass every person from the cruise ship several times as they wandered through Carambola Botanical Gardens, lush with a zillion plants Nikita had never seen before. Plants weren't exactly high on her list—other than the edibles she'd learned about during survival training—but the gardens were spectacular. Trails wound through the forty-acre patch of jungle revealing trees with leaves that were bigger than she was, in the form of fronds, twists, and massive banana leaves of green so pure it almost hurt to look at. Impossible flowers grew at every turn from tiny lavender-tinged stars to cascades of white-and-yellow orchids so alien looking that they *could* be creatures from another planet.

Zoe started making up wild science fiction stories about their evil plans to conquer the earth.

Drake joined in on the same theme.

In the poor flowers' defense, Nikita countered with wild tales extracted from Dr. Seuss about a lovely tropical princess and the flowers that tried to be as beautiful as she was when she walked among them each day.

The laughter was easy. She'd never been so thoughtlessly comfortable in a group. In a way, she walked beside herself, separate from the smiling woman with her hand tucked in the handsome gunner's elbow, laughing with trained killers and two tour guides. Who was this woman acting as if she was in love with the man beside her? Nikita knew it was herself, and yet it wasn't. Maybe she and not the flowers was the one wrapped up in a Seussian tale, trying to live up to an impossible standard.

Nikita knew the warrior. That woman she understood completely. This one—with the feathered haircut that fluttered every time she turned to look up at her man, whose stomach was sore with laughing rather than with inverted sit-ups, whose body was still loose with the memory of how he had made love to her—this one was a stranger to her.

Then Zoe had delivered the ultimate reality check.

"Let's go clothes shopping."

Nikita had decided she would rather die, but the tour guide whisked them ten kilometers up-island to Junk Boutique in French Harbour.

"This sounds promising," Nikita whispered to Zoe.

"For Esly. Her wardrobe is horrid. It just won't do if she's going to continue being with Drake Roman, Inc. We have standards."

Which was true. "But Junk Boutique?"

"We are a small island," Mercedez overheard her question

and replied with her cheerful but unstoppable charm. "We have several very good designers here. This is where they sell. Casual and couture. It is also on the center of the main walking street of our second largest and most pleasant town."

Through the morning it had become clear that Mercedez was practically adopting Esly. By now they appeared thick as thieves, leaning their heads together and laughing. It was almost as if Mercedez had found her missing daughter for a brief moment.

The shop's window, in a stone building that looked as if it just might have been here since the ships of the 17th-century buccaneers had filled the bay, included a cheerful array of trinkets and a very skimpy bikini that she could see was giving Drake ideas. Thankfully the shop was little bigger, though much better stocked, than the one on the ship. Nikita was able to use that as an excuse to sit out on the bench just in front of the store with the two men and the driver, letting Esly and Zoe go in with their guide.

Across the street was a short beach with a good bay.

"The largest fishing fleet in the Western Caribbean," Emmanuel nodded toward the boats anchored throughout the bay and along the piers.

The traffic and pedestrians of French Harbour swirled around them. Not with the hurry of Mobile or the frantic rush of Norfolk, Virginia, near DEVGRU's base. No one was in too much of a hurry to greet Emmanuel their driver, who rarely spoke more than a word or two but was apparently well known and liked. English, Spanish, black, white, brown—the populace was more mixed than a Navy mess hall. Fashions ranged from khakis and t-shirts to flowing caftans. Every person seemed unique, yet they all seemed to belong.

And, once she managed to get over the near miss of a life-threatening shopping trip with Zoe, she was able to appreciate that this too fit with Drake's plans—Mercedez was serving them very well. Every single person who called out a greeting to Emmanuel carefully inspected the people he was escorting. The island patois was hard to follow, but she caught snatches of questions.

Drake had introduced himself to the guides as a businessman seeking new opportunities throughout Central America. A businessman who had an entourage and required Altman and Esly as his putative guards.

Esly had walked off the ship standing tall. The cautious, carefully-spoken woman who had shared their suite since last night had stepped into her role, looking almost as fierce as Altman, especially after she pilfered a set of Altman's dark, wrap-around shades.

Emmanuel was very circumspect about his current customers, and that alone seemed to speak volumes to those who talked with him.

Esly emerged from Junk Boutique looking even tougher than when she'd gone in. The changes seemed minimal: sturdy boots, a light jacket with a military flair to it, and a brilliant yellow blouse with a low enough neck to accent her dark, creamy skin and generous cleavage. But the alteration in appearance was substantial. She looked tough and sexy at the same time. Maybe Nikita should introduce her to Sugar. Mercedez also emerged with a black clothing bag and wearing what Nikita now recognized as a very expensive smile.

Nikita couldn't help laughing and Mercedez only looked a little abashed—she'd taken them to her own store. But Esly looked both sexy and powerful in her new clothes, which said Mercedez was also good at what she did.

"I am hoping that it is okay I buy two dresses. Zoe said I must," Esly was saying.

Drake was nodding his okay, but she was looking at Altman.

"I look very good in these dresses. Perhaps I can wear one when we go to dinner tonight."

Nikita looked over at her commander. He eyed both Esly and the smiling Zoe cautiously, but kept his mouth shut despite the fact that he now had two women teasing him. Altman was a smart man. It was a no-win scenario.

"Now," Mercedez said cheerfully as Emmanuel loaded the dress bag into the back of the van. "Maybe we should all go swimming along with the dolphins. That is very popular with many people."

Nikita hadn't brought a suit. The string bikini in the window mocked her, but she ignored it. Or tried to. It was far too easy to imagine Drake getting her into it.

"Or perhaps we have done enough in public places for you," Mercedez winked at them all. "I know a very private beach of beautiful sand and tall palms trees where the swimming is far more casual."

Nikita opened her mouth hoping to come up with any other suggestion when she spotted Arthur coming toward them along the street.

She called out his name with relief as a welcome distraction.

* * *

At Nikita's call, Drake looked up in time to see Arthur's reaction: oddly pleasure, not dismay.

"I am so glad I found you, Mr. Roman," he bumbled through the locals going about their business and finally came to stand close in front of the bench they were gathered around.

"Why is that?" He tried to stamp down on his irritation at the interruption and knew he was doing a lousy job of it. The image of going swimming off a tropical beach with Nikita, with or without bathing suit, had rocketed to the top of his mission list. And now, of all irritating beings on the planet, he had to contend with Arthur. If he ended up being the key to all of this, Drake was going to turn in his Minigun.

"Norma has been pushing me for a way to help you. And I've been thinking on it very hard."

"I'm not buying your damned painting. Wait. *Norma* has been pushing you?"

"She can be a very persuasive woman, Mr. Roman, and she seems to have taken quite a liking for you. I finally thought of something this morning but you had already left the ship. That's why I'm so glad I ran into you."

Drake checked sideways, but Nikita simply shrugged. He suppressed a sigh that now he probably wasn't going to get to see what that shrug would look like in a bathing suit.

"Spill it, Arthur."

The man waffled from one foot to the other. "It isn't very much; I only hope it can help. I was told to make sure that Mr. Baer of GSI was informed that this painting was available for purchase." His stance stabilized as if he was now done.

"Who told you to sell it to Baer?" Drake was getting tired of this.

"I don't know."

Drake cursed and rose to his feet.

Arthur stumbled back and almost crashed into Zoe. Esly shot out a hand and clamped on to Arthur's jacket like she was clamping an unruly kitten by the scruff of the neck. She held him in place. Drake could get to like her.

"How can you not know?"

"That's not how it works," Arthur continued in a hurry. "We aren't actually part of the cruise line. My company contracts to run the gallery, present art education programs for the passengers, and hold auctions. We have stables of artists we buy from frequently as well as freelance artists. We try to make sure that there are paintings for every taste, including a few exceptional pieces."

"You're not saying—" Drake remembered that damn nude far too clearly.

"No. No." Arthur shook his head. "The technique is good though. Borrowing from both the Dutch Masters' depth and Art

Deco's clarity of line. I feel that the composition is somewhat lacking, however..."

He trailed off when he caught sight of Drake's expression and cleared his throat carefully.

"Items are accumulated, sorted, and distributed to the ships in containers. I get a provenance sheet on each piece and a cost. I make a commission on every dollar above cost that I can sell a piece for."

"And the provenance sheet said to sell this to GSI."

"Not exactly. Sometimes we have frequent travelers with known tastes and we try to make sure to have a piece or two from their favorite artist or style aboard. This was noted as a definite purchase for Mr. Baer—he buys every one and insists that he always sees them first. He pays rather well for paintings in this particular series."

"There's a series of these goddamn things?" Drake managed a deep breath but it didn't calm him. "Can we see the sheet?"

Arthur reached into his pocket and pulled it out.

"You're not earning points for proactive helpfulness, Arthur."

The man blanched white. Even hard-core method actors weren't so obvious. Maybe he was authentic.

Drake inspected the sheet, didn't see anything unusual except the note: *Definite purchase for GSI.* He handed it to Zoe, who struck him as most likely in their group to have a clue about something like this. She inspected it more carefully than he did, then shrugged.

"Is there anything unusual on that sheet?"

"Nothing," Arthur shrugged.

"Or the case it came in?"

"A simple cloth bag with a rigid protection board. It would be very unlikely that I ever shipped a painting to a client in the same bag it arrived in so I doubt if there would be more information there," then he blinked several times. "But I'll check if there's anything else that came with the painting. I can't imagine there was. I knew Mr. Baer would be aboard because one of that series of Myora's paintings was in this sailing's collection. Who makes sure that they are sent to me? I have no idea. Inquiries into how our buyers work is…not encouraged." He grimaced with the face of prior experience.

Drake nodded to Esly, who let Arthur go. He was so insubstantial that he seemed to waver at the sudden release.

"We need to see the painting," he couldn't believe he was saying the words. "Now."

"So, you *will* be purchasing it?" The overeager art salesman was back as if that's truly all he was.

"Don't push your luck."

"I can promise you an excellent price," Arthur seemed to realize that he wasn't making any headway and pulled out his cellphone, "I can have it delivered to your suite; my assistant is still aboard." He placed the call. "All set. It will be waiting for you."

"How did you find us here?"

"Oh," Arthur pointed at the boutique behind them. "I wanted to get something pretty for Norma."

"For Norma," Drake felt as if his ears were ringing and he couldn't make enough sense of it to answer the call.

"She's just the most wonderful woman, but she doesn't see herself as beautiful as she truly is—too many years of working the cruise ships can do that to you. I've been trying to show her otherwise."

"They have several stunning nightgowns. Very pretty, very tropical," Zoe prompted him.

"Oh my. Exactly the kind of thing I was hoping to find. I must be the luckiest man there is. Good day, Mr. Roman. Good day," he nodded to the rest of them and hurried inside.

"Is he for real?"

Nikita rose from where she'd remained on the bench and kissed him on the cheek. "First Sugar and now Arthur. I suspect they are both for real. You do seem to attract some very odd sorts, Mr. Roman."

"Present company included," he hugged her back and kissed her temple. Over the top of her head he saw the elegant bikini that would have looked so good on Nikita. He cursed to himself over lost opportunity and turned to Mercedez.

"I'm afraid that our day has been cut short by business."

Chapter 13

I hate that painting even more in daylight," Drake sat on the sofa. He couldn't stop staring at the hideous thing. The nude was so blatant. Too realistic to be ignored. It was almost as if a naked harlot was lying in their midst.

"You only hate it because you have taste," Nikita curled up on the couch beside him with her bare feet tucked under her. He had his arm over her shoulders and if Altman or Zoe had anything to say about it, they were keeping it to themselves.

Esly sat in her armchair, unaware of anything out of the ordinary—like a Night Stalker getting cozy with a Navy SEAL.

Altman inspected it again. "There's no card, no secret inscription carved on the frame, we don't have x-ray vision to see if there is actually a copy of *Dogs Playing Poker* underneath it." They had tried holding it up to the muted sunlight lost behind the heavy clouds, but learned nothing that way either.

Zoe tipped her head back and forth to inspect it. "Maybe her head is on another of his paintings and her missing foot on yet another. If it's a piece in a larger puzzle, we're nowhere."

"I can't believe that there's a series of these goddamn things," Drake managed a deep breath but it didn't calm him.

He went to the window and stared out. They were docked in Mahogany Bay, a narrow, deep-water inlet five kilometers from the town of Coxen Hole. There was room to squeeze in two cruise ships. Beyond the dock a small quaint "village" had been set up—half souvenir shops and half tour providers. Beyond that lay a forest as thick as and even more foreign to him than the Alabama one. Here all he could smell was the sea.

It would have been prettier if not for the high layer of thin, gray clouds that had moved all the way across the blue sky since dawn. It reached to the mainland, sixty kilometers distant across the turquoise water gone dark blue beneath that sullen sky.

"I know this place."

Esly was from Honduras, so he wasn't sure why she sounded so surprised. But then Drake turned and saw that she wasn't looking at the view, she was looking at the painting.

"What place?"

"It is *la cascada,* a, uh, waterfall near El Carbón. It is deep in the national park."

He hadn't even looked at the background of the painting as a picture, merely to see if it hid words or a map.

Drake grabbed his satellite phone and punched a speed dial.

"5E Tours," someone answered. "How may we help you today? We have special discounts on heli-diving, heli-jungle tours, and women's lingerie."

"Say what?"

Then the voice registered.

"Rafe!" Drake was so glad to hear his pilot's familiar voice that he forgot to use the lieutenant's title, which was just as well with Esly in the room. "How close are you?"

"Flying, driving, or walking?"

Drake looked at the phone and tried to make sense of the question. Finding no clue as to what game Rafe was playing, he put the phone back to his ear.

"We've been in place for a couple of hours, but we were told you were already off ship. I guess you're back. Been enjoying your luxury transport? It's a very pretty ship, by the way."

Drake stepped out onto the verandah and looked down at the dock. Nikita followed him out. She spotted them first, resting a hand on his shoulder to get his attention, then pointing. Most of ten stories below he spotted two guys sitting on a bench in the shade. Both wore outrageously loud Hawaiian shirts. The two of them appeared to be wrestling over the control of a phone.

"Look up and forward," he instructed them. He and Nikita waved and in moments they were waving back. "Be with you in ten."

* * *

"Damn, Nikita. You look like a major babe in that outfit," Rafe offered a wolf whistle.

Nikita wasn't sure how she could possibly be a "major babe."

"And Zoe, way hot!" Julian offered her a high five that she smacked hard.

"You two are awfully cozy." She followed Rafe's attention down to her hand with some surprise.

She'd come down the ramp with her hand tucked around Drake arm as if it was a completely natural thing to do. Perhaps because it had been a perfectly natural thing to do. This whole romantic whatever-it-might-be was getting out of control. Except it didn't feel as if it was.

"These two not so much," Julian pointed at Altman standing stiffly beside Zoe.

"And this must be Ms. Escarra. Our friend Parker has told us so little about you." Rafe bent low over her hand and kissed it.

"Hey," Julian protested. "Stop trying to hog the hot women."

Esly looked at Nikita in a bit of a panic.

"Do not worry, Esly. It isn't just you, they're always this irritating."

"I do not mind. Two such handsome men, I very much am not minding. Also, have no reason to complain. I am mostly happy that I am not dead yet and that I do not kill you, Nikita."

"Nor anyone else…according to *our* records," Rafe was suddenly serious, almost nasty. His flirt of a moment before was now schizophrenically set aside between one breath and the next. Usually he made it easy to forget he was the officer in charge of a forty-million-dollar war machine and that both he and his helicopter were known for their fiery temper.

"The only people I ever shoot was in the line of my duty," Esly raised her chin.

"Before you went to the fucking dark side and—"

"Can it, Rafe," Drake stepped right up in his commander's face. "Old ground, already covered. Moving on now."

Rafe glowered and Nikita almost wondered if they were about to fight over the woman.

But Julian gave Esly a reassuring wink. Then he looked at Drake, "What the hell happened to you, Duck-man?"

"What do you mean?"

"What do I mean? Standing tall, looking like you're ready to take on my fellow pilot to defend your women," Julian punched Rafe in the arm hard enough to receive a snarl. That was Julian's gift, he could always joke Rafe out of a mood. Nikita had seen it a number of times.

"Shit!" Rafe scrubbed at his face. "Sorry about that, but you're supposed to pick a goddamn side and stick with it."

"Yes," Esly nodded. "I know that now. But it was better than ending up dead in the streets. I already knew too much. If I refused when they said I must switch… You do not live in Honduras. Do not pretend that you know its problems."

Nikita liked that she said it simply, without anger or pushing back against Rafe's load of attitude. She could see the quiet-spoken police woman despite the pretty clothing they'd purchased for her.

"But something sure happened to the Duck-man," Julian went for the distraction and it served to finish shifting Rafe's attention.

His eyes finally focused on how closely they stood.

"I didn't do this to him," Nikita protested but didn't back away. "Drake did it to himself." It wasn't in her power to transform a man so wholly.

Zoe's sharp laugh was soon joined by Esly's.

"Oh, my friend, Nikita," Esly actually hugged her. "Of course you did. It is the power we women have on men."

"I'd rather shoot them," Nikita grumbled out. That was so much easier. Get assigned a target, complete with a long and bad history, then infiltrate, acquire, take down, and exfiltrate. This whole trying to understand the man beside her was much harder.

"We have the VIP helo at the local airport because we knew you were coming in today," Julian was explaining to Drake. "The rest of—" he glanced at Esly, "—our people are offshore."

Nikita didn't know of an aircraft carrier group in the area. So either a helicopter dock ship or a littoral combat ship was parked outside of territorial waters. Or Belize's waters, which were less than a hundred kilometers away.

"We'd like to go on a sightseeing tour today," Esly finally spoke up.

She hadn't struck Nikita as being stupid in any way. But she… was teasing Rafe just moments after facing him down.

Go, Esly.

"I would so love to see the pretty islands of Roatán and Utila from the skies. I have never seen Honduras from a helicopter."

"Lady," Rafe protested, "you know that we're busy here. Besides, there's a tropical storm coming. It's supposed to stay out to sea, but it's still going to make for some very lumpy air."

Julian caught on immediately of course, but Esly was able to string Rafe along for several more pedantic declarations before he noticed his copilot's big smile and figured it out.

* * *

Drake could think of far worse ways to travel than a luxury helicopter flown by two of the best heli-pilots in the military.

Whereas the whole maid and butler treatment in a cruise ship's luxury suite was actually creeping him out. It was like everyone was always watching him, the entire ship's complement. Nikita and Zoe's rumor campaign had definitely taken hold and he couldn't go anywhere without being nudged for exciting tales to fill the other passengers' boring lives. Thankfully, there'd only been one other like the banker who had actually tried to hire his clandestine services to deal with a competitor.

Word of the treadmill race, and many hints of the steamy aftermath, had also gotten out. That story didn't appear to need any help from Zoe to spread far and wide. He was propositioned in the dining halls, in the bars, and on the gangway by women ranging from a very sultry Frenchwoman who happened to mention she had just started *lycée* this year (how did the French look so mature when they were just starting high school), to an Italian grand dame offering him the keys to her Amalfi villa at any time—bringing along "the girl" was optional, but only if she liked the *right* kind of games.

Sanctuary had not been achieved by clinging ever more tightly to Nikita. For her part, she merely appeared amused, or perhaps bemused.

He'd taken on a mythic persona and the only ones who could see through it were all on this helicopter. And he wasn't even sure about that. He often caught Nikita looking at him, just watching, as if she didn't know him at all.

Once again he and Altman were in the back-facing seats.

"Okay, Altman. You've got to admit that we are two damned lucky guys," Drake nodded across the narrow cabin toward the three women.

Altman grunted something that might have been agreement, it might not. What did they do to people when they turned them into SEALs?

Across from them were three very attractive women who couldn't be more different if they tried.

In the middle sat the dark, sultry Esly. She wore the tough-as-nails outfit on a killer body.

Zoe was across from Altman, still just as cute as hell in the outfit she'd been wearing all morning—an airy silk caftan in wild tropical colors that was constantly falling off one of her fine shoulders. The plunging neckline could only be worn by a woman as lean as she was. And it just brushed her knees.

On Nikita it would be…he pictured it…then tried to picture anything else, but couldn't. On Nikita's taller, more powerful build, she'd reveal deep cleavage rather than an expanse of smooth skin. And it would land ever so high on her thigh. That he definitely had to see. He looked at her dressed in a long flowing skirt of woodsy colors, and the simple white blouse that said it wasn't about the clothes at all, it was all about the woman inside them.

And it was true.

They left Roatán and flew sixty kilometers across the storm-dulled Caribbean Sea. After they made landfall they flew the same distance again up into the rugged hills of eastern Honduras. Drake spent much of the flight chatting softly with Altman about just what it had taken for the first woman to become a SEAL. Slowly at first, but warming to the tale of his prize pupil, he revealed just how impossibly high Drake was shooting if he was going after Nikita.

Time to really *gear up, Duck-man.* Because going for her was Number One on his personal mission list.

* * *

"It is all so different from the air," Esly sounded deeply perplexed.

Nikita had finally switched seats with Esly so that she could look more easily out the window. Julian had fished out a small pair of binoculars and handed them back for her to use.

The rolling eastern mountains of Sierra Rio Tinto National Park were covered in trees completely foreign to Nikita. Southern Alabama was mostly river flood plains and bottomlands of the Tombigbee and Alabama Rivers. Even Cheaha Mountain, the highest point in the state, topped out at twenty-four hundred feet and had a resort lodge and RV park atop it.

The mountains of eastern Honduras climbed little higher, but they did it in steep slopes covered in dense jungle. Trails were few and roads fewer as they flew further inland.

Nikita had carried out missions in these kinds of jungles and they were hard work. It always seemed she spent half her time trying not to be bitten or even eaten. It was her first trip to Honduras, but she'd been plenty close. She'd had to shoot a variety of fauna: a cougar in Nicaragua, several charging wild boars in Guatemala, and there'd been a time in Panama where it had been touch-and-go as to who got who first—her shooting a Mexican drug lord brokering a major deal or the jaguar that had been stalking her hideout through the long, motionless afternoon.

She didn't like these jungles.

They were following the Sico River up into the hills as well as they could, but it meandered as it flowed, occasionally disappearing entirely in dense growth. The flat light of the overcast sky wasn't helping: hiding instead of revealing terrain and water.

She alternated between looking out over Esly's shoulder and Zoe's.

"You have changed him, you know," Zoe whispered without turning as Julian announced they were crossing from Sierra Rio Tinto to Sierra El Carbón National Park. It didn't look any different to her.

"We have gone too far. Make the pilot turn us back. We are very close. I have not been here since my first lover when I was sixteen, but I remember it well. I will know when I see it."

Drake passed Esly's instructions to the pilots and they circled.

"How have I changed him?" Nikita kept her voice low.

"The Drake Roman I know was always a follower. Good at what he does, damn good. Like he's born to it. But it still felt like he was just loafing."

"You have to be better than good to 'loaf' along in this crowd."

Zoe nodded her agreement, "He is. And if you doubt that, look at who one of the 5E's most eligible bachelors is attracted to."

"What…"

Zoe turned, her bright blue eyes only inches away. "You, you goof. Drake Roman is completely and totally gone on you. How many other female SEALs do you see in the military who qualified the hard way? None. Duh! Delta has what, two or three now? That puts you in a very elite category. I don't think he understands yet what it means that he's attracted to such an amazing woman. You really, really make me wish I could be more like you."

Nikita sat back and stared straight ahead. Between Drake's and Altman's seats she had a small view out the forward windshield. So far the flight had revealed more jungle-covered peaks undulating ever higher into the distance. They'd overflown a line of high-power transmission towers leading to a big construction site lower on the river. Now they were headed back that way.

She'd actually been envying Zoe her apparent ease with the world around her and with her own body. Again Nikita faced that strange dichotomy of the SEAL who knew exactly what to do with her body and the woman who didn't have a clue.

Esly and Drake were both leaning forward and looking down at something, probably still trying to trace the elusive river toward the unknown waterfall.

Drake Roman.

Zoe was right. Nikita had always liked him well enough, as much as she ever liked anyone. But now Drake stood out from the crowd. And not just in the ship's dining room, but in the crowd that included two top pilots, and maybe even Luke Altman. There was a focus, a drive that Drake had never revealed before.

Nikita had wondered at Zoe's original selection of each of their roles, placing Drake in the character of Head Mercenary. It was not a selection she ever would have made. Now she couldn't imagine it being anyone else. And if he was leading a contracting firm instead of flying for the 5E, maybe, just maybe she'd be willing to work for him.

Oh god, she was losing her mind!

There was no way she was leaving DEVGRU, not until she was too old to maintain the training level. And certainly not for a merc outfit, not if God herself was in charge.

But Drake was an amazing man to serve with. He hadn't been mad when she'd been injured, he'd been furious. When Rafe had threatened Esly—a team member in only the most tenuous sense—he'd tromped down on it. He commanded loyalty as easily as—

Esly's shout of excitement said that she'd finally spotted what they were looking for.

At the same moment, dead ahead, Nikita saw a telltale spark in the jungle.

"Incoming!"

Her shout had Rafe slamming the controls in a hard evasion to the north. "Where?"

"Downriver. Range two thousand meters, minus."

As he twisted the helo around and plunged toward the trees,

the side view opened to the east. They'd overflown somebody who now was very unhappy about their return.

"I'm guessing that we finally found what we're looking for," Zoe spoke up.

"I'm so thrilled," Altman tone was impossibly drier than usual as he actually teased her back. There was no time to be surprised.

Nikita could see whatever was coming at them still burning fuel against the dark clouds. And it turned!

Not an RPG—rocket propelled grenades didn't have guidance systems. This was a guided munition of some sort, but not a SAM. Surface-to-air missiles were generally supersonic and would have fried their asses already; an American Stinger or Russian Igla hustled along at Mach 2, ten times the speed of a helicopter. From just two thousand meters, they'd have been dead already.

The Bell 429 wasn't a DAP Hawk. There weren't countermeasures. Nothing aboard to return fire.

"It's following," she shouted.

Drake and Esly were now staring at it as well.

As the helicopter twisted down and away, she turned in her seat to follow it but lost it. No more heat trail.

"Too small to show on this radar," Julian called. A civilian Bell's radar was all about not hitting another helicopter or a massive squall line. Actually, their helo was new enough, it should be able to see one of those stupid hobby drones as well.

Which meant whatever was following them was very small.

Rafe began twisting and turning the bird in hopes of losing its track.

"Bank hard right and climb!" Nikita shouted out.

Zoe was forced against her as they carved the turn. Maybe, if her guess was right—

She was looking too high to see the explosion, but she saw the flash coming from close below them.

The helicopter pinged and rattled as shrapnel peppered the helicopter.

There was a sickening twist—the kind that reminded her of other helicopter crashes.

"Someone find me a landing zone," Rafe called out as warning alarms began bleating from the cockpit.

Everywhere Nikita looked—which was a wide range as the helicopter began spinning awkwardly—was jungle. Tall trees and helicopters were a lousy mix. She'd gone down once very memorably in an Alaskan cold-weather training mission and never wanted to do it again. The only reason they hadn't all died had been because they were on the verge of a scheduled night parachute jump.

Her team made it out, though one lost a foot to a bad tumble and a slice of the rotor blade. The two pilots had died high in the trees.

"Waterfall," Esly called out. "There was a large pool below a waterfall. Would that work?"

"If I can reach it," Rafe banked them carefully back toward where they'd been shot as he bled altitude. They were already below the ridgeline, soon they'd be below the treetops. At least they would be out of the line of fire that way.

"Whoever shot us is going to come looking for us," Drake was looking right at her.

She nodded, exactly her thought. "Julian, do we have a flare gun aboard?"

A moment later, he tossed a plastic case backward between the pilots' seats.

It hit Drake in the head as the helicopter slewed one way, bounced off Altman's lap as it carved the other direction, and Zoe managed to grab it. She popped the latches and turned it to Nikita.

As she was reaching for the flare gun, they almost lost it to a gut-wrenching yaw that meant the helicopter had almost no time left aloft.

"Shrapnel must have caught both the rear rotor and a main blade," Drake shouted to her.

"Perfect!" She managed to grab the bright orange pistol and the three flare cartridges. She shoved one in the gun and the other two deep into her pocket. She then clutched the weapon to her chest with both hands to make sure that she didn't drop it when they impacted. It was the same training that had let her hang on to the beer bottle in the bar fight—never let go of your weapon.

She'd enjoyed that fight.

The trees were now flashing close by either side of the helicopter. If a rotor blade clipped one, they'd be going down hard. *Trust the team. Not in your hands.*

Instead she thought about having a beer and a girl talk in a rowdy bar with Sugar. She actually hoped that she'd have a chance to do that. She'd bring along Zoe, maybe Esly too and—

A blade caught and the helo twisted hard. Flew backward for a moment, then continued around in a corkscrewing flight.

Trees...

The river running away from them...

More trees...

A massive waterfall towering over a hundred meters above them...

Trees...

Another view downstrea—

They plowed into the water, tail first. A horrendous shearing sound of ripping metal sounded close behind her.

The twist continued, tumbling the helicopter on its side.

The rotors beat water and shattered just as surely as if they'd hit concrete. Out at their tips they were spinning at nearly the speed of sound.

The helo flailed and jolted for a long moment, but the water buffered the motion.

With a last ratcheting grind, the transfer gears sheared. Then the racing turboshaft engines ingested a load of river water and died.

In slow motion, the helo tipped the rest of the way onto its side.

Zoe lay on her and she lay on Esly, their seatbelts only keeping their waists in place.

One heartbeat. Two. Three. The engines gurgled to a shattered halt.

All stable. As a bonus they apparently weren't going to blow up right away. She'd have to send Bell Helicopter a thank you letter.

"Go! Go! Go!" Altman shouted. He opened the high-side door, the downward facing one offered a clear view of rounded river rocks beneath the water.

In moments, they were out. No obvious blood or breaks.

She pointed at the First Aid kit floating in the water and Drake grabbed it as he followed her out.

"Nice landing, Dude," Julian's voice was thick with sarcasm as he climbed out the pilot's door.

Nikita could barely hear him over the roar of the waterfall. Instead of a clear fall, it spilled down over a massive, water-carved rock face thirty meters wide and twenty stories tall. A fine mist of spray filled the air over the broad pool at the base of the fall. Jungle crowded close to all sides. Even taking root up the rocky face to either side of the cascade. It would be a breathtaking view if she had time to admire it.

"Hey," Rafe replied as he crawled out of the cockpit favoring one wrist. "Any landing you can walk away from is a good one."

"You call that good? This helicopter ain't walking away from anything. So who is gonna tell the Army they have to buy a new one? It isn't me, I can tell you that much. The base commander is gonna be so pissed."

"Why?"

"Because we only borrowed it to go to Miami. I sort of didn't bother to tell him we were taking it to Honduras with us. It's his personal bird."

"Fine," Rafe tried to use his bad hand, which wasn't working. He did a tumble and flop into the water, then stood in the waist-deep current. "Then it's definitely you that gets to tell him."

The two of them kept at it as they were splashing toward the shore, though Julian had a solid grip on Rafe's upper arm to guide him along and keep him steady. The river was warm and not moving too quickly here.

She still had the flare gun in her hand.

"Herd them to shore," she shouted at Drake. "And get them behind something solid. Bind Rafe's wrist."

"Yeah, he broke it, just hasn't noticed it yet." He dragged her against him for a quick kiss. "Don't go blowing yourself up. I'll be pissed as hell if you do." Then he headed to shore.

No insistence that he should do this next dangerous part because he was the guy.

Nikita located the cap to the fuel tank. She cracked it loose, and fuel began to spill because of the mostly inverted angle of the helo.

Drake didn't even treat her like an equal.

She checked to make sure everyone was ashore and mostly out of sight. The timing on this was going to be tricky.

He treated her as if she was the DEVGRU warrior and he was the Night Stalker. Even a lot of her teammates didn't do what he'd just done. Drake actually treated her as if she knew what she was doing.

She sure as hell hoped she knew.

She popped the fuel cap all the way off and Jet A spilled out, adding a sharp slap of kerosene to the thick moldering jungle and brightness of the fresh water mist. Most of the fuel ran down the hull and into the open passenger bay door. A trickle of it spilled into the river as well.

The shore was too far away to trust that this would work from there. She had to sink the first shot.

She swam halfway toward shore.

No one in sight except for Drake, peeking around the side of a tree.

Nikita stood up, hoped this wasn't the last time she ever saw him, turned, and fired.

Chapter 14

Drake barely had time to cry out before Altman grabbed him from behind and dragged him back behind the tree.

Nikita had fired the flare gun nearly point blank into the helicopter's gas-filled rear bay.

Then she'd dropped as if cut down where she stood—and the helicopter exploded.

Bits and pieces of it slashed through the leaves overhead. To either side of the massive tree they were hiding behind, shrapnel zinged by like…like…shrapnel!

Large chunks of helicopter slammed into tree bark and stuck there, quivering with the force of impact. Half of a pilot's seat landed in the brush not half a meter from where Julian was splinting and binding Rafe's wrist.

Then the bits and pieces that had been blown upward began to rain down in a bright patter, landing all around their refuge.

Still Altman wouldn't let him go.

"Goddamn it! She's—"

Altman released him barely in time to save himself a hard elbow to the ribs. A last piece of helicopter, an unidentifiable shred of metal, slid off a higher branch where it had hung for a moment, and disappeared into a bush covered with impossibly blue flowers the size of his head.

Drake struggled back to his feet. The helicopter was shredded; only a few jagged edges of the wreckage stuck out above the water. A large section of the hull, still fiercely on fire, starting bobbing down the river. For a hundred meters downstream, spilled jet fuel burned on the surface, making the center of the river a streamer of flame.

Then, right in front of the conflagration, Nikita rose from the river's depths like one of those James Bond fantasy scenes. The cotton blouse was now sheer over her breasts, her hair slicked back in a wet look that reminded him of the shower they'd shared, and the skirt that clung to her legs was like an artist's afterthought.

She surveyed the burning remains of the helicopter, nodded her head, clearly pleased with herself, and began wading toward shore.

"Shit, woman! Are you okay?" She walked right by him when he tried to lend her a helping hand over the slippery rocks along the shore.

"Sure. I was afraid that if I missed and left a flare burning in the jungle due to a bad shot, they'd see it. These things aren't all that accurate," she held up the stubby orange flare gun. Nikita stepped from the river like a Navy SEAL despite the fact that she looked like a river goddess.

Before he could argue with her sense of urgency, he heard the heavy beat of a helicopter's rotor blades echoing up the valley. With the roar of the waterfall, it meant the enemy was close.

"Cover our tracks."

Thankfully, between the bare rocks and the soft mat of undergrowth, it was only the work of seconds. Drake dropped dead branches to cover their wet footprints over the rocks and Nikita spread leaves across a muddy patch. They withdrew into the woods only a moment before a pair of helos swung into view far downstream.

"Bury yourselves in case they have infrared."

Drake almost pointed out that the temperature here was at least body heat, maybe hotter by the way he was already sweating, so they wouldn't stand out, but thought better of arguing with a river goddess SEAL.

As he helped scoop branches and dead leaves over other team members, he wondered at his presumption for wanting to be with such a woman. She could have the pick of anyone anywhere. By what earthly reason could he even hope to be with a woman like her?

They slid side by side under their own cover; he made especially sure that her white blouse was well hidden.

Of course he wasn't a goddamn idiot. He was going to stick as long as she'd let him despite his inability to figure out why she let him.

The helos made one high pass, then one of them descended to barely ten meters above the burning wreckage. Bell TwinRangers, painted black with a gold racing stripe and no other insignia.

He could see Nikita reloading the flare gun.

"Don't even think about it!"

"Tempting though, isn't it?" Her smile looked particularly evil.

The TwinRanger hovered not thirty meters away, broadside to them. The cargo bay doors had been removed, making for a large opening that would be an exceptional target. An M240 machine gun was mounted on a swivel and by pure chance was aimed almost directly at them. Yes, it was very tempting. But it would be an easy shot in both directions.

Four-man squad: pilot, copilot, and a pair of gunners. They were mercenary stereotypes right down to black t-shirts and camo pants, black baseball caps, shades, and M16s.

Then he glanced at the second bird still hovering a hundred meters up, near the level of the top of the waterfall.

He nodded upward and Nikita looked aloft.

The second bird had a side-mounted M230—five and a half feet of bad-ass chain gun—and a 7-tube rocket launcher on the other.

"Let's not piss them off, what do you say?"

"Spoilsport!"

He nudged his hip against hers under the foliage, she nudged him back, and he couldn't help smiling. Together they turned back to watch the low-hovering helicopter's inspection of their crash. It would have helped if there'd been a body or two, but he'd rather his team stayed alive.

Apparently the lack of any bodies on fire didn't bother the bad guys for long, as the helicopter pulled up and away after less than twenty seconds.

No one moved until they were well clear.

"Well, that was fun," Drake sat up shedding leaves and branches. He brushed the worst of it out of Nikita's hair as others emerged.

"What the hell was that?" Rafe's arm was now bound against his chest in a sling.

"Raytheon Pike by how it behaved," it was the only weapon Nikita could think of that fit the performance parameters.

"Shit!" Altman was pissed. "That's leading edge. We only got those ourselves at the beginning of the year. If this GSI guy wasn't already dead, I'd fry his ass for selling those to unfriendly powers."

Drake hadn't even heard of a Pike.

Nikita took pity on him. "It's a sweet little laser-guided missile about the length of your arm that can be fired out of a handheld grenade launcher. Good to about two thousand meters. Proximity fuze. I'd hoped that last bank and climb would fool it."

"Might have," Julian agreed, "if we had a Black Hawk. Seven people is the TwinRanger's payload limit, plus it's hot so the air is thin, and our rate-of-climb sucked. Nice call, Nikita, even if it didn't work."

"What now?" Rafe's voice said that the pain was beginning to register. Nothing stronger than aspirin in the First Aid kit.

"Did anyone bring lunch?"

Everyone turned to look at Drake like he was insane.

"Either we can hike out through fifty kilometers of jungle filled with bad guys without a map or," he pulled out his waterproof satellite phone, "we can wait until dark and call in the rest of the crew to come fetch us."

* * *

Nikita would have preferred to go alone, but Drake had insisted on going with her and Altman hadn't shut him down. Instead he'd done his zero-expression face, leaving the decision up to her. Drake had proved his skills, but she was worried about his stealth—that took a lot of practice. Still, a second set of eyes would be useful.

To avoid any possible booby traps set in the jungle, they slipped a couple of logs into the river and then floated down the current with them.

"I imagined going swimming with you," Drake floated along beside her. "There was this bikini in the shop window that—"

"Wasn't going to happen," Nikita peeked over her log to check for any approaching rapids.

"But you're a SEAL."

"In a wet suit armed to the teeth. Not in a Drake-fantasy string bikini."

"Well, you in a soaking wet cotton blouse was pretty damned fantastic."

Nikita hadn't thought about that. She should have put on a bra this morning, but again, the unbuttoned look had seemed to fit her role better.

They drifted half a kilometer before Drake spoke again.

"Any crocodiles around here?"

"They're lousy at climbing waterfalls and we flew over several others on our way here."

"Exactly my point," Drake looked side to side fearfully. "That means that any that made it this far up river would be like the Special Operations Forces of the crocodilian empire."

Nikita palmed a faceful of water at Drake, who laughed.

Their laughter didn't carry them very far downstream. They came around a corner and quickly swam to the northern shore by mutual consent.

On the southern shore was a massive fence topped with multiple coils of razor wire. They dug in and watched.

Beyond the fence, the jungle had been sheared off—clear-cut for the construction site they'd flown over on the way out. The clearing stretched for hundreds of acres smack in the middle of a national park.

There was a well-worn pair of ruts along the inside of the fence line. They didn't have to wait long to see who was using it. More heavily-armed, black-t-shirt-and-camo guys cruised by in a black Toyota Tundra. They wore dark sunglasses and serious expressions.

"Pros," Drake whispered. He glanced at his watch so that he could measure the time between patrols. "All look like Americans with beards. These are far bigger guys than the natives we saw in Roatán."

"Fucking mercs," Nikita whispered back. "When we circled back to find the waterfall, they must have decided that we were showing too much interest in their compound and it was best to take us out."

"Tourist helicopter lost without a trace. And in other news at eleven…" Drake intoned.

"Yeah. Exactly the sort of contract you'd expect a merc to take."

"Can you really picture J-dawg or Sugar taking this deal though?"

Nikita glared at the compound for a long moment, hating it. If someone gave her a B-2 stealth bomber, she would carpet bomb the place. But…she'd liked the Titan people; it was hard not to like J-dawg when he was toting around a young Afghan girl on his shoulders.

"Hey, Nikita! Shake it off. No emotion, remember."

"I'm not shooting right now. I don't even have my damned rifle because of ship security. I *want* my rifle." And that's when she heard it in her own voice. "Shit! How can you stand to be around me, Drake? I'm a screwed-up mess."

"Yeah! But you're my *favorite* screwed-up mess."

Nikita had to think about it a bit. It wasn't like she had a long list of people she was close to, but that didn't make it any less true, "And you're *my* favorite mess, Duck-man."

"There!" Drake pointed. A rising wind out of the east had swung the trees aside for a moment. A three-story, steel-framework guard tower came into view for a moment. Once they'd spotted it, it was easy enough to see. Nikita tried to gauge how far they'd floated downstream from the waterfall. Close enough to two kilometers to answer the question.

"It fits. That's probably where they fired from. But what didn't they want us to see?"

Nikita pulled out the binoculars that Esly had held on to through the crash. She scanned the compound carefully, softly listing off what she saw.

"Five big excavators. Half dozen dump trucks. None moving. One of the earth movers is a burned carcass. I don't see anybody working. I don't even see any buildings. Nothing but a wasteland of churned soil." Which was a metaphor for her emotions that there wasn't a chance she'd be considering.

"Look at the hills."

She turned her binoculars but all she saw was jungle.

"No, just the general topography."

Nikita lowered the binocs, but still didn't get what Drake was on about.

"The current Honduran government approved a lot of new dam building, a whole lot of it. They did it without environmental impact statements and ignored a lot of agreements with towns and local tribes. There have been pitched battles back and forth ever since. They've got murder squads hunting down environmentalists—one article said that was now the job in the country with the shortest life expectancy. Huh!"

"What?"

"I didn't pay attention to where all the bad blood was. This must be the spot."

"Our unfriendly boys in black." Sometimes talking with Drake was almost like talking to herself. They simply thought the same.

"Probably."

"What about the hills?" But he saw different things than she did. Patterns. And she was learning that he was good at it.

"See how the rise on either side of the river sweeps back into ridgelines? It would be an ideal spot for a dam. This whole valley would be filled, right back to the waterfall and probably over it."

"Okay. Dam going in. Unhappy environmentalists. Mercenary kill squad…" she couldn't quite put it together.

"Not only set up by GSI, but probably bankrolled by them. Now someone wants to cut them out of the loop. Esly's buddy Daylin and his boys were brought in to clear away the upper level contractors as thoroughly as the environmentalists."

They watched as a helicopter came in from the south.

"More gun boys?"

"No," they were right at the limit of what she could see even with the binocs, "white shirts and black slacks. Suits."

"We need to know what's going on."

"No we don't. Just clear out the mercs."

The truck went by again. They were so stereotypical mercs that he couldn't tell if it was the same truck or not. He checked his watch: twenty minutes on the dot.

Nikita watched them go by and groused again about not having her rifle.

"They can always grow more mercs. We need to cut off the head of the snake, not just some of its scales. I need an in."

* * *

As if in answer to his prayer, Drake's phone rang. It was loud enough to make both him and Nikita jump, but far quieter than the river splashing over the nearby rocks between them and the compound.

"Mr. Roman?" It took him a moment to recognize the voice of the ship's hotel manager because it was so unexpected.

"Norma?"

"Yes, I'm glad I reached you. I have a very insistent party on the line trying to reach the occupants of Suites 612. I thought that might be of interest to you."

"Please patch them through," he considered warning her that she'd be safer if she didn't listen in, but that would be pointless and outside his control. Instead, "Be aware that I may lie a little."

She laughed nervously, then there was a loud click, "Here's your party."

There was no secondary click of her leaving the circuit.

"Daylin?" a male voice asked.

"No longer a factor," Drake lowered his tone more than normal, trying to sound nastier. It sounded good to him. Like Arnold Schwarzenegger's "I'll be back."

Nikita leaned in so that their shoulders were touching. He tipped the phone so they could both hear, but didn't quite dare to put it on speakerphone.

"Buck Baer?" The voice was disdainful. "I thought we made it clear that we were done with your services."

"He also is no longer a factor."

"Then who am I speaking with?"

They exchanged names and there was a short pause...perhaps the length of a quick Internet search.

"Mr. Roman. What is your intent here?" Apparently the disinformation plan was solidly in place as now Franshesco Gutierrez's tone was very cautious.

"I, shall we say, *acquired* all assets of Global Securities International. I am interested in continuing any mutually beneficial business relationships, but under my purview, *not* the former management's." All of his practice over the last days aboard ship at meals and in bars was paying off—he managed to say it with a straight face, or at least with a straight tone over the phone.

He made a face at Nikita, who shot him a thumbs up.

"Perhaps we could meet somewhere quiet this afternoon to..."

"I'm presently out on a private excursion."

"Ah, yes. Daylin did mention that you were traveling with your mistress before we, uh, lost touch with him."

Drake let all of the cold chill that washed over him spill into his voice. "Yours is not DR, Inc.'s only investment in the area. I can—" Nikita put a hand on his arm to warn him off.

I can disassemble you far faster than GSI put you together.

"I can meet you for drinks at eight this evening?" Drake wished that he had a cellphone tracker so that he could see if the person he was speaking with was presently at the construction site just across the river.

"That is...possible."

"Good. I will be at the front gate of the El Carbón dam site at that time."

"That won't—"

"As you know, I'm on a ship that leaves port later tonight. That is the only time I can spare, and I always do my own site risk assessments myself. I will meet you there. End of conversation."

There was a long pause. "I shall look forward to that. Ask for me; I will be there." And he was gone.

"Norma?"

"Ye-es?" the hotel manager's stutter of embarrassment at being caught was sweet.

"Could you please have my white Armani and a nice summer dress for Nikita delivered with a rental car to the town of El Carbón by nightfall?"

"Hey," Nikita frowned and Drake ignored her.

"I can take care of that for you, Mr. Roman." Much more in her comfort zone.

Nikita nudged her shoulder sharply against his in protest.

"Also a set of casual dark clothes from Nikita's wardrobe and..." he drew it out just to make Nikita crazy, which was clearly working. "Her black rifle case."

Nikita's smile finally made him able to picture the young girl reading her Dr. Seuss, suddenly happy to have her toys. She must have been a serious handful as a kid.

Couldn't just fall for some timid, stay-at-home babe, could you, Duck-man?

There was no response over the phone.

"Norma?"

"I will...take care of it personally, Mr. Roman."

"Thank you, Norma. It would probably be best if you made the car reservation in the name of GSI's former chief, Buck Baer."

"Mr. Roman?" her tone shifted enough that he knew what was coming next and didn't force her to ask the question.

"Yes, Arthur was actually very helpful today and appears to be clear of any intentional wrongdoing."

"Oh, thank goodness," the relief in her voice spoke volumes.

"I have to ask," and Nikita's look said he shouldn't, but it was too late to stop now. "You and Arthur?"

"He isn't the most...impressive of men," her voice grew softer than he'd yet heard, or ever expected to hear. "But he is a good man despite that and he's being very good to me. I'm glad he didn't do anything to get himself in trouble."

"He didn't," Drake couldn't think of what else to say. His parents had an A-plus marriage, as did a few military couples he worked with, but he didn't know many others who did. "Please keep who we are under wraps until after we're gone."

"Of course, Mr. Roman," and the hotelier was back. "I'll now see to everything."

He hung up and looked at his watch.

"Six hours until sunset. Oh, what shall we do with the time?"

"Hike back upstream without getting ourselves killed, bitten, or poisoned," Nikita eased back into the jungle away from the camp.

"Spoilsport."

* * *

No, Nikita told herself, *not a spoilsport. Sensible.*

Sensible because she'd wanted to have groaning sex right there beneath the eyes of the watchtower. Because she wanted to lose herself in his arms and not just for an hour or a day.

They clambered over tall roots that splayed in all directions. They backtracked around patches of foliage too dense to penetrate and jumped narrow, steep canyons carved by rushing streams heading down to the river.

What had been a twenty-minute float was a two-hour battle of hard labor to return through the fading sunlight that slipped past the high, leafy canopy and dappled the jungle floor. By the end of the journey, the sun was lost behind the heavy gray overcast.

Once they rejoined the rest of the team, the planning began.

As with almost everything else on this trip, Nikita decided that her role in the plan they put together completely sucked.

Chapter 15

The major sent out the two Little Bird helicopters to extract them from the twilit jungle.

Or to at least move around the pieces on the board.

Drake could only smile as Nikita kept griping about not going with LCDR Altman, but it was clear that her place had to be at Drake's side. Besides, if ever there was a one-man army for a special assignment, Drake knew that Luke Altman was it.

Then their Little Bird, nearly as silent as the night birds whose calls filled the forest, set him and Nikita down on the road a half kilometer outside El Carbón. He enjoyed the stroll through the descending darkness with Nikita. It was easy to imagine walking like this with her, making it a regular part of what they did together, talking about not much of anything.

He told her about his big sister, who stood five inches shorter than he did and just how much that continued to make her crazy.

She told him about the life with her mother before the Curtis

Contracting debacle had shattered her family. Even back then it had been mostly just the two of them as her father was always away on "assignment."

The wind, which had buffeted the Little Bird, was now building through the high trees, rattling the leaves together almost as loudly as the various birdcalls. Whatever they were, they weren't chickadees or cardinals. There was a moving cacophony of clicks, buzzes, throaty rattles, and other birdlike noises, warning of their progress along the darkened road—they certainly didn't sound like any birds from New England or even Alabama.

The small packs they'd been handed during the brief flight had lightened rapidly as they each drank several bottles of water and ate two meals' worth of rations.

By the time they reached the village, lit only by a few stray indoor lights, he wished he'd thought to grab a flashlight. The "main highway" through the region had turned into an agility test of stumbling among unseen potholes.

Their rental was waiting—and it had gathered a large circle of gawkers in the small town. No wonder. It was a town with only three buildings that were two stories high; the others were better than shacks, but not by much. Donkey carts, not cars, were the standard.

And there, in the center of town—as defined by the tiny cluster of buildings huddled together along the road—sat a shining black Toyota Land Cruiser. He and Nikita picked up their own following as well, mostly children eager to see the two white people who had walked into town along a road that stretched empty for over twenty kilometers before the next community, farther up into the interior.

Behind the Land Cruiser, a small white pickup was parked with two men sitting on the tailgate.

"Senor Baer?" The rounder of the two men struggled to his feet and asked.

"*Si,*" Drake nodded, hitting another third of his Spanish. He only remembered at the last moment that he'd decided to keep posing as GSI so that his own name didn't appear on any paper trail in Honduras.

The man replied with a long fluid cadence of which Drake didn't catch a single word.

Much to the man's consternation, Nikita was the one who answered with something that might have been questions or might have been music. He was going to have to learn the language just so that he could listen to her speak it so beautifully.

The man handed her the keys and a card and looked relieved to be rid of it.

"*Bueno,*" Nikita finally finished and turned to Drake. "He says that this is an armored version to B6+ standards. That covers us through all the 5.56 mm ammo and most of the 7.62, up to armor-piercing. Our clothes and gear are inside. We simply call this number and tell him where the vehicle is when we're done with it and they will fetch it back."

"Wonder what the insurance waiver is on this thing. Norma done good. Remind me to tip her well."

"Let's just be glad that J-dawg is paying for it, both the waiver and the massive tip."

"Roger that. *Gracias,*" he used up the last third of his vocabulary on the two men. They drove away as fast as they could as if there was going to be a gun battle right here in the middle of El Carbón. Unlikely, as they had gathered quite a crowd of locals by that point.

"I'd be more comfortable if we got out of town first." She went straight to the driver's door.

He thought it was amusing, until he saw the puzzled look on the crowd's faces. In this culture, the man would always be the one to drive. He stepped up and plucked the keys from her hand.

"But—"

"You're messing with my macho, woman." Her glare as she circled to the other side warmed his heart.

* * *

Nikita had wanted to go straight to her tactical clothing. Norma had even packed her boots and she was going to kiss the hotelier the next time she saw her.

"No," Drake had insisted as they changed by the soft wash of the dome light spilling out the back of the SUV on an empty stretch of dark, dirt one-lane. "We have an image to maintain. And you're the surprise."

That's why she hated her role in this. There was only so far she was willing to compromise.

Before putting on the dress, she strapped a Glock 19 on one thigh, her knife with three spare magazines on the other, and slipped the Glock 36 subcompact and its spares into a purse that Zoe had made her buy because there were no pant legs to hide an ankle piece. Now she felt halfway to human. If only she could think of a way to slip five feet of sniper rifle under her clothes…

Roman had pulled on a fresh t-shirt and slacks, strapped on an ankle piece (which she envied), and shoulder-holstered a pair of Glocks under his jacket. Then he leaned back against the open door and watched her. Steady, calm, and armed to the teeth—he looked so damn good. His smile said he knew it, too.

No.

His smile said she was standing naked except for her underwear and her weapons in the middle of a dark road in a hazardous country.

"Damn but you're a picture, woman."

"I'm not a fantasy poster-babe."

"You sure as hell are. What I wouldn't give for a camera at the moment."

"That would be good. It would give me something to break over your head, Duck-man." How was she supposed to keep herself from being dazzled by him? Nobody ever saw her the way Drake did. She almost wished that Norma had packed that ridiculous bit of La Perla frippery just so that she could pull it on at this moment and then tell him he wasn't allowed to touch her.

"If only we had the time," his voice was soft as he reached out and brushed a thumb down her cheek. Not her exposed breasts, not her bare waist, but her cheek.

She struggled with the unexpected tenderness as she wrestled the dress on over her head and her weapons. It made her feel… what? Desirable? Drake's every glance and gesture made her feel that. Exposed? Absolutely, as if he could see parts of inside her that even she couldn't.

But there was something else.

She turned her back to him, "Zip me." What stupid men had designed dresses so that a woman needed a man to get her in and out of them? Bastards.

Roman zipped her in, then slipped his hands around her waist and held her tightly—so tightly it was even harder to breathe than the dress' tight waistband made it.

Wanted? There was no question that Drake wanted her. Nor that she wanted him. She could finally accept that a man had gotten so far past her shields that she wanted him deeply.

"When we get out of this, Nikita, we're going somewhere and you're mine. Completely mine. You hear?" His voice was intense and his arms squeezed even tighter about her abdomen as he buried his face in her hair.

That's when she knew what Drake made her feel.

Loved. Sugar and Zoe had both said Drake was "gone" on her. She hadn't understood. Maybe they hadn't even understood, not fully.

He wasn't *gone* on her, he was in love. That was something she truly wasn't ready for. But the words that came out weren't careful or a rebuff. They were soft and…feminine.

"Yes, Drake. Completely."

Now she had a new question: why was that answer *not* scaring the crap out of her?

Chapter 16

You touch her and you're a dead man," Drake kept his voice low and calm.

The gate into the construction site was reminiscent of an army base guard station. Multiple stops, alternating concrete barriers forcing a slow, weaving drive to enter, massive floodlights fighting back the jungle darkness. And at the far end of the gauntlet, they'd been asked to climb out of their car.

When the guards went to inspect the inside, he'd hit the remote door lock on the key fob. The SUV had sealed itself with a smug click from all four doors and the rear hatch. There were items in there, like Nikita's rifle, that were best kept out of sight.

That hadn't exactly set the tone for a friendly welcome.

Then one of the guards had slung his rifle over his shoulder and moved in to frisk Nikita.

"I won't repeat myself. Do *not* touch her."

The guard glared at him, then made a point of looking at his three companions, all armed with M16A4s before sneering at him. The guard took the last step and raised both hands chest high to make it clear exactly where he was going to start patting her down.

"I tried to warn you."

When the man glanced his way, Nikita shifted into action.

In a blur Drake could barely follow, she pulled the man's KA-BAR knife out of his own sheath. With it, she slashed the carry strap on his M16. Snagged it by the grip with one hand as it dropped and aimed it at the guard who had been standing well back so that he could provide cover protection for the three closer guards.

She heaved his long knife, point first, into the ground, drawing everyone's attention down.

Then, on the upswing of her arm, she yanked the guard's SIG Sauer P226 out of his holster. She continued the upward motion and rammed the big pistol up under his chin hard enough to make him squeak.

While everyone was watching her in surprise, Drake pulled his pair of Glocks and rested the barrels on the temples of the two guards closest to him.

All four gate guards froze as if cast in concrete, their eyes shot wide.

"Nikita, can you please tell me why people just don't listen to a simple warning?"

"Lack of education, Mr. Roman."

"You," Drake nudged one of them hard enough with his pistol to draw blood that began to drip down his temple. "Give us one good reason not to continue the lesson." He'd finally found a problem with the Glock: because it had no safety, there was nothing to make a threatening click when he flicked it off.

"Because the tower guard will drop you where you stand," he'd gotten over his surprise and shifted to anger. The tower they'd observed from across the river, looming above the front gate, had actually blocked their view of the gate itself. He wished it was still afternoon and he was once again lying close beside Nikita under the trees. Now the rising wind blocked any sound of the nearby river.

"Really, that's your answer? Whichever one of us the tower guard targets first, the other one will still have time to kill at least two of you, but probably all four. You've got to do better than that."

A Mercedes sedan rolled toward them from inside the compound. It didn't come from a distance—one moment it wasn't there, the next it was already in motion with its lights on. Whoever it was, they'd been waiting outside the floodlit perimeter to see how the first meeting played out.

The sedan stopped twenty meters back and a man in a suit stepped out of the driver's side.

"What did I tell you boys about these people being guests?" He called out as he got close.

"They wouldn't allow us to inspect their car," the guard facing Nikita's M16 from too close a distance didn't sound happy about it.

"Or check them for weapons," the man with the dribble of blood easing down his temple was still pissed.

Drake ignored them and focused on the man. "Mr. Gutierrez, I presume?"

"Franshesco, please, Mr. Roman."

"Then I'm Drake."

Franshesco. One of the most prominent members of the Gutierrez family, with dirty fingers in far more than large construction contracts. They also controlled shipping, a small airline that specialized in moving very questionable cargo from Colombia to Mexico, and much more. He was into everything ugly in the country.

"What do I do with these?" Drake nudged his pistol once more against the man's bleeding temple, earning him a hiss of anger.

"I couldn't care. They're replaceable."

"Hear that, boys?" he asked the guards. "Next time you're

looking for work, contact Drake Roman, Inc. On second thought, don't. We're looking for people with skills." Then he made a show of reholstering his weapons slowly as if he had no worries in the world about the two angry and armed men standing less than a meter from him. It was a calculated risk but he figured that it made him look more like an arrogant mercenary. That, and Nikita was still armed to the teeth.

As a kid he'd always wanted to be a Wild West cowboy. Not cowboys and Indians or Pony Express, but a gunslinger on the streets of Tombstone, Arizona, had sounded good—sometimes on the side of the law, sometimes not, but always *The Blazing Guns of Justice*. It had sounded good to a kid anyway. That's how he'd gotten into acting, now that he thought of it. Funny that this was the first time he'd ever played the role of gunslinger. There was a certain satisfaction to closing that circle.

He let Franshesco Gutierrez come to him. His handshake was good and his smile appeared genuine on his dark face, but unlike Arthur, Drake would bet that the guy was a good enough actor to make any impression he chose. His suit had the perfect fit of custom-made and the watch was a very distinctive U-Boat, recognizable at ten paces away and worth over seven grand. He had the broad shoulders of a military man, but his walk said businessman with a passion for fitness. He was the sort of man who would pack a .44 Magnum long-barrel revolver because that's what Clint Eastwood had carried as *Dirty Harry*, the renegade cop.

The man was as smooth as an upper-crust Boston banker and probably just as trustworthy.

"This is my assistant, Nikita."

She offered him a tight nod, more of a twist of her neck, but hadn't yet eased off on her stance.

He recalled the sexy look of the outspoken Sugar, dressed in leather and firing a sniper rifle in an Alabama field. It was a good memory. But nothing compared to the quiet woman who had just disarmed a pair of heavily loaded mercenaries while wearing a white Marc Jacobs summer dress with a flowing skirt spangled with blue flowers. She was spectacular…and still not moving.

"We'll consider this lesson taught," he said softly.

* * *

Nikita couldn't let go.

These were exactly the sort of men Curtis had always hired.

Had her father been one of these? Was that *all* he'd been? Big, tall, Jack "Lumberman" Hayward—so called because he was built on the scale of Paul Bunyan—had always been her idol. But what if?

What if his refusal to speak at the end hadn't been to protect her, but instead had been the same raw, stubborn pride these idiots were portraying. Even the guard, up on his toes to ease the pressure of where she was jamming the barrel under his chin, was still glaring at her in fury at being outmaneuvered.

Had her father been so shallow? A part of her knew that for truth. He had only done two tours in Afghanistan, never climbing out of regular Army. Then a merc outfit. Not one of the good ones, which she finally had to admit existed and she knew which select few they were.

She finally looked across at Drake. A gunner for the Night Stalkers 5E. The 160th required five years in the service before you could even apply. He'd flown with the 10th Mountain Division for six, then fought his way up to the most elite helicopter company of them all.

Would her father have stood in front of Esly to protect her from Rafe's suspicions?

Would her dead fiancé?

Those questions earned her a *slim maybe* and a *not a chance.*

Drake *was* the man who a young Nikita had thought her father and Barry were. That she had struggled all her life to be worthy of. She'd fought merely to win the admiration of a dead father. Yet by doing so, she'd won the love of a true warrior.

These two guards in her sights—over-armed, over-arrogant—didn't deserve to walk the same dirt as…

"Nikita?" Drake's soft call was like a slap of reality.

She thumbed the magazine releases, dropping them out of both weapons, cleared the chambers, and let both the rifle and the handgun drop in the dirt. Turning her back on the men, she stepped over to stand close beside Drake. She didn't take his hand, because it would slow down their reaction time.

He didn't reach for her either, though under any other circumstances he always reached out for her when she was close. At first it had been strange; now she missed the simple intimacy.

But there was no question that this was where she belonged, standing side by side with him. In that moment she knew that she'd never find a better place to be.

"Perhaps, Franshesco," Drake continued smoothly as if she wasn't assimilating a new reality for her life, "you can offer us a tour of the situation before we discuss whether we can benefit one another."

"Why certainly," and he began leading them toward his Mercedes.

"Let's take our vehicle," Drake turned for the armored Toyota Land Cruiser. The safety of the steel box was a good tactical advantage and also a good reminder to get her head back in the game.

The first thing Nikita did after being put in the back seat behind Franshesco was to pull her purse weapon and aim it through the seat at his heart. She'd wager that when they'd armored the vehicle, they hadn't loaded up the seat backs. There was something slippery about him that she didn't trust at all.

* * *

Drake wasn't sure quite what had come over Nikita. Whatever the reason for the change, it had been amazing to watch. The guard who she'd disarmed had been so angry that Drake had been sure it was going to end in blood. The guard's blood.

Then, when she cleared and dumped his weapons in the dirt and turned away from him, he'd deflated like a popped balloon. Drake actually had to pull the Toyota around him as he continued to stand there with two firearms, two magazines, and a knife scattered about his feet. If they came back this way, Drake was glad that they'd be doing it in a vehicle rated safe to higher than an M16's ammunition.

As he glanced that way, he noted Nikita's position, with a gun to the back of Franshesco Gutierrez's seat. Whatever had changed in her, she hadn't lost her focus. She was as much telling him as threatening Gutierrez: *I don't trust this man.*

He heard her loud and clear; neither did he.

"There isn't much to see here, Mr. Roman." He pointed for Drake to follow the perimeter road, the headlights slashing narrow paths through the darkness. "We are having problems with the locals, but nothing we can't handle."

"What are you doing about the European banks pulling twenty-four million euros in funding off the project? I don't think that Sinohydro will continue building your dam without being paid. Also, I don't see that you have enough long-term collateral to offer them for the Chinese banks to step in. Your political environment is too unstable—they are notoriously conservative investors." That accounted for most of the article he'd read about the murders of two leading environmentalists only a week apart. He'd never thought he'd use those boring Boston-society parties that his father's parents had dragged him to, but without them he wouldn't have understood the financial implications and maneuvering. Apparently everything had a reason if he could only find it.

"We will find other funding," but Gutierrez didn't sound happy about it, perhaps his first honest emotion.

"In the meantime, your investments sit idle. I see that you have cleared the construction area, but have done minimal work since then."

"We are simply assuring the safety of our investments to date so that they will be ready as soon as additional financing is obtained."

Meanwhile, Drake was observing what he could. The perimeter fence, a work of military beauty near the main gate, rapidly tapered to little more than coils of razor wire as it ran along the deeper jungle. That explained the frequent perimeter patrols. Out here, eyes watched him from the forest. The headlights revealed a deer and a few specimens that looked like furry pigs. A flock of white bats flitted across the beam of his lights but were abruptly batted aside by a blast of wind. Didn't they know a storm was coming?

He reminded himself that the guard tower had been well enough armed to take out their helicopter from two kilometers away. Four or five guard towers could cover the whole area of the construction site…but he didn't see another tower as they drove. Security was a stupid place to cut expenses.

That told him a lot about Franshesco Gutierrez. Not only wasn't he military, but he probably didn't listen much to his security advisors, neither Buck Baer while he'd been alive nor whoever was on site now. Gutierrez was high up enough to be worried only about the money.

Drake knew in that moment that Gutierrez was going to find out what Drake knew and then do his best to get rid of them permanently. Drake Roman, Inc. wasn't being considered for anything. Instead they were being assessed for what scale of threat he represented.

No joke about the storm coming. Stray branches and leaves blew past his windscreen. When he could see the jungle, the trees were swaying heavily in the gusts.

So Drake kept the conversation light and matter-of-fact as they cruised the perimeter fence.

He had most of what he needed to know. Security was mostly concentrated at the point of entry and at least one alpha target was on site, sitting right now in his vehicle. Drake checked the odometer, had to remember it was in kilometers, and decided that the patrol's timing was correct for a single Toyota constantly driving the perimeter. There was bound to be at least one more vehicle somewhere, but not out on patrol.

No, taking out the mercenaries wasn't the challenge. The problem was Gutierrez and the other suits who had arrived on the helicopter this afternoon. How to remove them without just dropping a bomb on their heads.

He knew that the third helo was still here because the first call he'd made once they'd retreated into the jungle this afternoon was to Zoe's boss, Sophie Garcia, back at the 5E base on Fort Rucker. She had the Avenger drone aloft and on station above the construction site in under three hours. The clouds from the approaching storm had blocked the view, but they didn't slow down the radar in the slightest.

She'd reported two armed helos and one unarmed, all on the ground in the center of the site, well clear of the perimeter. But everywhere Sophia had looked, there were still no buildings.

He had to solve that first.

* * *

Nikita listened to the conversation, but couldn't make any sense of it. It was as if Drake really was looking to turn this into a serious business discussion. He acted as if the clock wasn't ticking and he had all the time in the world.

"You want to add three more towers, though I'd recommend five. I can source the steel for you. Your best price elsewhere minus ten percent."

"I notice your boys are still using the M16A4s. You should set them up with something decent. You know that the US military has almost completely phased them out."

"Your outer layer security is fixable, but it is only single tier. I'd suggest at least two more layers if you're having the kind of issues you've mentioned."

He offered a new earthmover at cost when their headlights lit up the burned-out one. "Engine fire," Gutierrez had explained, not that she believed him—it was scorched from one end to the other.

It was as if Drake was commenting on every single piece of their security. Then she realized that's *exactly* what he was doing. They had each taken an encrypted radio from the Little Bird. She'd tucked hers in the rifle case because there was nowhere to hide it on a dress. But Drake must have locked a frequency onto transmit and had just given a running narration to the rest of the team still aloft.

It gave her the creeps because it was shades of the militia that had tortured her father and Barry to death on an open frequency. But it also made her want to kiss Drake, the Duck-man was as sneaky as a DEVGRU SEAL.

Finally they dropped Gutierrez off near a small hut. Close by was a pair of Toyota pickups, another Mercedes, and the three helicopters. There was no way the people needed to man them would all fit in that shack.

That they weren't invited in was a very bad sign.

"Are you sure I can't run you out to your Mercedes at the gate, Franshesco? We are headed that way, after all."

"No, Mr. Roman. I'll have one of the boys fetch it for me. I have some business I need to take care of here. We will definitely be in touch. Thank you so much for coming to Honduras and introducing yourself."

They appeared to shake hands sincerely. Nikita climbed into

the front seat, keeping her sidearm ready, out of sight behind the still-open passenger door.

The instant the doors closed, Nikita practically shouted, "What the hell, Roman?"

He just stared out the window at the shack as Gutierrez went inside.

"Drake?"

"They're set up underground. These guys are ready for a siege. They're dug in."

"Then we have to dig them out."

"Or entice them. Too bad they're going to try and kill us first."

That was news to her. "Any time soon?"

"Not sure," Drake dropped the Land Cruiser into gear and turned for the main gate. "But I'd say yes. They don't want Drake Roman, Inc. any more than they wanted GSI. They think that hired guns equal security."

Nikita pulled the side lever and laid her seat down so that she could crawl into the back.

"Where are you going?"

"I'll be damned if I'm going to get killed wearing a dress."

Drake's chuckle made her smile…until she tried to figure out how to pull down the zipper on the back of her dress by herself.

Chapter 17

Drake stared at the gate from a few hundred meters out. "They're going to kill us sooner than I thought."

Nikita slid back into the front seat. He hadn't seen her looking like this since the Philippines. Camo pants and jacket, boots, and enough magazines of ammo on her vest to stop a small army—perhaps even a mid-sized one as she also had her long Tac-50 sniper rifle out of its case and propped in the foot well.

"There's the lady I fell for. Wondered where you'd gone."

"I got tangled up in some idiot he-man's idea of a wardrobe. Won't happen again so I hope you enjoyed it." He could easily hear her smile in the dark.

She shoved something in his lap.

"Here's your jacket, unless you want to be an Armani-white target."

A blast of dirt whipped against the side of the SUV, rattling it loudly, though the armored Toyota was too heavy to sway in the gust of wind. The storm was almost here.

He changed into the darker clothing as he continued to watch out the windshield.

Drake had doused the lights on the Land Cruiser the instant the glow of the main gate's floodlights came into view. Now they were parked atop a small clear-cut rise, looking down at their welcoming committee. The security was outlined in a circle of light that had been punched into the jungle's darkness.

The four guards all had their M16s off their shoulder straps and in their hands. He only saw one other up in the guard tower. They weren't watching the gate. Instead, they were all facing into the compound, waiting for his arrival, not knowing he was already here—in range of their weapons but hidden by the darkness. A distant crack of lightning said that ploy wasn't going to work much longer.

He turned on the windshield wipers as the first of the rain started to fall.

When someone knocked on the window, he nearly leapt out of his clothes. He risked turning on the dash lights. There was just enough glow to light Luke Altman's smiling face.

Drake rolled down his window, the only one that still operated after armoring. The fresh smell of rain washed in. He could feel the red dust of the Honduran soil being knocked down. Soon it would be slick and muddy, but after most of a day and an evening in the jungle, it was a relief.

"Hey, Altman."

"Hey yourself. Nikita, nice to see you in proper clothes again."

"Asshole," Nikita replied cheerfully.

"So, looks like they're waiting for you."

"Looks like," Drake agreed.

"I might have an idea on that."

Less than a minute later they were ready.

"Do it," Altman slapped him on the shoulder.

But Drake hesitated. He wasn't sure exactly why at first, but then he focused on what his instincts had seen before his thoughts did.

The every-twenty-minute patrol. He glanced at the dashboard clock.

If they were on schedule…

A minute later a black Toyota pickup was coming along the fence line, its lights refracting high off the raindrops before it fully came into view. The two guys in back were hunkered down in ponchos, not even pretending to look around them.

Drake waited, estimating the timing for both his SUV and their truck to arrive at the gate at the same time.

"Now!" He dropped the Land Cruiser into gear, checked one more time that the steering wheel was well tied off, then flicked on the headlights as he stepped clear. At just engine idle, it began rolling toward the gate.

He walked over to Luke and Nikita.

"Why are you lying down in the mud?"

"If you want to catch a stray round, that's fine with me," Altman said flat-voiced.

"Not with me," Nikita complained. "Get your ass down, Roman. So much to teach you, it's just sad." She was watching the unfolding events through the scope on her rifle.

He got down fast. His instincts were too used to being wrapped in a helo's armor.

"They've seen it. Raising their M-16s."

The Land Cruiser continued to idle forward, slowly gaining speed. It wasn't much of a slope, but it would be enough to make sure that it didn't get stuck.

When it was half the distance down to them, the guards opened fire. Their muzzle flashes were brilliant yellow despite the big floodlights shining above. The rounds sparked off the armor and bulletproof glass. A few ricochets whistled by overhead and Drake was glad he was lying in the mud.

"Changing clips."

They resumed burning rounds. The headlights finally went,

but the SUV just kept rolling. The pickup pulled to a stop and the occupants piled out to add their firepower.

"Watch the tower," Nikita announced.

A heavy machine gun began chugging away, its roar loud even at this distance.

"It's just a Mark 48. Still marginal against this armor. Looks like he figured that out."

"About time," Altman grumbled.

A streak of white arced down from the tower and onto the SUV. The Pike missile hit the driver's window and blew a massive hole in the side of the vehicle. As if that wasn't enough, the tower gunner fired a second round through the hole.

Unable to contain the internal blast compression, the entire roof and window section of the SUV flailed upward. The heavy door armor on the other side was all that saved the two sets of guards on the ground, keeping the Pike's shrapnel within the vehicle. But the force of the explosion was enough to bowl them all off their feet and send them tumbling.

The Land Cruiser veered off course slightly.

"Damn it!" The SUV was supposed to cripple the tower.

Instead of hitting the base of the tower as planned, it lodged in the storm fence between the empty Toyota pickup and the tower.

"That's why I came early," Altman pulled a small box from his hip pocket. He had taken supplies from the Little Bird this afternoon and floated downriver himself.

He dialed in a frequency and pressed a trigger. Two of the four legs on the tower blew out. In slow motion, the tower collapsed over the burning remains of the SUV, blocked the front gate, and the guard shack at the tower's top shattered the parked black pickup. The tower gunner dove clear at the last moment, but just lay stunned in the mud.

"Let's go!"

Together the three of them raced downslope through the

battering rain. They arrived before any of the guards had shaken off the effects of the double explosion so close by. In moments they had them cuffed with zip ties hand and foot. There were only two Hondurans among them, the rest were US ex-military or worse.

A bright crack of lightning illuminated one of the Little Birds landing just in time to help finish the job. He, Nikita, and Altman all grabbed night-vision goggles, then Drake pointed upward without looking.

"Nikita, floodlights."

In moments she'd shot them out.

He flicked on the power switch and his world went to the familiar thousand shades of green produced by NVGs.

He continued securing the downed and now blind guards.

Then the Tac-50 sounded again, a round hitting metal very close by with a sharp clang.

He turned in time to see Nikita's second Tac-50 round hit the Mercedes sedan. Head on in the engine block. A hiss of steam rose from under the hood.

* * *

"I have an idea."

"Hit me," Drake replied.

So Nikita did. His surprised yelp was only partial payback for making her wear a dress to a gunfight.

Esly had been on the Little Bird and was now kneeling on the least happy of the guards, who was facedown in the mud. It was the bastard Nikita had disarmed earlier—she should have shot him while she still had the chance.

Nikita walked up to him and at her nod, Esly turned his head to face her. She flicked on a flashlight for his benefit, not hers.

"Were you the shooter of the environmentalists?"

His eyes went wide at her transformation.

She placed the business end of her Tac-50 an inch from his right eye. The sniper rifle could throw a half-inch round well over a mile. At an inch, the bore would look like a cannon.

"I suggest you answer her question," Esly prompted him with a hard knee to the kidney. "She isn't as patient as I am."

Nikita clicked the safety off and braced as if she was about to fire.

"No! It was Hank. Not here! Not me!" His panicked accent placed him from New Jersey. "He's back at the underground base. Hank pulled the trigger on both of them; he insisted it was his right as leader. We were just patrol. All we did was track and secure."

Nikita kept the gun aimed at him.

"I swear. It wasn't me."

His right. Killing an innocent was—

Oddly, she didn't feel a desire to pull the trigger on the downed guard. She wouldn't have, he wasn't a sick animal to be put down. But in the past she'd have thought he was. Now he wasn't even worth her time.

She huddled back up with Altman and Drake as Esly finished tying everyone up. Ankles as well as wrists.

"We need to get this guy Hank out of his hole in the ground and have him come here."

"Easy," Altman shrugged. "But what do we do with him once we get him? And in order to flush him, we're going to spook off the people we really want. I don't have a plan for them."

Nikita gave a sharp whistle to Esly, who came trotting over. She wore a holstered sidearm, an ammo vest with a half dozen clips, and carried a loaded M16.

"Well, you didn't shoot us in the back," Drake told her. "Guess that means you're okay."

Altman's grunt made it clear that he'd been comfortable enough around her to not object to her arming herself.

Nikita ignored both the men. "Esly, how connected is Mercedez?"

"Are you joking with me? She is a woman who knows everybody and everything."

"Do you have her phone number?"

Esly tapped her forehead and smiled.

Nikita pulled out Drake's phone and handed it to her.

"What am I asking her about?"

She glanced at Drake and Altman, but they hadn't put it together yet.

"Ask her how to reach the most corrupt military commander at the nearest military base. Call it a hunch."

Drake smiled slowly as he caught on. "Gutierrez would definitely need the local protection of these guards, but he'd also have an ear inside the military. Let's see if we can't cut the whole head off this snake. And now that you mention it, I'd like to ask her a question myself after you're done with her."

Drake's look could have covered anything from calling in a bomber to pulling her into the darkness for a quick tumble.

It was the moments when he was being most creative that she couldn't read him.

Chapter 18

Once they had the information from Mercedez, Drake had placed his call, stepping away from the others to place it privately. He'd need an authentic reaction of surprise for this part of his plan to work. He also didn't want the others to reject it as being too stupid for words. Drake could see it in his head; he just hoped that the reality matched.

Because Altman spoke Spanish and Drake didn't, Altman then played the role of Gutierrez. He placed a panicked call to the military commander that Mercedez thought was most likely to be involved with siphoning money off a big construction project in his area.

Altman started nearly hysterical, then escalated from there.

Drake could only assume he was on script, since he supposedly was shouting something like: "Not just the local crazies. They have helos and are in-bound. Get up here now. Low profile. Only your most trusted. We can't risk exposure of your role in—" Altman hung up the phone mid-sentence.

Drake was going to start Spanish lessons the minute he got back to base. Maybe Nikita would give him private lessons; he liked the sound of that. Though he'd suggest somewhere drier. It wasn't a cold rain, but he was soaked right through. At least it wasn't Philippine monsoon—if he never hit that again, he'd be a happy camper.

As soon as Luke was done, Drake got on the radio up to Zoe. She had taken over running the Avenger drone from a small screen and set of controls rigged in the back of the other Little Bird.

"Black out their cellphones. I don't want the military able to call Gutierrez."

Zoe acknowledged and began working her drone magic.

Drake checked his phone. It took less than ten seconds before his two wavering bars of signal plummeted to *No signal.*

"How long do we have?" he asked Altman.

"I could hear him shouting orders in the background and he sounded seriously upset. La Ceiba to here in a Huey, which is about the most advanced helicopter they have in their fleet… Half an hour at the earliest, forty-five at the outside."

"The timing is going to be tight. Let's go with Stage Two now. Time to take out the rest of their security."

Drake walked over to the pile of gear that Esly had gathered as she stripped off the guards' gear. He picked out a radio and keyed the mic.

"Main Gate to Base! Main Gate to Base! We've got a problem here." He copied the New Jersey accent of the trussed-up guard.

Altman pulled out his sidearm and fired six frantic shots into the jungle.

Esly unleashed her M16 at the fallen tower's shack for half a clip on full auto. She must have hit some stored munitions, perhaps the stockpile of Pike missiles, because the shack suddenly shredded itself and a fiery plume shot several stories up into the night sky.

Drake turned off the radio and tossed it back on the pile. "I think that should do it."

"Oops," Esly didn't look the least bit sorry, but she did put a fresh clip in the rifle.

Drake clicked on the encrypted radio to the Night Stalkers team circling above them. "Zoe, you can jam their radio frequencies now as well."

"On it," he heard a quick rattle of keys on the keyboard. "There. Our encrypted radios are in a different frequency band, so we should be fine, but they're blacked out."

"Roger that. Okay, Esly. This part is up to you and Altman. Nikita and I have to run."

Esly gave him a hand sign that might have been a "Hurry Up" military signal or might have been a fist pump prior to starting a happy dance.

He grabbed an M16 and a stack of magazines for himself, and a couple of the guard's jackets. After a quick stop to make sure Altman was clear on what was happening, he chased after Nikita, who was already halfway to the horizon.

Drake wished she hadn't shot the Mercedes sedan; he could certainly use it at the moment. The rain, slashed at him by the hard-gusting winds, pounded so hard on his head that it almost hurt. He couldn't wipe his eyes fast enough to clear the water streaming out of his hair. Maybe Philippine rain wasn't so bad.

* * *

Nikita waited, crouching by the burned-out earth mover. She considered giving Drake a moment to catch his breath when he reached her, but where was the fun in that?

She started to rise but then saw the two Toyota pickups racing by along the perimeter road and settled back down. There was no way for them to see her, as she and Drake had been directly moving across the construction site because it was the shortest distance rather than following the road. And between the rain and their own camouflage clothes, they probably wouldn't have been seen at three paces, never mind three hundred.

"They're moving awfully fast," Nikita knew that would be a logistical problem for Luke and Esly, dangerously narrowing their engagement time.

"Should I have stayed and waved a Caution sign at them or something? I don't see a way to slow them down."

Nikita dropped into a prone position and swung out the bipod legs on the Tac-50. She'd done so much training in so many weather conditions that the increasing rain only crossed her attention as a blurring of her sight lines. Rain didn't affect something as big as the rounds the Tac-50 fired.

"You're kidding me, right?"

She ignored him and focused on the first pickup in the line, then the front half of it, then the front right tire, then the leading edge of that tire. Using the markings in the scope, she used the typical length of a quad-cab full-sized pickup to estimate the distance. At nine hundred meters and a target the size of a truck tire, she didn't need to factor in much for temperature, humidity, or Coriolis effect. The wind was the major factor, kicking in the high twenties out of the southeast.

Nikita tracked the leading edge of the tire long enough to get a feel for the truck's speed as it jounced along the rough road. At its current speed, it would travel twenty-two meters in the full second it would take her bullet to fly the distance between them—almost exactly three times the truck's length.

She swung her rifle ahead more by instinct than thought, fired, and worked the bolt. But she wouldn't have to fire again. It had been clean. Keeping her line of fire centered in the scope's field, she saw the tire enter her field of vision just in time to have a hole punched in its sidewall.

The truck stumbled badly. The driver was good enough that he didn't flip and roll despite the rough ground. But it slowed them abruptly from sixty kilometers an hour to fifteen. The truck following close behind them nearly rammed into the back, skidding wildly in the mud to avoid a collision.

As they straightened themselves out, the two Little Birds descended out of the night sky and turned on blinding searchlights, one fore and one aft.

In moments, Altman and Esly appeared to disarm the mercenaries.

Nikita watched long enough to see Esly boot one in the balls particularly hard after she tied him up. Apparently she'd found Hank.

Drake tapped Nikita's shoulder and they were up and running again.

"Shit, woman! How did you make that shot?"

"I could teach you."

"But then you'd have to kill me?"

"No, then you'd be a SEAL."

* * *

Drake would have laughed if he'd had the breath. He'd been able to match Nikita on a treadmill, barely. Over open terrain he was flat out when she was still in graceful-gazelle mode, carrying the rifle that was almost as long as she was and weighed twenty-five pounds to his M16's nine with the ease of a relay racer's baton.

"What direction will they be coming from?"

Not able to spare the breath, he pointed the M16 due west. That was the direction of La Ceiba military base.

Nikita veered in that direction and he followed her.

They'd been racing toward the helicopters parked near the shack that covered the entrance to underground. Now they were running west. Fifty meters, a hundred, two hundred.

"This should do it," she spoke as if she was finishing a morning stroll, not a hard 3K run.

She lay on the ground facing west.

He lay beside her, but facing the other direction, back toward the parked helicopters.

Drake stared at them for a long moment before he saw the problem…nothing was moving. "They're staying in their bolt hole."

"Now what, genius man?"

"Genius man?"

"Would you prefer Mr. Mercenary Man, sir?"

"Sir?" Drake nudged an elbow against her ribs. "I like the sound of sir."

"Maybe try a panic call from Hank?" She ignored him.

"I can fake a random guard's voice, but I don't think we can play that card twice. Besides, I didn't bring one of their radios because I have Zoe blocking their frequencies."

"Well, we have about five minutes to flush them out."

How to flush a rabbit out of its hole? Going in the front door would just drive them in deeper. Or out the back door. The problem was, he didn't know where the back door might be.

Had they built underground because it was a convenient and safe place for their construction headquarters, needing only a simple couple of rooms? Or was it a complex arrangement for other purposes? How could—

Then he had it.

He patted the nearest part of Nikita, which turned out to be her splendid behind, earning him a sigh of exasperation.

Then he tucked in the earpiece for the encrypted radio.

"Zoe?"

"Here, Duck-man."

"Do you have anything on your Avenger drone that you could rig to act as a ground-penetrating radar?"

"Would an *actual* ground-penetrating radar do, or do you want something else?"

"You brought—"

"You didn't say what we'd need, so I had Sophie load up everything I could think of."

"I could just kiss you."

"If you do, Nikita would pound the shit out of you. So keep it to yourself, Duck-man."

"Roger that." Nikita made no response from close beside him. "We're right on top of a rabbit warren here. I need to know where it goes."

"Give me a couple minutes. My baby is up at forty thousand feet."

"You have thirty seconds."

"Stingy," Zoe complained. But it was well under thirty seconds later that he heard the loud *whoosh* of the Avenger slicing by close above them. She must have descended under full thrust. It was amazing she hadn't ripped off the wings with that maneuver, but that's why she was an Avenger pilot and he was merely a DAP Hawk crew chief.

For a full minute, it swept back and forth making multiple passes. For a full minute, he lay there trying not to be driven deeper into the mud by the blasts of wind-driven rain. If it was this bad here, Roatán and the ship—over a hundred and fifty kilometers deeper into the storm—must be getting hammered.

"These are rough, but it looks as if there's a small complex and it runs south, away from you and toward the jungle, but doesn't reach it. On the last pass I did a thermal scan and I don't see that anyone has come out."

"Okay. Drop a pair of JDAMs on their backdoor."

"How about a few SDMs instead? The radar and the jamming packages took up too much space and payload for me to carry any of the bigger weapons."

"A pair of small diameter bombs should serve my purpose

just fine." At two hundred and fifty pounds each, they'd shake the place hard without doing much damage.

"SDMs. Wow!" Nikita spoke loud enough to be heard over the ripping wind while they waited for the next pass of the Avenger. "They *have* put you in a bad mood."

"They tried to kill, then kidnap, you. Then that guard was going after your breasts and I'm sorry, I have prior claim to that territory."

"*That territory?*"

"Your breast territory. I have rights of sole passage until you revoke them. No two-bit mercenary hired hand gets to trample all over *my* territory."

Nikita's reply was smothered by the pair of bombs that struck a few hundred meters to the west. Great fountains of dirt shot upward, lit in the darkness by the central explosion like a blooming night flower. What kind of flowers did Nikita like? He didn't know.

Considering that she was a DEVGRU SEAL, probably exploding ones just like these.

Dirt spattered down all around them along with the rain, but nothing big was thrown this far.

He waited for nine heartbeats, then on the tenth saw a stream of people scrambling out of the hut and racing to the parked helicopters.

"Bingo!"

"Good timing," Zoe announced over the radio. "I have three birds incoming from the west that must be Gutierrez's military connection. Ten kilometers and closing."

The trio of Gutierrez's own Bell TwinRangers began cranking to life. The timing of the meeting between the two helicopter groups was going to be too close. Nikita's Tac-50 had an effective flash suppressor. His own borrowed M-16 didn't—and they'd be able to see where his shots were coming from.

That would ruin the whole play.

He draped the guard's jackets that he'd taken into a jumbled pile in front of him, weighting them in place with a couple of stones. Then he nudged the muzzle into the folds of the jacket and flipped the firing mode to semi-auto. He'd just have to hope that the jackets hid his muzzle flash.

"In sight," Nikita whispered.

"Hold…hold…hold," the first two TwinRangers crawled aloft. These were the two armed patrol ships that had flown out to check on their downed 5E helicopter at the waterfall. The VIP craft was still waiting for the last people to board.

"Tell them to hurry," Nikita whispered. Both helicopter groups had to be aloft and nearby at the same time for this to work.

"Remember not to actually shoot them down."

"This is crazy."

"You want to face five heavily armed helos with a rifle?"

"I'm not that crazy."

"Just crazy in love with me?" Wow. Time for another one of his do-overs. His timing sucked.

"*Definitely* not that crazy," but she didn't sound upset. "Damn it, Roman. Don't make me laugh when I'm about to shoot at multiple gunships loaded with corrupt military."

Laughter wasn't exactly the response he'd been hoping for.

The third of Gutierrez's helicopters—the transport with the suits aboard—made it aloft. The two gunships were hovering fifty meters up.

"Go!"

* * *

Nikita began plinking at the three helicopters incoming from the military base. Firing a half-inch round out of a high-precision sniper rifle, it was actually hard *not* to shoot them down. It should be two shots right through the windshield. Dead pilot and copilot. Crash. Done.

But that wasn't Drake's master plan.

So, instead, she shot at one of the skids and missed. The wind had continued to pick up and was playing havoc with the bullet's and the helicopter's flight paths.

She worked the bolt and aimed for something bigger. She dropped a round on the FLIR camera in the front. It would knock out their night-vision camera, but it shouldn't go through the frame and kill anyone.

Nikita could hear Drake firing down by her feet. *Snap!...Snap! Snap!*

She chose another helo and shot it high in the windshield. Her round would either skip off the windshield or punch through into all of the electronics directly over the pilots' heads.

It took surprisingly few shots before Drake called hold.

In moments the military Hueys and Gutierrez's TwinRangers were in a full-fledged battle directly over where he and Nikita lay in the mud.

It had been so simple. The two groups of helicopters had approached each other with their radios out of commission due to Zoe's jamming. Add in a nighttime rainstorm and a panicked evacuation.

A few shots head-on at each group of helicopters with no detectable origin, and they'd each assumed the worst and attacked each other.

"There goes one," Nikita called out as one of the military's Hueys appeared to stumble in the air. It didn't autorotate down, it plummeted.

Drake tapped her shoulder and led her racing back the way they'd come.

As they circled behind the parked earthmoving equipment, a helicopter flew close above them. The blast of wind said that it was far bigger than any of the helos currently fighting it out in the storm, but the sound was odd, far more like a washing machine flying away from them than a five-ton DAP Hawk flying toward them. It settled on the mud for the briefest of moments and she and Drake piled aboard.

She was glad to be sitting once more on a hard steel deck instead of the red mud of Honduras that had penetrated her every pore. She was sopping wet.

Someone at the crew chief position handed her a headset.

She recognized one of the gunners from the 5E's big Chinook helicopter but couldn't remember his name at the moment.

"How goes the battle?" she asked over the intercom.

"The locals," Julian called from the front seat, "are tough contenders this year. They're not to be put down lightly, sports fans. Each side is down one bird, and I mean down as in hard. Nobody walking away from those."

Nikita looked out the open cargo bay door, but the battle must be on the other side of the aircraft. The DAP Hawk was circling back out of the way. She dangled her feet out the door and over the abyss.

Someone—Drake—snapped a harness around her waist. She felt him tug it to make sure that she was securely attached to the frame. Then he slid his feet out beside her. For a moment they both just sat with their rifles across their laps, staring out at the wind-torn darkness.

She leaned her shoulder into his and just listened to Julian's play-by-play as the DAP Hawk jounced through the turbulent winds.

The Honduran Navy was down to one as the second bird autorotated into deep jungle, snared high in the trees, and exploded long before it hit the ground.

Julian's slow circle brought the construction site back into view.

Drake pointed an arm.

Three helicopters spinning and twisting across the sky. Actually two doing the dance and one hightailing it out of there.

* * *

"Gutierrez," Drake knew he was right. "Julian, we can't let that third bird escape."

"I'm not supposed to shoot them down. Any suggestions?" But he climbed, circling wide around the continuing battle, and laid down the hammer to chase the departing aircraft.

Drake looked down at the M16 in his hands. That wasn't the answer.

If the military won, they would declare themselves heroes. If they lost, well, they'd probably be declared heroes anyway.

But if Gutierrez was shot down, there would be far too many questions. He was too important. Everything could come to light. But if he escaped, he would just start all over again somewhere else. Still, there couldn't be any cause to look beyond a conflict with the military.

Drake watched the last two helicopter pilots battling it out. Neither was Night Stalker caliber, but they knew their machines. Their battle was lit in strobe flashes of lightning and distorted by sheets of rain. The drops stung his legs where they dangled out in the DAP Hawk's slipstream, but neither he nor Nikita pulled their legs in.

Instead they watched.

Watched until the military Huey made the first mistake. Apparently noticing that Gutierrez's aircraft was slipping away, it turned to shoot him down.

The remaining armed TwinRanger raced directly at it with a fusillade of fire streaming off its side-mounted M230 chain gun.

Realizing his mistake, the military pilot carved a hard turn to bring his own weapons to bear, but they were too close.

The two helicopters tangled their rotor blades as they passed. They twisted and slammed their tail sections together as they sped by one another. A moment later, they were both gone from sight, plunging into the river at unsurvivable speeds.

So much for the military solving the problem. Now Gutierrez was free—unless Drake could stop him.

Stop him but make it look like an accident before they lost him in the storm.

The storm!

"Julian."

"Yes, Mr. Roman of the dangerous reputation?"

"Screw you."

"You wish. Only the finest of the ladies get to play with this body."

"Julian," Drake started over. "Is he following the power lines?" Drake could picture the tall transmission lines climbing the hill toward the interior, away from the storm.

"He's right over them, following their break in the jungle to keep out of sight."

"Does he know we're here behind him?"

"No, he's now flying at a standard cruise speed."

"What happens if we fly over him?"

"Not much."

"I mean *right* over him. Like a couple meters."

Chapter 19

Family mourns loss of Franshesco Gutierrez in storm-related accident.

Nikita read the headline on the suite's bedroom television screen again and tried to feel sorry about it, but she couldn't. The bodies of Gutierrez, two bankers suspected of drug running, and a dirty chief of police known for his generous payoffs were found in the crashed helicopter. Of course none of those details were listed, but command had confirmed who they'd been.

"Why was the entire head of the snake onsite for a meeting?" she asked Drake where he lay beside her.

"Because," he poked a finger in her shoulder, "they were worried about the great Drake Roman coming their way. Your rumor campaign was big enough that it got back to them somehow and must have scared them spitless."

Nikita remembered the moment that their DAP Hawk had overflown the Bell TwinRanger. A flash of lightning had strobe-lit the moment. The down-blast of the DAP Hawk's massive rotors disrupted the air flow over the much smaller Bell helicopter, and its blades had lost all lift.

Another flash, this time of man-made lightning as the helo snagged one transmission line with one skid, twisted, and laid the tail across the other. It had lain there for a long moment, arcing and flashing with light, before the rotor sliced one of the massive wires and then the aircraft plummeted down into the clearing. There had been no explosion, but they had landed on a boulder field from fifty meters up. There was no question of survivors.

The newscast flipped to the next news item and Drake chuckled beside her.

"Show off," she accused him and he didn't argue, instead pulling her more tightly against his side. Nikita snuggled as she joined his laugh.

Police sergeant goes undercover to unmask environmentalists' killer.

Nikita couldn't help smiling back at the image of a grinning Esly, soaked by the rain, standing with her M16 over a dozen well-bound mercenaries. Drake's move of calling in the press had been a brilliant way to make sure the entire site's security detail was taken out of operation. Apparently the guards had tried to tell stories of the 5E team, but Esly had simply said, "Others who wish to remain anonymous for their safety offered some assistance." It made it sound like a locals' movement seeking retribution for the killed environmentalists, which would only make the whole event more popular.

President declares Esly Escarra a national hero.

"He didn't have a lot of choice, did he," Drake asked the screen rhetorically.

Tropical storm Kyra gives coast glancing blow.

They both sat up as the images flashed across the screen.

The ride back to the ship had been a wild one as the storm

buffeted the Roatán coast. It had been a dozen times more violent on the island than it had been up at the El Carbón dam site. At midnight, in the heart of the storm, they had fast-roped down from their helos onto the top deck of the cruise ship as it wallowed and bucked against the pier despite its protected harbor. She and Drake from the DAP Hawk, Altman from one Little Bird, and Zoe from the other. With no one the wiser, they'd reached their suite. Drenched, filthy, but back in their suite. A quick call to Norma and they were all logged as being back aboard—much earlier in the evening.

Drake had declared it would be best if they were found here. Less chance of an official connecting their leaving the ship with what had happened up in the hills. He had proven himself as a strategist so many times that no one questioned his judgment anymore.

But no one had slept until it was reported back that the three helos had flown through the storm wall and safely landed on their ship in the relative calm of the eye.

The newsfeed shifted from showing the mainland to footage of the islands:

French Harbour had been hammered.

Fishing and tour boats were cast up on the beach, others were sunk at their piers.

Houses had been damaged.

Then Nikita saw the palm tree rammed through the front window of the Junk Boutique.

She was up and half dressed before she knew it and Drake was right there beside her.

Out in the main suite's living room, Altman and Zoe were also dressed for hard work.

At the ramp, the ship's attendant tried to convince them to stay aboard. "The seas are too rough for us to leave today, but we *strongly* suggest that all passengers remain aboard."

They brushed past him, though it took a while to find a truck making its way toward French Harbour that they could hitch a ride on.

Where Drake led, Nikita and the others followed. He was a sergeant and Luke Altman a lieutenant commander. Drake was actually the lowest ranked of the four of them, but there was no question who was the leader.

They arrived at the Junk Boutique ready to go to work. Mercedez was inside with a mop. She was in a good mood despite the damage, "I am better off than others. It is only broken glass."

As a team they managed to pull the tree back into the street. Emmanuel found a roll of thick plastic in the back room and they soon had it tacked over the window. Then Mercedez shooed them on their way with a sincere hug for thanks.

The sky was still overcast, but the rain was no more than an occasional spatter and even that tapered off as they worked along the street.

When they reached the harbor itself, Nikita saw that it had been the worst hit. It wasn't long before Altman found the local tour divers and began going down with them to help refloat sunken boats. Nearby, Zoe used her magnetic charm to turn the people working at random along the beach into a team that dug half-buried boats out of the beach sand and hauled them back into the water.

Nikita stuck with Drake. They lifted, moved, dug, and mostly consoled people until her muscles burned, but still they didn't stop.

When they managed to get a restaurant put back together enough to make food, they were served the first lunch. Zoe and Altman soon joined them and they sat out at the end of a pier with their feet dangling over the turquoise water. The harbor waters were active without being rough. The fishing boats that survived and those they'd been able to refloat or relaunch bobbed at their moorings once again. A group of children were making a game of swimming out to floating plastic furniture and hauling it onto the beach.

"What next?" Nikita would be content to sit here all day, her shoulder brushing Drake's each time one of them lifted a conch fritter for another bite. It was hard to imagine being anywhere other than at his side.

"I don't know," Drake said softly.

She'd meant what was next after they'd eaten, but Drake wasn't scanning the beach for the next task, he was looking at her.

"You tell me."

The conch seemed to stick in her throat as she looked up at his dark eyes. The subject of the future hung between them. She turned away before the sadness overwhelmed her.

In perfect irony, the midday sunlight finally broke through the parting clouds and the turquoise water seemed to turn golden.

If this was like any other mission, they would return to US soil and she'd catch the next flight to Virginia Beach. As much as she enjoyed working with the 5E, they had accounted for less than ten of her missions over the last year. Without them she'd fought piracy in the Persian Gulf, tracked kidnappers across Africa, taken down terrorists in Indonesia, and any number of other missions.

"I could," it hurt to say, but she forced it out, "switch—"

"Hey," Zoe's shout interrupted their whispered conversation. "I know that boat."

Nikita looked up as a massive black motor yacht idled into the harbor.

Zoe jumped to her feet and finally managed to flag them down. The boat turned and headed for the pier.

They all rose to their feet to catch lines and greet them.

Nikita couldn't bring herself to finish the sentence. She loved being a DEVGRU SEAL. But life without Drake Roman—she didn't know if she could face that.

* * *

Drake pulled Nikita tightly against him as Jared's boat finished nosing alongside the pier. Drake buried his face in her hair and kissed her on the temple.

If a man ever needed proof that a woman loved him, it just didn't come any higher than what she'd been about to say.

He whispered for her alone, "If you *ever* even hint at leaving DEVGRU for me again, you're really going to piss me off. Just so you know."

She turned her face into his shoulder as if hiding there. "Then what do we do?"

Drake smiled, "I have an idea on that one." But he wasn't ready to give it a voice yet.

Nikita looked up at him and, after a long look, gave him a kiss that promised a lifetime if he could just figure out how to make it happen.

A massive hand crashed down on his shoulder, "Damn, military!"

Jared had a hold on both his and Nikita's shoulders and was shaking them like clothes on a line during a storm.

"Hey, mercenary," Nikita shot back, but her smile said she was no longer reacting to her past. Drake was so proud of her. How in the world was he supposed to tell an ST6 SEAL that he was so proud of her it made his chest hurt?

Jared shook them some more. "You weren't kidding about the whole 'being invisible' shit. Been watching the news feed and there isn't even a goddamn hint you were there. That was damn sweet work. Damn sweet."

"I think," Sugar eased up beside him, "that may be the highest praise I ever heard from J-dawg."

Asal nodded her agreement from close beside them.

Drake handed her his plate, which had one more conch fritter on it. She nibbled a corner, paused, and then began eating it happily.

"I got the names and faces of those mercs," Jared was practically effusive. "They were all GSI hires, which means they were bad news anyway. Can't believe you caught Hank Jaffer; I've been after that bastard for years. I spread the word that if any of those assholes ever get out of Honduran jail, Titan will be taking down any outfit that hires them—all the way down. They're blacklisted for life."

Drake slapped a hand down on Jared's shoulder, partly to stop the dual-shaking thing he was doing. A group of men and women lined the rails of the boat and looked down at the proceedings. The men were like miniature Jareds, a wide variety of types and all military tough, though none of them were as big as their boss. The women didn't look any less dangerous.

Nikita went up on her toes and actually kissed Jared, which shocked him into silence and thankfully made him finally let go of their shoulders.

Sugar gave Nikita a sideways hug, "Knew there was hope for you, Swimmer Girl."

"Hey," a voice called from up the pier.

Drake turned to see Esly striding along it.

"Do you have proper entry stamp for that boat?"

Nikita and Zoe threw their arms around her and the three women hugged.

All he got was a punch on the arm.

"What's it to you?" Jared growled.

"Careful, Mr. American. You are now talking to the Roatán Island Chief Minister of Security."

Drake laughed. "Mercedez *is* well connected."

Esly joined his laugh. "Yes, she had the mayor create this job for the new 'National Hero.' My duties are to ensure that the Bay Islands, including Roatán, remain safe for tourism no matter what disaster is the mainland. So," she turned to Jared and scowled at him. "Tell me if I should trust these people or no. They look like bad element to me."

Jared simply glowered, not able to hear the tease.

"I wouldn't trust them," Nikita was the first to speak.

"Not for a second," Drake crossed his arms over his chest.

"You wouldn't believe the kinds of things these guys do," Zoe chimed in cheerfully.

Altman simply stood beside Zoe with his arms crossed as well.

"Unless…" Drake trailed it out.

Jared glared down at him.

"Unless they were willing to help pitch in on the post-Storm Kyra cleanup."

Jared looked out over their heads and inspected the waterfront.

Drake saw him register the damage the storm had done and the people struggling to put their town back together. Without appearing to notice what he was doing, he reached an arm around Sugar's waist and pulled her tight against him.

"And if I was?" But despite his grumble, there was no question he'd be joining in. His true emotions were always clear on Sugar's face and Drake could see how proud she was of her man.

Drake knew exactly how she felt as he hung on to Nikita.

"Got room for four temporary Team Titan members?" Drake nodded at the others. "A couple of days' hard work together and we would go a long way to getting these people back on their feet."

Drake didn't need Sugar's glowing smile to tell him he'd done it right.

It was Nikita's laugh that really mattered. The merry sound proved that over these last days they had finally broken the past's hold on her life and now she'd be glad to work side by side with a military contractor, at least a good one like Titan.

They'd fixed her past, but his future—their future—was still a huge question.

Chapter 20

Nikita leaned on the bow rail of Jared's massive boat as it eased out of French Harbour.

The town was still damaged, but it was no longer broken and she could feel the ache of every day of the hard work, deep and good in her muscles.

Drake's arm was warm around her waist. It was just the two of them, leaning against the rail watching the harbor slide away.

Norma had left all of their clothes and gear at baggage claim at the Roatán airport before the cruise ship was finally cleared to continue its voyage. She'd done a fair job of covering how glad she was to have them off her boat.

Jared was now delivering them to the seaside airport for the flight home.

"I'll miss this place." The setting sun illuminated the tropical colors of the buildings—pink, pale blue, apricot—they all glowed in the warm evening. Most of the boats were back at the moorings and piers. There were even tourists venturing into town from whatever latest cruise ship had come in this morning.

"We'll be back," Drake said softly.

Nikita was torn with a ton of questions. *We?* That was the biggest one, but she didn't know how to face it. She'd thought of little else as they worked side by side over these last days. It had been at the forefront of her mind when she'd collapsed into the luxurious bed aboard—because Jared definitely traveled in style—shaking with exhaustion. It was her first thought when she awoke.

But she'd been afraid to give it a voice. Drake had been right: she couldn't leave the SEALs. *What* she'd done to get there—the why no longer mattered—was as essential a part of her as breathing. The problem was, Drake Roman was an equally essential part.

Unable to voice that question, she faced a simpler one. "When? How do you know we'll be back?"

"Because Esly said she'd track me down and kick my ass if we didn't honeymoon here."

Nikita started to laugh at the first part of his statement, then nearly strangled on the second part when it registered. When she looked over at Drake, he was no longer watching the shore but was looking at her instead.

He was right, there was no question. Not about marrying him and not about where to honeymoon. And now she finally knew what to do with that crazy La Perla lingerie body suit. As her sole concession to girldom, she'd wear it under her dress white uniform on her wedding day so that he could discover it when he undressed her on their wedding night.

"When?" Nikita barely managed to repeat the question now that it meant so much more.

"I'll take that as a yes."

All she could do was nod.

"Then I think the day I qualify would be a good one. A double celebration."

"Qualify for what?"

Drake looked out at the golden water for a long time before answering.

"I spoke to Altman and to my commander. There's a DEVGRU training course starting in a couple weeks. They both approved my transfer and application, but I told them it needed one more sign-off."

Now it was Nikita's turn to stare out at the water, but she couldn't see it past the blur in her eyes. She and Drake would be together for life. A husband-and-wife Navy SEAL team, the first one. With that future, none of the past could possibly matter.

She turned and kissed him as the sun settled behind the distant mainland, casting red across the coming night sky. *Red at night, sailors delight…*

"I'll take that as a yes, too."

Nikita didn't even bother with the nod this time.

This time she knew exactly where the tears were coming from, and they were pure joy.

About the Author

M. L. Buchman has over 50 novels and 40 short stories in print. Military romantic suspense titles from his Night Stalker, Firehawks, and Delta Force series each have been named *Booklist* "Top 10 Romance of the Year": 2012, 2015, & 2016. His Delta Force series opener, *Target Engaged*, was a 2016 RITA nominee. In addition to romance, he also writes thrillers, fantasy, and science fiction.

In among his career as a corporate project manager he has: rebuilt and single-handed a fifty-foot sailboat, both flown and jumped out of airplanes, and designed and built two houses. Somewhere along the way he also bicycled solo around the world.

He is now making his living as a full-time writer on the Oregon Coast with his beloved wife and is constantly amazed at what you can do with a degree in Geophysics. You may keep up with his writing and receive a free 4-novel starter e-library by subscribing to his newsletter at:

www.mlbuchman.com

About the Author

If you enjoyed this title, you might also enjoy:

Target Engaged (Delta Force #1)

Carla Anderson rolled up to the looming, storm-fence gate on her brother's midnight-blue Kawasaki Ninja 1000 motorcycle. The pounding of the engine against her sore butt emphasized every mile from Fort Carson in Pueblo, Colorado, home of the 4th Infantry and hopefully never again the home of

Sergeant Carla Anderson. The bike was all she had left of Clay, other than a folded flag, and she was here to honor that.

If this was the correct "here."

A small guard post stood by the gate into a broad, dusty compound. It looked deserted and she didn't see even a camera.

This was Fort Bragg, North Carolina. She knew that much. Two hundred and fifty square miles of military installation, not counting the addition of the neighboring Pope Army Airfield.

She'd gotten her Airborne parachute training here and had never even known what was hidden in this remote corner. Bragg was exactly the sort of place where a tiny, elite unit of the US military could disappear—in plain sight.

This back corner of the home of the 82nd Airborne was harder to find than it looked. What she could see of the compound through the fence definitely ranked "worst on base."

The setup was totally whacked.

Standing outside the fence at the guard post she could see a large, squat building across the compound. The gray concrete building was incongruously cheerful with bright pink roses along the front walkway—the only landscaping visible anywhere. More recent buildings—in better condition only because they were newer—ranged off to the right. She could breach the old fence in a dozen different places just in the hundred-yard span she could see before it disappeared into a clump of scrub and low trees drooping in the June heat.

Wholly indefensible.

There was no way that this could be the headquarters of the top combat unit in any country's military.

Unless this really was their home, in which case the indefensible fence—inde-fence-ible?—was a complete sham designed to fool a sucker. She'd stick with the main gate.

She peeled off her helmet and scrubbed at her long brown hair to get some air back into her scalp. Guys always went gaga over her hair, which was a useful distraction at times. She always wore it as long as her successive commanders allowed. Pushing the limits was one of her personal life policies.

She couldn't help herself. When there was a limit, Carla always had to see just how far it could be nudged. Surprisingly far was usually the answer. Her hair had been at earlobe length in Basic. By the time she joined her first forward combat team, it brushed her jaw. Now it was down on her shoulders. It was actually something of a pain in the ass at this length—another couple inches before it could reliably ponytail—but she did like having the longest hair in the entire unit.

Carla called out a loud "Hello!" at the empty compound shimmering in the heat haze.

No response.

Using her boot in case the tall chain-link fence was electrified, she gave it a hard shake, making it rattle loudly in the dead air. Not even any birdsong in the oppressive midday heat.

A rangy man in his late forties or early fifties, his hair half gone to gray, wandered around from behind a small shack as if he just happened to be there by chance. He was dressed like any off-duty soldier: worn khaki pants, a black T-shirt, and scuffed Army boots. He slouched to a stop and tipped his head to study her from behind his Ray-Bans. He needed a haircut and a shave. This was not a soldier out to make a good first impression.

"Don't y'all get hot in that gear?" He nodded to indicate her riding leathers without raking his eyes down her frame, which was both unusual and appreciated.

"Only on warm days," she answered him. It was June in North Carolina. The temperature had crossed ninety hours ago and the air was humid enough to swim in, but complaining never got you anywhere.

"What do you need?"

So much for the pleasantries. "Looking for Delta."

"Never heard of it," the man replied with a negligent shrug. But something about how he did it told her she was in the right place.

"Combat Applications Group?" Delta Force had many names, and they certainly lived to "apply combat" to a situation. No one on the planet did it better.

His next shrug was eloquent.

Delta Lesson One: Folks on the inside of the wire didn't call it Delta Force. It was CAG or "The Unit." She got it. Check. Still easier to think of it as Delta though.

She pulled out her orders and held them up. "Received a set of these. Says to show up here today."

"Let me see that."

"Let me through the gate and you can look at it as long as you want."

"Sass!" He made it an accusation.

"Nope. Just don't want them getting damaged or lost maybe by accident." She offered her blandest smile with that.

"They're that important to you, girlie?"

"Yep!"

He cracked what might have been the start of a grin, but it didn't get far on that grim face. Then he opened the gate and she idled the bike forward, scuffing her boots through the dust.

From this side she could see that the chain link was wholly intact. There was a five-meter swath of scorched earth inside the fence line. Through the heat haze, she could see both infrared and laser spy eyes down the length of the wire. And that was only the defenses she could see. So…a very not inde-fence-ible fence. Absolutely the right place.

When she went to hold out the orders, he waved them aside.

"Don't you want to see them?" This had to be the right place. She was the first woman in history to walk through The Unit's gates by order. A part of her wanted the man to acknowledge that. Any man. A Marine Corps marching band wouldn't have been out of order.

She wanted to stand again as she had on that very first day, raising her right hand. "I, Carla Anderson, do solemnly swear that I will support and defend the Constitution…"

She shoved that aside. The only man's acknowledgment she'd ever cared about was her big brother's, and he was gone.

The man just turned away and spoke to her over his shoulder as he closed the gate behind her bike. "Go ahead and check in. You're one of the last to arrive. We start in a couple hours"—as if it were a blasted dinner party. "And I already saw those orders when I signed them. Now put them away before someone else sees them and thinks you're still a soldier." He walked away.

She watched the man's retreating back. He'd signed her orders?

That was the notoriously hard-ass Colonel Charlie Brighton?

What the hell was the leader of the U.S. Army's Tier One asset doing manning the gate? Duh…assessing new applicants.

This place was whacked. Totally!

There were only three Tier One assets in the entire U.S. military. There was Navy's Special Warfare Development Group, DEVGRU, that the public thought was called SEAL Team Six—although it hadn't been named that for thirty years now. There was the Air Force's 24th STS—which pretty much no one on the outside had ever heard of. And there was the 1st Special Forces Operational Detachment—Delta—whose very existence was still denied by the Pentagon despite four decades of operations, several books, and a couple of seriously off-the-mark movies that were still fun to watch because Chuck Norris kicked ass even under the stupidest of circumstances.

Total Tier One women across all three teams? Zero.

About to be? One. Staff Sergeant First Class Carla Anderson.

Where did she need to go to check in? There was no signage. No drill sergeant hovering. No—

Delta Lesson Number Two: You aren't in the Army anymore, sister.

No longer a soldier, as the Colonel had said, at least not while on The Unit's side of the fence. On this side they weren't regular Army; they were "other."

If that meant she had to take care of herself, well, that was a lesson she'd learned long ago. Against stereotype, her well-bred, East Coast white-guy dad was the drunk. Her dirt-poor half Tennessee Cherokee, half Colorado settler mom, who'd passed her dusky skin and dark hair on to her daughter, had been a sober and serious woman. She'd also been a casualty of an Afghanistan dust-bowl IED while serving in the National Guard. Carla's big brother Clay now lay beside Mom in Arlington National Cemetery. Dead from a training accident. Except your average training accident didn't include a posthumous rank bump, a medal, and coming home in a sealed box reportedly with no face.

Clay had flown helicopters in the Army's 160th SOAR with the famous Majors Beale and Henderson. Well, famous in the world of people who'd flown with the Special Operations Aviation Regiment, or their little sisters who'd begged for stories of them whenever big brothers were home on leave. Otherwise totally invisible.

Clay had clearly died on a black op that she'd never be told a word of, so she didn't bother asking. Which was okay. He knew the risks, just as Mom had. Just as she herself had when she'd signed up the day of Clay's funeral, four years ago. She'd been on the front lines ever since and so far lived to tell about it.

Carla popped Clay's Ninja—which is how she still thought of it, even after riding it for four years—back into first and rolled it slowly up to the building with the pink roses. As good a place to start as any.

* * *

"Hey, check out this shit!"

Sergeant First Class Kyle Reeves looked out the window of the mess hall at the guy's call. Sergeant Ralph last-name-already-forgotten was 75th Rangers and too damn proud of it.

Though…damn! Ralphie was onto something.

Kyle would definitely check out this shit.

Babe on a hot bike, looking like she knew how to handle it.

Through the window, he inspected her lean length as she clambered off the machine. Army boots. So call her five-eight, a hundred and thirty, and every part that wasn't amazing curves looked like serious muscle. Hair the color of lush, dark caramel brushed her shoulders but moved like the finest silk, her skin permanently the color of the darkest tan. Women in magazines didn't look that hot. Those women always looked anorexic to him anyway, even the pinup babes displayed on Hesco barriers at forward operating bases up in the Hindu Kush where he'd done too much of the last couple years.

This woman didn't look like that for a second. She looked powerful. And dangerous.

Her tight leathers revealed muscles made of pure soldier.

Ralph Something moseyed out of the mess-hall building where the hundred selectees were hanging out to await the start of the next testing class at sundown.

Well, Kyle sure wasn't going to pass up the opportunity for a closer look. Though seeing Ralph's attitude, Kyle hung back a bit so that he wouldn't be too closely associated with the dickhead.

Ralph had been spoiling for a fight ever since he'd found out he was one of the least experienced guys to show up for Delta selection. He was from the 75th Ranger Regiment, but his deployments hadn't seen much action. Each of his attempts to brag for status had gotten him absolutely nowhere.

Most of the guys here were 75th Rangers, 82nd Airborne, or Green Beret Special Forces like himself. And most had seen a shitload of action because that was the nature of the world at the moment. There were a couple SEALs who hadn't made SEAL

Team Six and probably weren't going to make Delta, a dude from the Secret Service Hostage Rescue Team who wasn't going to last a day no matter how good a shot he was, and two guys who were regular Army.

The question of the moment though, who was she?

Her biking leathers were high-end, sewn in a jagged lightning-bolt pattern of yellow on smoke gray. It made her look like she was racing at full tilt while standing still. He imagined her hunched over her midnight-blue machine and hustling down the road at her Ninja's top speed—which was north of 150. He definitely had to see that one day.

Kyle blessed the inspiration on his last leave that had made him walk past the small Toyota pickup that had looked so practical and buy the wildfire-red Ducati Multistrada 1200 instead. Pity his bike was parked around the back of the barracks at the moment. Maybe they could do a little bonding over their rides. Her machine looked absolutely cherry.

Much like its rider.

Ralph walked right up to her with all his arrogant and stupid hanging out for everyone to see. The other soldiers began filtering outside to watch the show.

"Well, girlie, looks like you pulled into the wrong spot. This here is Delta territory."

Kyle thought about stopping Ralph, thought that someone should give the guy a good beating, but Dad had taught him control. He would take Ralph down if he got aggressive, but he really didn't want to be associated with the jerk, even by grabbing him back.

The woman turned to face them, then unzipped the front of her jacket in one of those long, slow movie moves. The sunlight shimmered across her hair as she gave it an "unthinking" toss. Wraparound dark glasses hid her eyes, adding to the mystery.

He could see what there was of Ralph's brain imploding from lack of blood. He felt the effect himself despite standing a half-dozen paces farther back.

She wasn't hot; she sizzled. Her parting leathers revealed an Army green T-shirt and proof that the very nice contours suggested by her outer gear were completely genuine. Her curves weren't big—she had a lean build—but they were as pure woman as her shoulders and legs were pure soldier.

"There's a man who called me 'girlie' earlier." Her voice was smooth and seductive, not low and throaty, but rich and filled with nuance.

She sounded like one of those people who could hypnotize a Cobra, either the snake or the attack helicopter.

"He's a bird colonel. He can call me that if he wants. You aren't nothing but meat walking on sacred ground and wishing he belonged."

Kyle nodded to himself. The "girlie" got it in one.

"You"—she jabbed a finger into Sergeant Ralph Something's chest—"do not get 'girlie' privileges. We clear?"

"Oh, sweetheart, I can think of plenty of privileges that you'll want to be giving to—" His hand only made it halfway to stroking her hair.

If Kyle hadn't been Green Beret trained, he wouldn't have seen it because she moved so fast and clean.

"—me!" Ralph's voice shot upward on a sharp squeak.

The woman had Ralph's pinkie bent to the edge of dislocation and, before the man could react, had leveraged it behind his back and upward until old Ralph Something was perched on his toes trying to ease the pressure. With her free hand, she shoved against the middle of his back to send him stumbling out of control into the concrete wall of the mess hall with a loud clonk when his head hit.

Minimum force, maximum result. The Unit's way.

She eased off on his finger and old Ralph dropped to the dirt like a sack of potatoes. He didn't move much.

"Oops." She turned to face the crowd that had gathered.

She didn't even have to say, "Anyone else?" Her look said plenty.

Kyle began to applaud. He wasn't the only one, but he was in the minority. Most of the guys were doing a wait and see.

A couple looked pissed.

Everyone knew that the Marines' combat training had graduated a few women, but that was just jarheads on the ground.

This was Delta. The Unit was Tier One. A Special Mission Unit. They were supposed to be the one true bastion of male dominance. No one had warned them that a woman was coming in.

Just one woman, Kyle thought. The first one. How exceptional did that make her? Pretty damn was his guess. Even if she didn't last the first day, still pretty damn. And damn pretty. He'd bet on dark eyes behind her wraparound shades. She didn't take them off, so it was a bet he'd have to settle later on.

A couple corpsmen came over and carted Ralph Something away even though he was already sitting up—just dazed with a bloody cut on his forehead.

The Deltas who'd come out to watch the show from a few buildings down didn't say a word before going back to whatever they'd been doing.

Kyle made a bet with himself that Ralph Something wouldn't be showing up at sundown's first roll call. They'd just lost the first one of the class and the selection process hadn't even begun. Or maybe it just had.

"Where's check-in?" Her voice really was as lush as her hair, and it took Kyle a moment to focus on the actual words.

He pointed at the next building over and received a nod of thanks.

That made watching her walk away in those tight leathers strictly a bonus.

Other works by M. L. Buchman:

The Night Stalkers

Main Flight

The Night Is Mine
I Own the Dawn
Wait Until Dark
Take Over at Midnight
Light Up the Night
Bring On the Dusk
By Break of Day

White House Holiday

Daniel's Christmas
Frank's Independence Day
Peter's Christmas
Zachary's Christmas
Roy's Independence Day
Damien's Christmas

and the Navy

Christmas at Steel Beach
Christmas at Peleliu Cove

5E

Target of the Heart
Target Lock on Love
Target of Mine

Delta Force

Target Engaged
Heart Strike

Dead Chef Thrillers

Swap Out!
One Chef!
Two Chef!

Firehawks

Main Flight

Pure Heat
Full Blaze
Hot Point
Flash of Fire
Wild Fire

Smokejumpers

Wildfire at Dawn
Wildfire at Larch Creek
Wildfire on the Skagit

Deities Anonymous

Cookbook from Hell: Reheated
Saviors 101

Angelo's Hearth

Where Dreams are Born
Where Dreams Reside
Maria's Christmas Table
Where Dreams Unfold
Where Dreams Are Written

Eagle Cove

Return to Eagle Cove
Recipe for Eagle Cove
Longing for Eagle Cove
Keepsake for Eagle Cove

SF/F Titles

Nara
Monk's Maze
the Me and Elsie Chronicles

Don't Miss a Thing!

Sign up for M. L. Buchman's newsletter today
and receive:
Release News
Free Short Stories
a Free Starter Library

Do it today. Do it now.
http://www.mlbuchman.com/newsletter/

CPSIA information can be obtained
at www.ICGtesting.com
Printed in the USA
BVHW04s1205220418
514082BV00001BA/97/P

9 781945 740138